FINAL RE

by

John Behardien

Duncurin
Publishing

Duncurin.com

First Published in England MMXVI

Duncurin Publishing
Monton
England

Duncurin.com

ISBN : 978-0-9935169-0-0

Book Design: Sheepie

DEDICATION

For Emmie and Lottie.
Final Year !
With all my love.

WITH THANKS

My sincere thanks to the following very talented people.

Cornerstones for first-draft advice: cornerstones.co.uk

Patrick Fahy: for wonderful copy editing: patfahy@lineone.net

Jamie Runyan: another super cover: design@reese-winslow.com

An amazing cover photo: courtesy of Yen Baet: YenBaet.com

Other Books By John Behardien

Crack In the Code
Stars' End

The Last Great Gift

Dawn Over Vancouver
All That Time Allows (for release 2016)

Final Horizon
Final Request

One Life Many Moments (for 2016/17 release)

CONTENTS

Chapter I

Silent Assassin

It was a cold and unsparing November's evening. The day had started dull and wet, but was then followed by clear skies. As the light faded, precipitously falling temperatures made the ground treacherous, especially to stiletto heels, and unforgiving to bare legs and shoulders. A few women, who sought comfort more highly than displays of glamour, had chosen substantial outerwear. Most significantly, the anticipation that percolated through those now approaching, with barely restrained excitement, was undimmed by such a lesser consideration as the English weather. Had they been aware, however, all would have agreed that there wasn't such a thing as a good day to die.

The great and the good, the moneyed and the influential, together with those who simply aspired to be one of those things, all converged at this time and place; each one eagerly clutching a prized invitation. This was the day, each year, when the doors of the American Embassy were thrown open. A carefully selected group of friends, those who wielded power and those who, it was hoped, could be subjected to benign persuasion had been invited.

All but three had one thing in common; they were guests of the richest and most powerful country that the world was yet to see.

One of the three had been sent by faceless others on a glorious mission to exchange his life for those of as many non-believers as possible. This violent act of loathing and revenge would be emblazoned on the very souls of those who were present that night − even as the perpetrator ascended into Paradise. His instructions were to get as close to the US ambassador as he could; to then wait until capitalist infidels surrounded him, before triggering the explosives that were laced with nails and shards of metal. By such means, all who bore witness would learn not only of the hatred in which they were held, but also that no place could be considered safe at any time. The remaining two were volunteers. Having chosen to attend, they understood that only two outcomes now presented: either to stop the unseen, unknown person, or else die along with others in the attempt.

Miss Clancy hugged Toby's arm. She'd selected a beautiful off-the-shoulder and low-cut ball gown, which enhanced her figure perfectly. The gorgeous, spiky shoes brought her height to within a whisker of the level needed for her to be able to engage him eye-to-eye. She'd given off a shiver at least once but she knew that Toby would never ask her if she were cold. Although he was someone who'd known her all her adult life, he'd never presume to remind her of any human frailties whatsoever. Such things belonged to a former life: one that she neither chose to acknowledge nor to dwell on − even at times such as these. In a similar vein, she accepted that the last thing she would expect to be offered was his jacket. Studying his firm yet handsome features, she could tell that he was nervous. The little dimple that appeared in a perfect midline of his well-defined chin only when he was either worried or scared – as now – being very much in evidence. Not that it wouldn't surprise if one were scared, though Clancy could never admit to harbouring this emotion – especially to herself. She knew that suicide attacks of the type that their endeavours had suggested was in prospect tonight were the hardest ones to detect and defeat, especially given the slim window of opportunity available to them.

She chanced another glimpse in his direction; just before he became suspicious of the interest she held in him – thereby revealing her own fears. She realised that after all these years she'd never thanked him. It was perhaps, only what she deserved, to have these thoughts intrude when their lives were in the greatest danger, when she was trying to concentrate. Indeed, there were so many things to thank him for, this was one possible, but not the real, reason why she'd never even attempted it. The security he'd given her, the opportunities, the chance in life, a safe haven, the unconditional love and so many more things that she'd lost count. She, by way of thankless exchange, had given him absolute hell and it must have seemed on many occasions in the past that she hated him and his very being for having all the things that she did not and for being the person that she wasn't – and could never be. She realised that if things went badly tonight she'd never have the chance to tell him something of her thoughts that were crystallising within.

She was then compelled to think of her morbid fear of ending up maimed, being horribly burned, losing her sight or a limb. The female agent could only hope that if she were to die along with hundreds tonight, it would be quick, clean and final.

She shrugged. No doubt Toby would think this a shiver, but it was a simple means of re-aligning her own thoughts. She applied her acute mind to the job in hand.

Her eyes shone like discs of molten caramel, just at the verge of incandescence. The smile beamed outwardly upon those who had occasion to catch more than a fleeting glimpse of her. The striking woman laughed in a carefree manner disguising her fear that their target was not only unknown, but also, most likely undiscoverable, to them. Her bright and vivacious demeanour captivated, totally, the men and women who bore witness. Some glanced, a few stared, but all who saw her were compelled to look again as the handsome couple arrived at Grosvenor Square. All the while, the pretty eyes took in far more than those with lesser powers of observation could barely begin to match. Searching desperately for more clues, she scanned the hundreds who were arriving for anything that might reveal the identity of the person who'd been instructed to kill and mutilate as many innocents as possible.

Knowing that security would be all pervading and intimidating, Miss Clancy accepted that this wouldn't save them – any of them. Doing her best to appear star-struck, she took in the presence of the security guards, their arms folded purposefully in front of their muscular torsos. Each of them made an attempt, but failed, to fit in unobtrusively; their identical dinner jackets serving only to make them stand out more. She smiled flirtatiously to reveal the even array of beautiful teeth as her head came back, just a little, to give flight to the glorious tresses that shone in the available light.

Noting the frames that housed the metal detectors, her eyes glimmered, as might the sun rising on the milky dawn of a new day. The young woman gave a little laugh, like a butterfly soaring on a summer's afternoon. She espied the security cameras both before the metal detectors and beyond them. A slight hint of ozone wafted through the entrance as the sensors fizzed with the moisture in the air and mixed uneasily with the vast variety of perfumes and aftershaves that guests had sprayed themselves with. Furthermore, she surveyed the small queue that had built as the guests waited patiently, but excitedly, for entry after being scrutinised for weapons, explosives or honed blades. The animated hubbub of conversation seemed to subside the closer the throng got to being admitted. Pausing, she too waited, the excitement plainly visible on her face, as might a medal winner; the one who would be third to be called to the podium. Miss Clancy calculated that she would have to be precise with not only her own positioning, but also his.

Neither Miss Clancy, nor Toby were unaided, however.

"We are all set up here, Miss Clancy. Rupert and I are using the images from your neck cam to scan everyone and match them against the guest list. I'm afraid it's going to take time." came the disparate voice, through the earpiece that looked like one of a pair of diamond-stoned earrings, while they shone with an intensity to match her feigned mood.

Smiling again, she whispered in the general direction of the microphone, which was suspended round her neck, disguised as a beautiful necklace that complemented the earrings. "Understood; just do the best you can."

Tim, in the surveillance van sounded more nervous than she and he was parked more than a mile from the scene, well away from the potential fallout created by even the largest blast. "If you could perhaps turn just a little to use the camera to scan the crowds, we'd be able to get through them faster."

Toby studied her carefully, he wondered if this would be their last mission. The beautiful dress she sported was almost a statement of defiance in itself: if her life were to be plucked from her prematurely tonight, then she would go out looking fabulous. Time was very much against them and he could only surmise that she felt as nervous as him. "Everything all right, Clancy?"

"Fine, Toby," she understated, "just wish we had a bit more to go on. There are hundreds here."

He winked mischievously in her direction, "Three hundred and ninety, including us, Clancy."

"That makes me feel so much better, Toby. Only three hundred and eighty eight to go."

Miss Clancy, breathed in slowly, this had the effect of slowing her heart and helped her to focus. Holding Toby's arm as they began to move, she slowed his stride imperceptibly − her timing, as always, nothing if not perfect. The couple just in front of them cleared the security scanner − noiselessly. She knew it was time. Glancing up, briefly, at the surveillance camera, she moved forwards and seamlessly urged Toby to do the same. She watched as the quivering red beam from the camera held them dead-centre.

"Good luck, Miss Clancy," came from the voice in her ear. She wondered if it would be the last voice she'd ever hear. The metal detectors lay just ahead.

"Thanks, Tim," she managed quietly, before tugging her partner's arm with more force than the barely perceptible movement would suggest.

Flashes fired in succession from the official photographer and one or two pressmen, as the elegant pair presented themselves just before the entrance. As she became bathed in the vivid stroboscopic lights, some wondered if the striking woman was a film star. How she desperately wanted to close her eyes against those bright lights − each flash making her think of a bomb blast. She knew, however, this luxury would be denied to her. The metal detector loomed large in front of them; its circuitry not subject to the distractions exhibited by mortal men.

The open smile disguised, once more, the words she offered to her companion. "Come on then; too late to back out now." They moved forwards a few more paces. She then whispered unequivocally in his direction.

"Kiss me!"

"What?"

"*You* heard correctly, now please do as I ask, and quickly!"

Toby did as he was told, just as he always did when faced with an imperative from Miss Clancy. He'd learned not to question, or doubt her at such times. His mouth moved towards hers; the full lips that shimmered, as they seemed to manipulate the subdued light to their all-consuming advantage. She continued to walk forwards as he positioned himself to comply with her request. Their lips met in what appeared to observers to be a longed-for, yet breathless, kiss.

"Wow, Miss Clancy! Are you two doing what I think you're doing? Me and Rupert are blushing here." appeared in her earpiece.

Their lips remained locked; she gripped him, as if handling a high velocity rifle while faced with a particularly difficult shot, which she was attempting on the move, without a bipod. Her preoccupation precluded a reply. Carefully, she now spun her escort anticlockwise as they went through the security portal in their conjoined state. The ostentatious display of spontaneous endearment hid and distracted in equal parts – just as she'd hoped. Red lights flashed and a klaxon sounded, the second they attempted their passage. The loud noise intruded upon her slightly less than the camera flashes. Only then did she suspend the gentle rotation, their lips parted as she pushed him almost nonchalantly forwards and now beyond the detector and the cameras. Her gloved left hand came up to frame her disarming laughter, which had appeared seconds after her feigned shock and surprise.

"Oh, silly me. I am so sorry," she said, doing her best to look embarrassed.

Her uncommon looks and coyest of smiles were sufficient to quell scrutiny and suspicion at its birth, even from the most diligent and observant of security agents. She opened her small, slim clutch bag.

Tim's gaze remained locked on the images being fed from the camera around her neck, like a crucial scene in a thriller that the audience couldn't take their eyes off. "That was wonderful, Miss Clancy. Really foxed them."

"Quiet," she hissed, "can't you see, I'm concentrating here."

"Sorry, Miss Clancy, I'm just getting giddy with the excitement."

"Well, save your giddiness for later – if we come through this."

A bemused but inquisitive look appeared on Toby's face, "Pardon?"

"Oh, nothing, it's our mission surveillance chief getting carried away."

He smiled, as he finally registered the conversation that had been conducted through the most critical of the moments in passing through security: and it wasn't over yet. The alarm continued to sound. People stared at her, just as she knew they would; the best way of hiding something was in plain sight. From the opened clutch bag she guiltily, but obviously, drew out a metal glasses case. It shone in the stark overhead lighting of the foyer. The clutch bag she passed to Toby. Pushing him tenderly with a raised flat palm, she surreptitiously moved him and, most crucially, the bag further beyond the range of the detectors and the cameras. She held up the bright case as she raised both arms, signifying her willingness to be searched. She, then, offered it up as a crucial exhibit to the security agent as a further example of her innocence. Laughing with just the right degree of embarrassment, she was still holding her arms up. Having passed the case on to the security guard, she attempted transit through the metal detectors, once again. Smiling more confidently, she noted beguilingly that it, at the second time of asking, bore silent witness to her movements.

The spellbound guard gripped the glasses case, caressing it between thumb and forefinger as if he'd just been given a rose, while he informed her that she could collect it from him later.

"That's fine," offered Clancy, smiling bashfully in his direction, without revealing that she wore glasses neither for near nor far vision.

Observers that day would only have seen the vivacious young woman with a pleasant and bright demeanour, who was clearly determined to have a wonderful time. Women looked enviously at her and men espoused similar feelings whilst looking at him – the lucky chap. In any event only a machine, but not one person, had detected the deadly assassin, who was preparing to act against an anonymous stranger – if there were still time to do so.

Two white-gloved embassy staff stood either side of the vast double doors that stretched so high that could easily have served as gates to an HGV depot had they not been painstakingly crafted in American Walnut. As she passed through the entrance, Clancy took an involuntary deep breath.

Toby smiled while he looked at her, having anticipated her reaction. "Impressed, eh Clancy?"

"Rich toffs," she muttered in his ear. "Have you no *ordinary* friends? Friends who have ceilings in their front rooms below thirty feet?"

He laughed again as she allowed him to guide her further into the impactful grand room.

She looked down; being aware that the delicate shoes she wore had passed on to a different surface. Discovering a magnificent marble floor, tiled in a contrasting check pattern, she saw ahead of them that this gave way to a detailed mosaic, set in the floor, making up the image of the Great Seal of the United States.

The vast and palatial room had served its function; to impress one's friends and intimidate one's enemies – at least that was the intention. Continuing to link Toby, they slowly circulated and mingled round the elegant stateroom. All the while, they both looked keenly for clues that might lead to the person they were there to find: the subject of their mission. By accentuating her normal precise walk, she rotated her torso slightly from side to side so as to bring as many as possible within the field of view of the camera – fashioned to look like jewellery round her neck. People were still filing in. Any bomber would wait until he or she could destroy as many lives as possible. So many people even in such a large space: casualties would be very high.

"Well, that went well," he concluded.

"Told you, we'd be fine," she returned, confidently.

"Nice touch that kiss; really distracted them. Only you could have done that, Clancy, good work." Toby reflected that despite his knowing her for so long, she still found new ways to surprise and enthral him. Something she did unfailingly with every man she met. He delicately touched his lips, the same ones that had met hers. She smiled delightedly by way of reply. More people stared at the striking couple as they slowly walked forwards.

"I can see you on the surveillance cameras," came from her earpiece. "Rupert, here, has hacked into the embassy secure feed. We should have more images soon. Cover the room as quickly as you are able. I'm afraid we have lots to get through."

Reflexively Clancy dipped her chin a little as she replied, "That is the understatement of the night, Tim. Now, please let us concentrate on the task in hand."

"Sorry, Miss Clancy."

"Tim! Shush!"

"Sorry, again," he offered, somehow hoping that a whisper would be less intrusive.

A few minutes of relative calm went by. Clancy did her best to walk slowly not wanting anyone to have a clue as to the urgency of the situation. She realised that if she started rushing then panic would not be far behind. Moreover, if their target saw them before they did him, he might set off his device without delay.

Clancy realised that they had to look logically at their task if they were to succeed. "Try to locate the ambassador. I suspect he is the one they would dearly like to place on their spiteful revenge list."

"Very well, Miss Clancy, we are paging all the cameras as quickly as we can. We'll centre on him."

A waitress offered them a flute of champagne, which he accepted and she declined. She did accept a canapé which she ate slowly as her sharp eyes scanned the expanse. Gripping Toby's arm once more, she rotated towards the side of the stateroom with pairs of marble pillars making up a colonnade, which ran to its lofty heights and formed supports for the soaring vaulted ceiling. Just for the moment, a moment that could have cost a hundred lives, Miss Clancy was distracted by the series of pictures of American presidents mounted on the wall space between the substantial columns. Mercifully, her camera continued to render images as she moved. Tim continued to pore meticulously over the same. For a second or two she could have sworn that she detected the hint of a smell of oil paint, no doubt coming from the most recent picture, that of President Obama.

"Miss Clancy?"

"What now, Tim? I am working here."

"Forgive me, Miss Clancy, but can you see the waiter off to your right? He has at least three vests on."

"Yes?"

Nervousness crept into Tim's voice. He knew that the female agent was trying to concentrate, but he adjudged what he had to say wouldn't wait. "It's a cold night, even colder for some, especially if one is not used to an English winter? Can you see the remains of stubble from someone who has tried to shave, but is not in the habit of doing so regularly? Also this man, even allowing for his three vests, is podgy. Waiters, and I've met a few over the years are all slim. They walk miles in a day. They are as fit as female Serbian volleyball players. This chap is no waiter. Furthermore, I wouldn't be seen dead in a waistcoat that was so ill-fitting. Facial scanning software is running. It will be done in a few seconds."

Miss Clancy held her breath; she gripped Toby's arm like a balancing pole as if walking on a wire suspended over Niagara Falls. "Tim, forgive me. I think you have something."

Most vitally, the waiter wrestled uneasily with the loaded tray of glasses of champagne as if it were an unaccustomed, if not novel, thing for him to do. Moreover, Tim was correct, his waistcoat bulged in all the wrong places.

By means of significant effort, Tim succeeded in scrubbing his voice of any vestige of tension or doubt. "Yes, confirmed; facial recognition software shows ninety-eight per cent certainty. We can't match him to the official list. Horizon control agrees; instructions are to proceed. Live rounds are authorised. I repeat; live rounds are authorised."

"Understood, Tim."

"Just don't miss and shoot the ambassador," offered their mission controller, brightly.

"If I shoot the American Ambassador, rather than this scum bag, then Toby will cancel my Christmas bonus."

"He wouldn't do that would he, Miss Clancy?" Tim returned with concerned tones.

"Look, Tim, if I shoot the Ambassador we'll all be down for a good waterboarding session for several Christmases to come. Now quiet!"

"Oh, a joke, yes I see, Miss Clancy, sorry."

Once again, she turned and pretended to be locked in animated conversation with her consort.

"No facial match, mission is authorised," she whispered in Toby's ear.

She was already looking beyond Toby, however, as she assessed her target. Her appearance was that of a young woman whispering endearments in her lover's ear, but disguising very different sentiments. Toby saw her slim long fingers reach gently into the compact clutch bag that he'd returned to her. It looked as though she was searching for a lipstick or handkerchief, perhaps. She held the bag tightly against her torso, but the end pointed firmly towards the waiter.

"Did you bring your Glock?" interrupted, once more, the voice in the earpiece.

"I told you," she sighed, whilst summoning more reserves of patience, "that it would need a silencer and *that* would make it too big and heavy."

"But, don't you always use a Glock?"

"No, I do not. I use any gun that will allow me to complete the mission. Or, come to that, a nice sharpened blade, or even a blunt club, like the one I've been known to use on those who keep interrupting me."

Finding the gun within her handbag, she knew she had to shoot, and do so accurately, from within its confines. Such a shot would also have to be as quiet and unobtrusive as possible. She accepted that no clue must be given as to where the volley had come from: at best, no one was to be aware that a bullet had been fired at all. This is why she'd chosen her weapon with care, because its special cartridge generated very little noise when fired. As an added bonus, it was compact enough to fit in the small bag. Furthermore, when used with the dedicated cartridge, it did not require a silencer.

"Are you sure that Russian gun is any good? What's it called again, a 'sin to mash'?"

"Ha, I think you mean a Tsiniitochmash PSS, silent self-loading pistol."

"Sounds double-Dutch to me, especially as a chip lover. What if you miss?"

At a pre-arranged signal, Toby effected a loud and ostentatious sneeze. Clancy fired at the same time, just glancing for a second or two away from her companion and on to her target.

"I never miss," she offered unequivocally, as the gun went off.

A slight 'phutting' noise was all but contained by the bag. As a further precaution, any sound was almost totally masked by his efforts at generating the sneeze. Anyone who might have been observing the waiter at that point was also distracted at the same time.

The waiter suddenly grabbed his right thigh and dropped the tray full of champagne flutes just before he collapsed in agony on the floor. A loud piercing cry that was clearly not English issued from his lips as he went down. Most people there present thought that he'd simply stumbled. He, however, as well as Clancy, Toby and their surveillance agent, knew otherwise. The polished marble floor was now strewn with pools of fine champagne and also peppered with shards of expensive crystal. His dark trousers, for the time being, masked the patch of blood as it began to spread slowly.

As he hit the floor he had managed to put his arms out in an attempt to protect himself. Miss Clancy acted just as quickly. Some of the shards of glass had cut his palms, which added to his distraction and general misery. Once again, Toby was ready to sow confusion, and cleared his throat, so that he was ready to say. "My God, this chap's collapsed. Man down!" he offered at the top of his voice, but by this time he'd simply confirmed the obvious. Now taking full advantage of the chatter and bewilderment that rippled around the room, this was all the time Miss Clancy needed in order to rush over to the disabled waiter, her face a perfect study of concern.

"Oh, the poor man," she called, to the room as a whole. She bent over the waiter and approached very closely.

"I'd stay down if I were you, or my next bullet will be somewhere between your ears," she advised without a blink or a falter of her slowly beating heart. He complied; the pain from his leg and the splinters of glass that had cut him ensured that any other response was highly unlikely.

She came even closer and then reached under his waistcoat with her right hand. At the same time, the left appeared to be comforting the prostrate man, but in reality was restraining his free hand and preventing him from activating the electric switch. Moreover, the agony visited on him as he writhed on the floor had long since precluded any other intentions. In seconds her exploratory hand had found what she was looking for: the detonator, which had been pushed into the cake of explosives. Whilst maintaining continually the illusion of helping the hapless man, she removed this thus making the charge completely safe.

With an expression of sympathetic concern on her face, she quietly offered him words widely at variance with such a vision. Whispering carefully but clearly, she ensured that only he could hear the threats she now conveyed. "Stay down, or I'll finish you. Make a move to get up or to run and it will be the very last thought you are aware of. Also, you've no idea who shot you. It could have been anyone," she suggested with an air of menace. All the while, she continued to smile sweetly at him. The resolute manner of her voice held very different overtones that left him in no doubt as to what would befall him if he failed to comply.

Dark eyes looked back at Miss Clancy, but were modulated with a mixture of pain and hatred. Her shot had missed the femoral artery at the top of his leg but by happy accident had grazed the femoral nerve, which ran in close proximity. Although bleeding was minimal, the pain was intense.

Suddenly, she recoiled in horror. "My goodness, this poor man has been shot!" At this point, she stood abruptly, her hands framing her mouth in shock, and effectively disguising the surreptitious bomb defuse. This was made still more dramatic by the hysterical scream she effected and the swooning, nauseated look she crafted on her face. Her elbow came up as she made as if she were going to faint, like a silent-movie matinee idol. She moved away quickly and Toby dutifully came forwards to comfort her, just as the security guards stepped in.

Once more her head was filled with Tim's voice. "I think you are in the clear, Miss Clancy. Don't worry, nobody would believe that a pretty girl like you could have actually gone and shot someone."

As the security forces moved to unbutton the waiter's clothing, the suicide vest was revealed. The curious onlookers gasped collectively as the ugly thing came into view. He continued to stare after Clancy as she and Toby quietly moved away into the approaching crowds. As they did so, a wave of mounting excitement was spreading around the room.

Within seconds the Chamber music stopped and this was replaced by a very different noise like a herd of wildebeest discovering a watering hole after many parched miles. In that moment, soft power of pressed flesh and gentle persuasion met the firm power of the clenched fist and the application of physical force. A different security team had clearly been deployed and these rushed in complete with battle tunics, Kevlar bullet-proof vests, helmets, tinted visors and shortened assault rifles. They immediately split into two groups, one of which found the ambassador and escorted both him and his wife back to their private chambers. The other, larger group stood either side of the waiter who, not only continued to moan, but also began to chant in an unintelligible tongue as he rocked from side to side in pools of champagne, blood and shards of crystal glass.

More people displayed a mixture of intrigue and horror while an animated but terrified buzz passed through the gathering. There were a great many important and powerful guests present that night: those who, above all, preferred to remain discrete, if not anonymous. Although they had all anticipated a pleasant evening, most of these now accepted that they had no place in being close either to a suicide vest, or to someone who was prepared to use it.

Swear words in over a hundred tongues coursed round the room. Several invitees saw this as being a signal for them to depart, not wishing, for personal reasons, to be associated with either such dangers or such publicity. They quietly, but quickly, dispersed into the crowds of people who had no need for such considerations; who'd approached purely to see what the fuss was. Some of the security guards drew their weapons as a couple of the others removed his waistcoat. They could see that the detonator was absent. Mercifully, they'd come across an incompetent suicide bomber. A few minutes later, medical help was called.

Toby and Clancy joined the number of those who sought concealment as they, too, melted into the background. If gaining an entrance had been a formal affair most suddenly realised that leaving would take on very different proportions. More significantly, for many present on that occasion, an evening that began with so much excitement had quickly changed into one that had then taken on more febrile proportions and it was all to do with the desperate intentions of one man.

Clancy smiled to herself, Toby picking her thoughts up, for once instantly, as she contemplated that rich and powerful people would not take kindly to having their egress subject to any constraints whatsoever. The Americans, however, had very different ideas and more security agents now joined those on the exits.

In scenes much beloved by Clancy, who was always fascinated by how the behaviour of rich people could degenerate into those reminiscent of a pub brawl. She gripped Toby's arm in that moment more with excitement than tension as she laughed, "This should be good. People would pay money to see this. I think it would make good TV; we could call it 'Toff Tantrums'."

"Don't get too involved, Clancy, that is a loaded gun you are carrying and we still have to get out ourselves."

"Shush, I'm listening."

Finding her mood infectious, he nodded towards the exit. "Look there's the Comtesse de Lyon, let's see how she gets on?"

"How dare yu tell me zat I cannot leave? Stand back zis moment. I zee you 'ave let the ambassador's mistress leave. Just ooh do I 'ave to sleep with to be allowed to go on my way?"

The Americans were now in a difficult bind, with the prospect of insulting many of those they'd tried to impress. As always, they'd put contingencies in place. The security guard smiled but retained a matter-of-fact air. "If I might see your invitation, ma'am?"

The Comtesse managed to hand over her invite whilst still retaining her offended overtones.

The guard looked at the invite and said simply. "Sorry, madam but if you'd just stand over there for the moment."

"Don't yu know ooh I am?"

"We do ma'am, we know exactly who you are, but if you'd just stand over there, momentarily?"

A diatribe of expletives in perfect French then came his way, causing even Clancy to blush. Upon seeing that he wasn't going to budge, she complied though still retained her anger.

The Chinese Ambassador then came forward and upon presenting his invitation was waved though immediately. The Comtesse then resorted to shouting her disgust and asked if he, too, had slept with the ambassador!

Miss Clancy stood behind two young women who were as excited as she in watching the spectacle.

"So, how does that work, then?" said one to the other.

The second woman showed the first her invite. "Look, all the invites have a colour code in the corner. They can then tell who the bigwigs are and those they can afford to upset."

The first woman then said, "I don't know what she's complaining about, she isn't a real Countess, she's just bedded more rich people than most."

Both giggled behind black-gloved hands that came up to disguise their merriment. The second woman then noted more high profile guests amongst those trying to take their leave.

"I think that's George Bush, he's been waved straight through. And look, I'm sure that's Tony Blair over there. Surely they won't make him queue, with the American friends he has."

With boundless delight Miss Clancy whispered in Toby's ear, "Look they've let Blair out before David Cameron and there's Corbyn over there, he'll be here till morning, at the very least!"

Doing his best to engage with her mood, Toby observed, "After turning up in just a lounge suit, no doubt they'll charge him with having dreadful dress sense."

Tim continued to monitor the scene and he had spotted an escape route. "Miss Clancy, towards your left; the chap with the glasses case, he's not taken his eyes off you."

Just as they left the queue, Clancy saw the Romanian defence secretary throw down his dinner jacket in a fit of temper and then take a swing at one of the guards. Although nobody could decipher the words he shouted, they didn't sound very nice. Two more guards came forward to restrain him while he added his disgust to the shouting still coming from the Frenchwoman.

"Come on Toby, time for us to leave?"

She walked straight towards the security guard who'd kept the glasses case.

"I wonder if I might collect my glasses case?"

He returned in a clipped English accent, "Of course, Madam."

Clancy pointed to the metal detector, the one she'd entered via not an hour before. She asked beseechingly, " I don't suppose we could duck out through there, could we? I promise, I didn't shoot anyone."

"Of course Madam, Sir, how could I refuse?"

As they went through the detector, but this time in reverse, once again it went off. She waved the glasses case at her admirer and smiled sweetly at him.

"Miss Clancy, can I detect a little fib?"

"Only a little one, a white one, Tim, which, as you know is permitted when for the greater good."

"Ah, yes thought I'd missed that," he returned.

More than once that evening she'd found ways to impress her partner, "Clancy, just what do you do to all these men?"

"Nothing, Toby, that they don't want me to do to them." This in a nutshell, as Toby considered much later, was surely the essence of a beautiful woman. People would gladly open doors for such a person and this was by no means limited to a literal sense.

She and Toby moved without hesitation. As they walked through the exit and away from the embassy, a Jaguar XJ, long wheelbase, swept in and stopped to collect them. The driver rushed out of the car in order to help Miss Clancy with the long evening gown. Toby looked bemused as he caught him staring at Clancy, this being all the excuse he needed.

Tim was ecstatic, "Woo, woo, nice work you two. What wonderful shooting. That little gun you packed came through after all."

"Which reminds me, we are due at the shooting range tomorrow, I believe, Tim. I'm keen to see you in action," Clancy advised.

"Does that mean I might be allowed out on another mission?"

"Well, just make sure you are there on time, as we need to see how your skills are coming along. However, by your performance tonight, I can't see why not."

"Wish I could shoot like that."

"All in good time, Tim. I will see you at the range tomorrow, as agreed. Remember, I want you there bright and early."

"Wouldn't miss it for the world, Miss Clancy."

Whilst Toby and Clancy made their exit, several spilled chaotically down the entrance steps at complete variance with their more sedate arrival of just a short time before. Others, ones who'd been looking forward to the function all year, left with more reluctance. Moreover, some had been waiting all their lives to receive a precious invitation. In truth, the arrival of so many members of the security forces had long since destroyed for just about everyone any enjoyment from the evening. Many had feared exactly what had been planned by the waiter-in-disguise, before some well-informed, unseen and unknown person had taken definitive action.

They could only wonder about that person. He was, no doubt, an undercover American security agent, who'd protected them: a quiet unsung hero. Indeed, it must be a highly decorated, but covert spy, who was used to stepping in to save his country from harm and embarrassment. Perhaps, he'd been keeping the baddy under surveillance and had been ready to strike at a moment's notice. Many held concern for that pretty girl who'd had the shock of her life when she'd realised that he'd been shot. The poor woman had looked dreadful as the grim discovery dawned on her. They could only hope that such an unexpected and brutal finding had not damaged her delicate constitution.

Toby and Miss Clancy sat in the back of the Jaguar as it slowly moved off. They both gave a collective sigh of relief. Neither could be sure how close a call it had been – perhaps it was one of those things that it was best not to know. In any event, and for now, they would both live to fight another day and Clancy looked forward to a quiet conversation with Toby.

As the pair were driven away, the car accelerated briskly and was soon swallowed by the all-concealing night. Tim continued to pose questions that poured from her earpiece. She looked at Toby and shrugged her shoulders as if summoning more reserves of patience in an attempt to satisfy an inquisitive child.

"Why didn't the Americans deal with this?"

Clancy laughed. "They didn't even know! Our client would have been ruined by the fallout if a bomb had gone off in there."

"Ooh, sounds a bit 'cloak and dagger', if I am not mistaken."

"Yes, I suppose it does, but that's what we do and we got what we came for. Our client will be delighted. She will settle our invoice in full and, hopefully, add a nice bonus out of gratitude for a neat, tidy operation. More importantly, she is someone who, how can I put this, is a good person to have on our side."

"I suppose in this business we need one or two friends in high places?"

"That we do, Tim. Our organisation needs patrons with influence just as much as the next business does, and it never hurts to make a friend or two as we go forward."

"Yes, I am beginning to see."

"Ah well, for now, it's time for home. I'll let you get back to your plate of chips and your volleyball. Great work, Tim, I would like to thank you and what an excellent mission controller you make. Thank you, too, for your wonderful surveillance and support, Tim. I hope to see you, ready for some shooting, bright and early?"

"Thank you for your comments. I'll be there. Good night, Miss Clancy, Toby."

"Good night, Tim. No speeding in the surveillance van. It would require a lot of explanation if the police stop you and want a look inside." came from the bemused young woman. The microphone went dead, as Tim cancelled the signal feed.

"I can't believe you still have him calling you 'Miss Clancy' – why don't you just tell him your first name?" queried Toby.

"Ooh and spoil the fun, he's having the time of his life."

"He and you, too, I suspect, eh Clancy."

The car stopped next to the magnificent F-type, and Clancy moved to exit, as the driver quickly presented to hold the door.

"Goodnight, Toby," she offered just after she'd kissed him. "Thank you for all *your* help and support, as always."

"Wouldn't have wanted to miss it," he offered as he reflected what a pleasure it was to watch the skilled and resourceful, female agent in action and up close. "We'll meet up after his gun training session and you can give me some feedback?"

"With pleasure, goodnight," she said, as he hugged her. Still with the smile on her face, she went towards her F-Type, finished in pure white. Just as she walked away, he powered down the window and called, "Take your own advice, eh Clancy. Try to keep the speed to two figures as you head north."

She nodded, but her mischievous smile revealed a much closer hint as to what her speed would be on the quiet late-night motorway.

"Besides, I'm amazed that you can drive in those high shoes."

"Look, I've told you, you shouldn't notice what I wear," she returned, as she advanced one of the gorgeous shoes forwards.

"Don't get arrested for speeding, will you? I'm not sure the policeman's heart could cope with seeing the contents of your clutch bag."

"He should be so lucky. Besides, he can look in the bag all he wants, just as long as he doesn't want to look in my boot!" Toby now looked horrified as he remembered the assortment of weaponry she kept in her boot. She smiled, sensing his discomfort. "Don't worry, he'll never catch me. Goodnight."

For weeks to come the Americans would pore over their security images, searching for clues as to who had shot the bogus waiter. The CIA were brought in from the outset. The staffing agency that had recruited him found that the genuine waiter, who had passed all their security checks, had been replaced by the terrorist, who was intent on destroying himself, together with as many innocent people as he could take with him. When the footage from the numerous cameras failed to demonstrate how the imposter had been shot, they resorted to questioning him. He informed them that he was working alone and he had no knowledge as to who'd shot him. They asked him about the girl that had come over to him, but he became even more vague. In fact, whenever they mentioned her, he kept repeating only that he knew nothing. They recognised the partner she had attended with as someone who received an invitation each year and whose security credentials were unimpeachable. They realised that such a line of enquiry was fruitless and they went back to studying their guest list and security tapes. Going through the events of that night again and again, the identity of the person who had acted in this way, and saved a great number of important people, continued to elude them.

It was with a mounting feeling of absolute dread that the 'truth' came upon them. Their uncomfortable conclusion was that the British secret service must have intervened but had done so without them being aware. The CIA understood that there would be serious repercussions if this were found to be the case. They tentatively put out feelers to British Intelligence, asking them if they'd mounted a covert security operation that night. The Americans were relieved of further embarrassment when the British informed them that they had no information regarding such an operation. This in turn, generated further relief, as they failed to understand how such a high profile organisation could have mounted such a mission right under their noses, without their knowledge. It was only then that they realised that they were no further on with their investigation. The question as to who had taken action remained unanswered. This meant that they couldn't even begin to answer the next question – *why* someone had intervened, for them, only then, choose to remain in the shadows.

Meaningful though all these events were, the Horizon team believed that they had earned a moment's relief; even a measure of self-congratulation. Unfortunately, this was to be short-lived as the most significant event occurred later that night.

Toby brought up the secure video-link to their client.

"Her Majesty's Government is once again indebted to you, Mr Richmond. We are especially pleased that the threat was neutralised invisibly and without casualty."

"That's our pleasure, Dame Helen."

"Please accept my thanks but as usual no official recognition of either our or your involvement will ever be made."

"Of course, Dame Helen, this is the way we prefer to work, as you know."

"We will transfer funds direct from the Treasury in the morning and I shall see to a significant bonus being included, as a token of my personal thanks."

"You are too kind Ma'am."

"Not at all, Mr Richmond, we are so pleased to have a dependable and discrete group such as you and your team upon whom we can call for our tricky dilemmas."

"Of course, Ma'am."

"Goodnight then Toby and well done once again."

"Ma'am."

After closing down the link he decided to prepare his dinner jacket for the dry-cleaners. A little inauspicious hand-written note popped out of his pocket. He'd never set eyes on either the note or the handwriting before. Assuming that it was simply an old scrap of paper, he nearly screwed it up and flicked it in the bin. On many occasions in the days ahead when the body count climbed, extinction faced the entire organisation and it seemed that his life's work lay in tatters at his feet, how he would wish that he'd done exactly that. Sadly, the nightmare would retain him, and others, within its cruel embrace and offer him neither an awakening any time soon, nor the prospect of a bright dawn to follow.

This is what he read:

'Sir, please forgive my unannounced and unsolicited means of communication. Please also forgive this hastily assembled note. I came to the Ambassador's ball tonight to beg the US for assistance in rescuing my daughter, who has been kidnapped along the northern border of Nigeria, where we live. My enquiries suggest that she has been abducted into Niger and it bears the hallmark of a warlord, who abducts women in this way and then sells such captives into servitude, drug running and prostitution in Western Europe.

The Americans are unable/unwilling to help me. I was about to leave when I happened to notice both you and your glamorous accomplice. The more I watched the more impressed I became. That precision shot she carried out from the little bag she carried and the planning that must have been brought into play to not only discover such a threat but to neutralise it, all under the noses of the Americans, has left me deeply impressed.

I wonder if you represent a private agency that I could retain in order to free my only and much-loved daughter?

For the purposes of our discussion here, I can command limitless resources and am only too happy to utilise them all, if need be, in order to get her back safely.

Time is of the essence. I wonder if I might ask of you that you could call me in complete confidence on the number below?

I have no wish or intention of exposing you or your actions to the Americans or anyone else and your secrets shall remain my secrets, even if you choose not to accept my heartfelt request of you and your people.

I look forward to hearing from you and shall be at your disposal for a meeting at a time and place of your choosing.'

Mitral Nukumobo

CHAPTER II

Wide-range Shooting

The following morning Clancy arrived at the agreed time of 7 am. She wore a brown leather pencil skirt, just on the knee, and a fine-cashmere 'V'-necked jumper in powder blue. The flawless panels of soft hide had been beautifully stitched, serving to enhance her slim, svelte form. She'd also chosen a pair of really high shoes that brought her up to the same height as Tim. He couldn't help but stare. After an uncomfortable minute or two, she spoke. She looked down.

"Look, Tim, these are legs," she kicked one forwards to add some levity, before moving on to the more difficult subject matter that she needed to address, "I'm sure you see ones just like them, as most people have a pair. Even you, I guess, must have a couple of legs, somewhat similar, under those trousers?"

Tim hung his head as he reflected quietly to himself that this was not quite true as, in his opinion, her legs were the sexiest things he'd seen grace a woman in a long time. Sensing something of his thoughts, she nodded and smiled; then tried a different tack. "We'll be working together, sometimes very closely, Tim. You are just going to have to try to put such feelings to one side," she offered, knowing that careless or uncontrolled thoughts could only jeopardise their future professional relationship.

"Perhaps, if you take a good look now, and get it out of your system?"

"I'll do my best, Miss Clancy, I am sorry."

Her smile was not unfriendly, but had taken on an edge of formality like that of a teacher, having controlled an unruly class. "And so, to our exercises this morning, Tim. That's if you are up to a bit of shooting?" He nodded by way of affirmation and looked sheepishly as he failed to meet her steely gaze.

She positioned her earplugs and also wore spectacles against the flash and the hot shell casings being ejected. As soon as he had followed suit, she produced her *Glock 19* and began firing at once. Firing each round in rapid succession, she emptied a magazine of fifteen bullets into a static target some fifty metres away. Each shot was perfect, despite the fairly long range.

"Nice shooting, Miss C, Tim offered."

She raised her hand; attracting the attention of the operator, in order to refresh the target. "Now then, Tim, let's see how you do?"

He followed suit with the fresh, but identical, target. His action was a lot less smooth and he took much more time between shots. As soon as he'd discharged the entire magazine, she walked towards him. Nodding approvingly, she said, "Excellent Tim, your scores are really coming on. I can see I'll have competition."

He acknowledged her encouraging words, but recognised that they were there to do just that – encourage him. She then fired another clip into the same target he'd used. One by one, the bullets landed just to the right of each of his; the bullet holes had been made as precisely as if a ruler had been used.

He stared as if he'd seen something he couldn't quite believe. "Wow, Miss Clancy, that's amazing. I don't think I'll ever be that good. Also, just how did you manage to shoot so accurately with the gun in that tiny bag, and an unfamiliar one at that?"

"I've told you, you need to sense the gun as being part of you. Learn to feel it almost by second nature. The gun has become part of you."

"But how did you get *that* good?"

She contrived an Australian accent. "Oh yew know, us Kangaroo hunters, we only get one blinkin' shot befaw that Roo 'as bownsed roit outa there."

He laughed, "No, I don't believe you have trained on culling kangaroos."

"Roit on mite," she assured him.

"Do you ever use laser sights?"

"No, not really." She hesitated for a moment as he had, clearly, been doing some research and, perhaps, seeking the views of the other agents. Her smile persisted for almost a minute, like steam on a window, before she became more serious and looked steadily at him. After the slight pause, she was ready to answer some of his questions.

"In my view, they only add more clutter and weight to a gun. You can either shoot or not. Adding these modern gizmos won't suddenly make you a better shooter. No amount of paraphernalia is going to turn a poor shooter into an expert marksman. Remember too that many laser sights put a red dot on your target. It might look good at the cinema but do you really want to warn your opponent in this way? Also, if you can instinctively estimate the range and a little bit of the cross wind, for windage adjustment, you will feel more confident. Given that, you'll be able to shoot out to further distances in adverse conditions. Talking of those who cull kangaroos, for instance, they have to be able to fire accurately and quickly. If they needed lots of gadgetry, their target would be long gone. For a distance shot, then, a good shooter would, perhaps, need some magnification from a decent sight, to collect a bit more light, and very little else. Learn, above all, by the *feel* and not by what instruments tell you. The other thing is that, more often than not, you may be shooting under poor conditions. In addition, you may have to return fire before you have had the time to set up. If you are an experienced shooter who has not relied on all that technology, then the sooner you'll be able, in a tight spot, to open up. The other point to bear in mind is that a really advanced sniper rifle won't turn a bad marksman into a good one. It *may* help a good shooter to become a great one, perhaps."

He fired off some more shots.

"Not bad," she said.

"Try this." She moved behind him. Her long legs stretched back against the pencil skirt as she stood in close proximity, mirroring his stance and his shooting arm. Holding him round the waist with her left arm, her voice dipped by a semitone as she almost whispered in his ear. Her right arm followed his. Her chin was practically in contact with his right cheek as she came so close that it felt as if she were staring down the sight with him: precisely what she'd intended.

"Look, relax, the gun is now part of you. A little more," she said, nudging him gently, "don't hold your body so tense. Also, watch your breathing. Some shooters hold their breath as they fire, others, like me, breathe out slowly." He felt her soft breath on his cheek; she pushed against his hand carefully as she despatched a couple of shots.

She sensed him tightening through his torso as she held him. His muscular tone stiffened, the opposite of what she'd intended. She could also detect his respiration rising and becoming shallower as he failed to moderate it; his palm had become slightly moist.

He attempted to relax, to rein in his breathing, as he'd been taught. The more he tried, the more control moved further away from him. Her perfume, with its bright floral highlights, filled his head and his senses; he caught a slight waft of the shampoo that she'd used to wash her hair with that morning, also the smell of hide coming from the delicate soft leather of her skirt. Sensing the cashmere jumper caressing his arm as she clenched herself so closely to him, he could also feel those stunning, toned legs against his. All his efforts at self-control having failed at this point, he started shaking.

"Sorry, Miss Clancy, can we try something else?" he suggested.

She released him from her delicate embrace, not able to meet his eye as he turned. "Yes, of course, Tim," she agreed, becoming aware that her desire to show him some of the finer points of gun control had been a mistake; and had unwittingly distracted him, just at the point where he needed more focus. Training with Toby would have been very different, she realised, finally. Perhaps they'd known each other for so long that neither was fazed by the close proximity of the other.

"Forgive me, Tim, I'm so used to working alongside Toby. Come on, let's try our luck with the moving targets and see how you fare there. Just wait here a minute, I'll need to change for the rough and tumble of the moving targets." Tim thought for a moment just how Toby, or any man with a pulse, come to think of it, could fail to be affected by a woman who looked like that, felt like that and smelt like that – under any circumstances. He then shook his head in an attempt to restore his concentration.

She returned a few minutes later wearing a more functional one-piece suit in a dark-blue colour made of a heavy twill fabric that rustled a little as she walked. She'd also selected a pair of New Balance trainers, in a lighter blue. He could see the tiny Union Jacks emblazoned on them. The long hair had been tied back giving more prominence to her high cheek bones. For the first time he realised he could see Miss Clancy in a more realistic light. Not so much the vivacious woman but evidently the keen-eyed marksman who having identified her target wouldn't hesitate to bring it down. He knew, in that moment, this was a discipline that he, too, thirsted for.

She moved on to a different section of the giant warehouse that had been specially converted for such training. They called it their 'shooting shed'. The moving target section involved a timed trial. The aim, to dispose of as many hostile targets as possible: at the same time avoiding deliberately-placed decoy and friendly objects. Points would accumulate for hitting the kill zones of the enemy targets as the clock ticked by remorselessly. A simple score was then calculated, taking into account all these factors. Each contestant was allowed to use no more than two clips of bullets.

Clancy went first. Repositioning her goggles, she waited for the trial to start, as signified by a loud beeping noise. Her legs were held slightly apart, giving her a firm stance, as she gripped the revolver two-handed; she readied it for action in front of her. Safety was set to off. The lighting dipped. Smoke generators started up. Confusing sound effects rose to a crescendo, in order to provide as much distraction as possible. Navigating through the programmed assessment smoothly, she fired single kill shots to each hostile target so as to conserve her ammunition, thereby achieving maximum scores by neutralising as many threats as possible. Moreover, as she charged through the exercise she made full use of any cover that was available and at all times put herself in the best possible position to not only fire but also to get the best out of each bullet. False targets or friendly images appeared in an unexpected and random pattern. She steadfastly ignored those not representing a threat; continuing until she'd finished the simulation: both her allotted magazines were empty.

The whole thing was then reset, which took a few minutes. Tim waited nervously. Observing the impossibly high score that Clancy had notched up, he checked his gun, removed the safety and went in as soon as the beeper went off. Having made a mental note of her methods and also her progress; he attempted to emulate her. As each target sprang into view, he despatched it with a single kill shot. His timing and progress was excellent as he found his rhythm. Shot after shot was discharged quickly and cleanly; his score rose steadily and his time was not far behind hers. Suddenly, a target of a little old lady with a walking stick appeared. He turned, crouched down slightly and fired a perfect shot straight through the decoy's forehead. The friendly target fell forwards and hit the floor with a loud thudding noise that seemed to echo through the new recruit's consciousness. The klaxons activated intrusively, lighting levels came up to full brightness and smoke effects stopped as large fans provided extraction.

Clancy walked in to the target zone. She held out the printout showing the results from his timed trial.

"Tim, that was *not* bad. You did so well. Your shooting was accurate, and it was also fast."

He hung his head; he clearly wasn't ready to take any positives from her assessment.

"Until I killed the old lady with a head shot."

She touched his elbow in an attempt to get him to look at her. "And forgive me, but did I hear," she now cupped her other hand behind her ear and crouched down so that he could see her even though he still looked down, "that this is your *first* attempt, first as in even less than two, at this very difficult trial. *Very difficult* as in no way easy?"

He smiled but briefly and even managed to look at her, just for a moment. "I know I can do better, Miss Clancy."

She now nodded; her melodic voice dipped a little. "And so you shall, Tim, with more practice."

He ejected the empty magazine and placed it with the Glock on her upturned palm. He then made a fist with one hand and punched it into the open palm of the other. He looked down again. "I'm so disappointed."

She smiled again and touched his chin forcing him to look up. "That much I can see. The old lady is there to make us all *think* and to make us *all* better shooters. You aren't the first to shoot her and I'm pretty sure you won't be the last." Clancy now pointed to the plywood image of the old lady. "I'm sure you won't be surprised to learn that this is the tenth one of these that we've made? We all know her so well that she's been named, 'Mildred the destroyer'."

Tim now laughed as he saw the large hole that he'd created in the middle of her head. "Yes, seems like she took some damage."

Clancy laughed, too. "Oh, I think she'll be back, looking as innocent as ever. Remember, keep cool; your anger and disappointment have no place here; they are emotions that will confuse and slow your marksmanship, not enhance it. Your body stiffens under such influences, breaking up the natural rhythm of shooting that you began so well with." She now crouched, once again holding the gun as the precision instrument it was, in her hands, in front of her. "Be the shooting *machine*. By controlling your emotions, the accurate shots will flow as if by second nature from your revolver." She clicked the trigger on the empty gun, rhythmically. "This is the key: the way to win the battle. It will come as you practise, I promise. Remember, too, Tim, I helped build this simulator. It's all very new to you. A few months ago, you'd never fired a gun and yet here you are, working with the *finest!*"

She smiled, hoping he'd excuse her deliberate exaggeration and lack of coyness as an attempt to bring up his mood. Rather than laugh, as she'd hoped, he agreed with her self-assessment.

"And I am working with the finest," he said.

She paused, just for a moment, thinking that his marksmanship would be more than adequate; she now just had to worry about the rest – his confidence and self-belief. Knowing that this would be a discussion for later, she decided not to take him up on this: for now.

"Come on, let's move to the long-range shots and see how you fare with these."

"No doubt, you'll paste me at that, too."

She smiled, "Come on, then, I'll use my left hand."

"You'll still beat me."

"Mm, perhaps that's another thing you need a little bit of."

"What's that?"

"Positivity and self-belief. Each shot needs a little bit of you to go with that bullet. If it's full of *negativity* and defeatism, how can you expect it to find its target?"

"You talk as if it's alive."

"If you can, at least, accept that there may be something in what I am saying, then you'll be a better shooter. I think I should say, an even better shooter. These little nuances, a little pause perhaps in the practice of shooting can separate, in my *humble* view," she emphasised, "the good from the *great* shooter. Just look at your half-way scores in the moving targets. Until you shot the old lady, they were a whisker behind mine. I can't see anything there to be unhappy with."

"Except shooting the old lady, perhaps?"

"Well, next time I am sure she will come through unscathed. Though, be careful, because they do tend to move her about a bit, and have her pop up in front of the bank robber with the assault rifle!"

Entering a 4-digit code gave her access to a reinforced, secure, locker containing several high-precision rifles, together with an assortment of sniper scopes. This allowed the new recruits to try different models. Clancy showed him how to prepare one of them, and also how to use the sniper scope. Demonstrating different types of rifle, she allowed him to try each one. Furthermore, she had brought along her own, which was a custom-built version, specifically tailored to her requirements.

"Use a few different rifles and get the feel for them. Once you have an idea of which you prefer, then we'll order one just for you."

"Wow, sounds expensive."

"Well, Tim, remember self-belief, you'll be worth every penny. To Horizon, you already are."

He lay prone next to her, as targets were prepared at the maximum distance of just less than a standard football pitch. As he lay alongside she couldn't help but notice his shoulder muscles and toned upper torso.

"Tim, have you been working out? You look great."

He blushed uncontrollably, an especial danger with one who had fair skin and pale-blue eyes.

"Just a little, Miss Clancy. I figured that now is a good time to get myself fit."

She continued to look with some amazement and more than a little admiration. "Well, Tim, if I may say so, it really suits you."

He rattled the gun as he moved the bolt action, in an attempt to divert her from her inquisitive expression.

Taking the hint, she produced a clip of bullets. "These slot in using the bolt action, one at a time. This creates more precision, both for the rifle and for you."

"Really?"

"Yes, in chambering each round, one needs to really think about each and every shot. There's none of this spraying with a hail of bullets that one sees in the movies. For us, in the lore of the sniper, each shot counts. And, sometimes, you may only have one shot."

Some time later, they walked out of the large shooting shed that was disguised as a sound recording studio. ITV assumed that the BBC owned it, and the BBC assumed that

ITV did. Moreover, because it was a sound studio, no one ever thought twice about the noises emanating from there at odd times of the day. It sat between two equally large TV sound studios in Media City.

Once again she held up his score sheets, pointing excitedly. "Tim, what an amazing score sheet. Your rifle work is superb. I can see that I'll have very little to teach you."

Once again, he looked down at his feet rather than at her. "Just the old lady to work on."

Miss Clancy looked away, she could see that he was fixated on one tiny error among a set of score sheets that anyone would be proud of, including most of the other agents.

He looked back at the shooting shed as they walked away and over to the café. He tucked his hands in the pockets of his jeans.

"You have some impressive facilities. This little lot, even if it's rented, must cost a small fortune. In fact it seems to me that no expense has been spared."

"Well, either thank, or blame, Toby for that. He firmly believes that in order to be the 'finest', we all need the best equipment, together with continuous on-going training."

"But the overheads must be enormous?"

"That they are. Long ago, after losing his entire family, Toby made a decision as to what was important in his life; without doubt you can tell that having pots of money standing in bank accounts wasn't what he chose."

"But surely, one man can't afford all this?"

"Pretty much, yes." She began, nodding. "Don't forget that our missions generate significant revenue, and he ploughs it all back in. Remember, too, that the people we invoice are not on their uppers. Furthermore, they are often *very* generous when we come through. I appreciate it's a pretty exclusive club, but the scrapes they have a habit of getting themselves into call for special and discreet intervention. They are then suitably, and eternally, grateful. Sometimes, even more important, are the favours we can, on occasion, call in. For instance, when we do the long-range shooting, out in the open, we use the Army range. Not just anyone gets to do target practice on there. Toby cultivates a lot of friends, contacts, and people with influence. On some of our difficult missions, it shows. Outside intervention can make the difference between success and failure. Don't let his quiet and understated appearance fool you, he has a lot of 'pull', shall I say?"

He passed a quick exploratory look in her direction. "So, can I ask, did my Dad settle an invoice?"

"Mm, I am sure we will talk about that another time. I can say, however, that there are some operations when running a profit is not the primary objective. Toby was determined to go forward with the mission to do with Alexis, for instance. When I looked at the costing for that mission, there was no way it was going to wash its face. He still wanted to go ahead, and that's when I knew."

"Knew?"

"That she was going to be so important to him. I saw it before he did!"

"And how do you feel about that?"

"Delighted, for sure. She is a lovely girl."

Clancy now looked at him carefully. She anticipated his next question. All she had to then do was remind him that he already knew the answer. "I believe that I told you.

Remember, when one has a losing hand, one has to play each card to its maximum effect."

"I know, I know, you told me. I just couldn't believe it when I read the transcripts from that undertaking. It all seemed so real, and yet you say it was only to bring about a certain set of events?"

"That's about it, Tim, and it worked beautifully. I am sure if you would like to check my probability figures, you will see that the strategy I followed was marginally going to be more effective than all others. I won't lie, however; it was a close call. Ultimately, I went with my instinct, I suppose. "

"Yes, but how can one predict human behaviour and emotion in that way?"

"A lot of the time we can't; it's perhaps a bit like the difference between shooting with lots of paraphernalia strapped to one's gun, or just feeling the wind on one's cheek and loosing off the shot anyway."

"Yes, Miss Clancy, I think I am beginning to see. I just have so much to learn, and I can't even sort the basics like shooting."

Tim bought the coffees. Clancy sat watching him as he paid the barista. The pretty girl kept staring at him and even though he'd scanned his contactless card she couldn't help but engage him in more conversation.

"You are new round here, aren't you? Do you work for the BBC or ITV?"

"No, not exactly. I've been brought in more as a consultant."

"Ooh, I knew you were someone important. Does that mean you'll be popping in from time to time?"

"Yes, I will. In fact, I think you'll see me regularly."

She almost whooped with delight. "Ooh, I can't wait. I'm Janet by the way and it's so nice to have met you."

Looking more than a little embarrassed, he shook the offered hand and was even more aware of those queuing behind him. "I'm Tim, Janet, and I'll be back, as they say in all the best movies."

Janet cooed with delight, once again, and as Tim left the counter she darted a poisonous look in Clancy's direction.

Clancy sat facing him in the coffee shop; he remained somewhat crestfallen. She was keen to promote a much more positive stance. "Wow, Tim, it seems you have a fan."

Tim shrugged but dipped his posture and his voice as he replied. "I can't see why, Miss Clancy. That young woman doesn't know me. I can't see what she'd see in me anyway."

Clancy looked at Tim, she could see exactly what the female assistant could see in him. Without doubt, looks were not his problem; she realised that his self-belief was a fragile thing and it had clearly been damaged rather than built over the years. She knew that he was twenty-eight, the same age as she but he'd clearly had a very different upbringing.

"Very well, Tim, I can see Janet over there needs no convincing. Maybe it's just you we have to work on. Your marksmanship is really coming on." She now enumerated things he should be pleased with as she indicated them using her long fingers. "You have taken to it quicker than most. Please remember, too, that we won't be entering you for the Olympics. You just have to be a *good enough* shooter, as are all the other agents. There are so many skills to learn that you may excel in other areas. For my money, and as regards the shooting, I think you'll just get better and better. Book a few more training sessions and I think I will have trouble keeping ahead of you." She touched his chin lightly, so that he looked up and, inevitably, over at her. She smiled back at him like a big sister showing her brother how to ride without stabilisers – or so she hoped.

"What's more, you can manage a fast rate of shooting and you are accurate when on the move, which is a very difficult skill for many to acquire. Anyone can hit a target with a well set-up rifle, under controlled conditions. However, if one takes them out into the field, one can soon see it unravel. This is where I think you will come into your own; under real-life conditions, you will shine."

"I don't think I'll ever be as good as you."

"Just how do you know *that?*" a slightly exasperated look appeared on her face, as she feared that his low mood centred on defeatism – an emotion she could not hold with.

"But you, you Miss Clancy, are amazing. An amazing shooter, I mean," he lied, on the verge of admitting much more.

"Tim, I've been doing this for quite a few years now. Practice, practice." She tilted her head, doing her best to engage with his downcast eyes. "We shall see how you develop with time. Some of us are better at some things than at others."

"Why do I get the impression that you, Miss Clancy, are simply good at everything?"

She laughed; her light mood, which refused to be dragged down by his negativity, was infectious as he tried to smile back.

"Now, Tim, I'm sure you know that can't possibly be true. Perhaps, when you've got to know me, you will see some of my many deficiencies! It may well be, there are simply too many for me to list here."

He stared, once again for a little too long, at her mesmerising brown eyes; trying, but failing, to find the slightest flaw with the prettiest girl he'd set eyes on. Although they looked deep brown now, there were times when her eyes looked lighter, approaching hazel or even amber. One thing remained: at all times, they looked amazing. She blushed and glanced away. A second or two later she was ready to respond, deciding that the sooner the better, if their working relationship was to survive: if he was to continue in their organisation.

"Tim, don't think I'm not flattered. I see the way you stare, and I am truly fortunate to be held in such esteem."

Pausing in that moment, she floundered in searching for the most appropriate words. She grasped that navigating through this would strengthen or destroy their future work together. Rather than attempt to clarify such thoughts, she tried a different tack.

"You realise we'll be working closely together; you, me and many of the others. Each mission will mean a different team being assigned. You have already seen how we allocate agents to specific missions, often at short notice, depending on their location and their skill-set. We might need a shooter, or someone who can hack a computer and so on." At that point, she let the pause open expectantly. A moment later he complied, as he grasped her logic.

"Yes, I know I stare a little too much. I am sorry. I am making you uncomfortable."

Clancy laughed, "No, not at all! It's just that the others are noticing."

"Yes, I'm sure they are saying that I fancy you."

"Well, probably not that," she lied. "I don't mind; as far as I am concerned, you can stare as much as you like. It's you I am thinking of," she continued to lie. "When we are deployed on missions, the others need to know you are in there with them and not drifting off or thinking of other things. The members of a given team need to be able to count on you and you on them. Their lives and, ultimately, yours, with some of our more active operations, as well as the success of the mission, will depend on each person carrying out his or her job to the letter. Besides, I am sure you won't want the embarrassment."

"Yes, yes you are correct, I am sorry Miss C. I'll do better in future, so that you and they, will be able to count on me, I promise."

"Don't beat yourself up about it. I'm sure we'll be okay."

"I would like to say, I am so pleased to be a part of the team; it means a lot to me. For the first time in a long time, I believe I can be a part of the whole and also, in some small way, make a positive difference to the outcome. You were correct in what you said, when you brought me out of that gambling den; my life was going nowhere pretty quickly. I am sorry I was so flippant with you when you gave me your card. I am glad that I kept it and took up Horizon's offer."

"That's more like it, Tim." She rewarded him again with another smile.

"So, may I ask, how did you meet Toby?"

She paused before choosing her words carefully, "Well, let's just say he pulled me from a train wreck."

Tim laughed, "Oh okay then, don't tell me if you don't want to."

The conversation moved on. It was to be much later however, deep in the night, that he realised that she'd allowed the release of a tiny, but vital, piece of personal information. Having thought she was joking, he failed to pick up the signs; the darted look and the pause, followed by the more searching look she gave him. Sensing that he hadn't grasped what she was telling him and why, she'd quickly moved on the topic of conversation as they sat at the table.

That night, as he drifted in and out of sleep, with time for quiet reflection, he realised what he'd missed: something crucial. What was more, it was a tiny piece, something important and concrete, that she was ready to gift him. He could have kicked himself, for he knew that Miss Clancy revealed only what she was ready to; and even then, at a time of her choosing. He wondered how long it would be before she afforded him another chance. The solitary bright spot in front of him was the fact that he was learning: painfully slowly perhaps, but learning nevertheless. In any event, he wasn't going to waste the greatest opportunity that had come his way in a long time: as he had with just about everything in his life up to this point. He then thought that given time, if he quietly got on with his training and learning the ways of the Horizon organisation, sooner or later he'd be ready to man up, take the plunge and simply ask her.

They finished their coffees. Tim waved to Janet, who looked crestfallen that he was leaving but did manage another look of undiluted poison in Clancy's direction.

"Well, Tim, I think Janet there thinks she has competition," Clancy continued just as Tim thought that he should be so lucky. "Let's go over to the offices; I believe Toby wanted a quick word."

They went up to the top floor and waited outside Toby's office. They could see he was in conversation with, no doubt, a client. On seeing the two of them waiting, he approached and invited both of them in.

The thin chap in the impeccable suit stood as they entered.

"Clancy, this is Mr Nukumobo, who is seeking our help with a difficult situation in which he finds himself."

"Ah yes, Miss Clancy, I saw you last night at the embassy. May I say, what wonderful shooting."

Clancy nodded but still looked a little suspicious. This stranger appeared to either know or have been told quite a bit and she knew it wasn't like Toby to reveal details of any of their missions to anyone. Sensing her concern, Toby came round from his desk. "Mitral, this is Tim, one of our newer recruits."

A long hand came forward with prominent, bony fingers. "Tim, yes I am pleased to meet you. You are very lucky to be working with such people."

"I believe I am, Mr Nukumobo," Tim replied without a moment's hesitation in pronouncing the unusual surname.

Toby took them all through to the meeting room where Tim sat next to their visitor and Clancy sat facing. Toby went to find some coffees and left the three of them talking.

Sensing Clancy's reluctance, their guest sought to gain her confidence while Toby organised the drinks.

"Miss Clancy, I was lucky enough to be in the embassy last night. I'd gone there to see if I could persuade the Americans to help me with a difficult problem. I know that when I have gone, Mr Richmond will want to discuss this with you in private. He has told me that he has no intention of helping me without your agreement. By sheer chance I was able to see how good you were with the gun and also how professional is your organisation. The Americans won't help me, and I was wondering if Horizon would be able to assist me?"

"Well, we will certainly take a look, Mr Nukumobo and if we are able to help you, then I am sure that's exactly what we will do."

"I saw your wonderful skills, courtesy of looking the right way just at the right time. I hope you realise that I have no business in revealing to others, regardless of your decision today, just what I saw."

"It's gratifying to learn that Mr Nukumobo."

"And you Tim, I see that you are a new recruit. May I ask what you were doing before you were signed up?"

"Oh, just wasting my life, it has to be said, Mr Nukumobo."

"Ah in that case, Tim, I can see that things have changed or are about to change for you"

"I do hope so, Sir."

Clancy could not let such an exchange pass without comment. "Tim was detailed to mission surveillance last night, Mr Nukumobo, and I can reveal that our success in finding and disarming the bomber was in large part due to his efforts."

The tall African nodded, having seen something in that minute that few could see. "I can tell that the team works very effectively together and I must congratulate you all."

At this point Toby returned with a tray of coffees and Mr Nukumobo stood up.

"You have been most kind, Toby. I know you will have a lot to discuss with Miss Clancy. It might be best if I leave the two of you to do so in an unimpeded way." As he shook hands with them all both Clancy and Tim stood, too.

Realising that their visitor was as diplomatic as he was observant, Tim told him that he was just leaving and would go down in the lift with him. Before he left, Toby gave Mr Nukumobo a card and advised him that they would come to a decision that day and inform him straight away. The white card, embossed with a delicate tracery of metal oxides, glinted in the intense lighting of the meeting room. He also informed the tall, slim gentleman that the number displayed on the card was available internationally twenty-four hours a day.

Toby sat next to Clancy and pushed a coffee in front of her.

"How is our latest recruit doing?"

"Oh, he's coming along very well. He is a bit hard on himself and very negative. However, I'll soon beat that out of him. I think he'll easily make the grade."

"He still seems so much in awe of you, Clancy. Is he managing to handle it all? I catch some of the looks he gives off in your direction. Do you think he is going to fit in? I overheard a couple of agents gossiping on how he has a crush on you."

"Oh, really?" she lied, doing her best to retain the surprise in her voice though in truth she had detected much the same.

"So do you think he will be able to step up to become agent material?"

"You know, Toby, I think he will. I have given him a bit of a pep talk. He really wants this and I have indicated to him that, if he is to be a success, then his personal feelings need to be held in abeyance."

"And do you think he is up to that?"

"I do hope so, Toby, as I think he will make a good agent. He was excellent last night and his shooting is really coming on. I think he has a good feel for what is expected of him. He certainly has that desire to fit in and do well. I am sure the rest we can sort."

Toby nodded with some finality indicating that he now wanted to seek her views about their visitor.

Clancy nodded towards the chair that their visitor had vacated. "He's no pushover, Toby. Just what did he see?"

"Well, Clancy, it seems just about everything. The funny thing is that he was there almost by accident; he'd gone to beg the Americans for help. They'd turned him down flat, not wishing to get involved."

"And we do?"

"You will be the judge of that, Clancy."

"So what do we have?"

"Ah, yes, Miss Nukumobo. She was captured in Nigeria last week, near the border with Niger along the northern edge. I'm afraid it's a bit lawless. Lots of girls have been abducted and we feel it's probably the work of one man. He and his band of *heroes* sell the girls into prostitution in Europe, drug running or into modern day slavery. Miss Nukumobo is the only daughter of Mitral Nukumobo, the chap who has just gone."

"Yes, I know, I can smell the money; no doubt one of your rich, toff friends?"

Toby laughed. "You may know him as the owner of *Stulag Steel and Fabrication*, which is Nigeria's foremost steel producer. He was trying to get a team together to pull her out, but he needs our help. He needs people he can trust, that's why he came to Blighty. He has a vague idea of her whereabouts but the chap that took her is very influential and people become tight-lipped when asked about any of his 'business' adventures.

We think she's probably been taken with lots of other girls over the border into Niger. It's a tricky assignment, I'm afraid, but I think it's something within our capabilities. How do you feel?"

"Very well then, Toby, I can see it's dear to your heart. I can only agree. I'd really like to run down some of these bastards who feel they can operate above the law. I'll get the planning team in tonight and brief them. We will start running up some metrics. Do you want to get out there, as soon as, and liaise with Mr Nukumobo? You may be able to fly back with him if you hurry. I know you hate slumming it on commercial airliners, sitting next to those who have fewer than ten rooms in their homes."

Toby ignored, as usual, her dig at those she liked to describe as his 'posh' friends.

"Yes, Clancy, time is of the essence, I'm afraid. Such girls are usually treated appallingly and badly abused. Many of them who fall in some way short of the grisly plans in store for them simply disappear. Mitral will fund our entire operation and provide a significant bonus should we get her out in one piece. He will also pay a bonus for every additional abductee we can set free."

"Okay then, Toby, you get to the airport with him. When I have calculated some rough outlines, I will assemble a team of agents and brief them tonight. The other pending cases can wait for a few days. Perhaps we can look at them as soon as we have rescued the steel magnate's daughter?"

"That's great, I'll just grab a few things. Stevens is available, so I'll take him with me and we can then start sending back information as soon as we can unearth some. I'll phone Mitral straight away to inform him that we will accept the mission. I am sure he will help with transport and local information. In any event, I will gain as much intelligence as I can and do my best to check it for authenticity. I will then send what I have uncovered back to you here before you fly out with the strike force."

Toby stood and walked to the door. "Thank you for this, Clancy."

"Toby, that's my pleasure. Also when you have a minute, and I accept that you haven't if you are going to catch Mr Nukumobo, then I need to talk to you."

"Oh, about anything in particular? Is it about Tim, do you think he is in trouble?"

"No, it's not about him and it will wait; it's waited long enough and another few days won't hurt."

He paused, having known her for so long he could sense the importance of what she wanted to say. Under ordinary circumstances he'd have sat down there and then and asked her to clarify. She was correct, however, now was a good time to intercept the steel magnate and gain some much-needed information. He looked at her with a little unease, "I'll get going then, Clancy, I'll be in touch as soon as we have landed."

Clancy sat down at the table and stared out over the old docks of Salford Quays. Toby seemed almost grateful that she'd agreed to the mission, which meant that he too could see the inherent dangers. She also worried about Tim. She could see that uncertainty over Tim's presence in the organisation was having a destructive effect on the whole team. It had even reached as far as Toby and it wasn't like him to pick up on what she'd assumed were purely temporary problems, which would have been resolved, if given time: a luxury that she no longer had. She knew there and then that the situation with regard to Tim was more urgent than she'd foreseen. Certainly, she couldn't just assume that Tim would sort himself out and all the others would just pat him on the back and welcome him. If Toby had made mention of the gossiping undercurrents, then it must be pretty widespread.

She realised then that she was either going to have to try a bold manoeuvre to settle it, or accept Tim's departure as being the only way forward. She knew what she was going to have to do. It was a high-risk strategy with little by way of safeguards that she could put in place. Clancy realised, when all was said and done, that there was, at this juncture, no alternative. Fortune favoured the bold, or so she'd been told. It was time to put this maxim to the test. One further thing assisted her at this point; Mr Nukumobo seemed to get on very well with not just Toby, but Tim too. She would use this to her advantage in the plan that was forming quickly in her mind. Without doubt, she'd have to lie to everyone, but it wouldn't be the first time she'd done such a thing – especially for the greater good.

CHAPTER III

Time of Trial

A few hours later, Clancy was going through a summary of the planned assignment. She had assembled the fairly large team, including those that had been available as well as those who could be diverted from other operations. Twenty people watched her as she outlined the mission. She walked in front of the giant screen, rather like a general planning a spring offensive. She paced up and down, her voice carefully and clearly summarised each of the salient points in turn.

"Here is a picture of Santhi Nukumobo. She is being held captive by a gang of degenerates led by this man, Mr Mdombku, who is a self-appointed leader in Niger. He likes to go by the title of 'Excellency'. What he is excellent at," she paused a little, letting the words sink in, "are some obscene and distasteful practices that trade in human misery for his financial benefit and, no doubt, other things too horrible to go into here. What we would like to do is throw a spanner in his works, if at all possible." She clicked her hand-held control so that a picture of the despotic leader of the organisation they were interested in appeared. "He lives in a large, palatial establishment in southern Niger and has a penchant for highly lucrative cross-border raids into Nigeria where girls are abducted right under the noses of their families and also the authorities. He acts with impunity. The police are unable or unwilling to take action. This is because they are frightened of reprisals against themselves and their families or are bought off with derisory sums of money. The girls are then either used for prostitution or, his favourite, sold as modern-day slaves into Western Europe. We are hoping, on this occasion, that he has taken the wrong girl. Her father has retained us to go and get her. As an aside to the main mission, we are planning to free as many captives as we can find and return them to their loved ones. It's time this hero of modern manhood receives his comeuppance, although it's unlikely he'll be there in person as he usually has others do his dirty work for him. Disrupting this, by putting a few of his cronies out of action, we hope will make him think again and see the error of his ways. At the very least, we hope that he will realise he can't just do what he wants while trading on the abuse and misery of others for his own gratification and financial gain.

"Santhi is our main target. It goes without saying that it's vital that we get her out safely. I am going to assign one of you to be her personal close-protection agent." Clancy now looked keenly at the rank and file of the agents as they all wondered who was about to be given this key role. She went on. "As she is pivotal to the whole mission, this person will be the one we all support while he goes in to get her. Once she has been located and, hopefully, freed, then we will expand the operation to release as many of the girls as we can, if not all of them." Her voice dipped by a semi-tone; here it was, the most important role was about to be assigned and several of the more senior agents licked their lips or swallowed hard with anticipation. Her line of sight traversed the room until she saw the person she wanted. She then walked a little way towards him. "Mr Nukumobo has asked for someone he knows to be in this role. Therefore, the agent I have in mind is you, Tim. Do you think you can do this for me?" Not for the first time, she'd chosen her words with care and neither a hint of the gamble she was about to take, nor uncertainty, crossed her business-like expression.

Clancy thought for a minute that he was going to look round as she watched him. It then swiftly dawned on the new recruit that she really did mean him. Several of the other agents quickly glanced in his direction, attempting to see something of what she'd evidently seen. Tim became aware of the weight of stares upon him. Many observers considered that it was unusual for such an inexperienced agent to be given a crucial responsibility. Everyone there present could only wonder why this should be so. Some harboured other thoughts, but did their best to dismiss them. Only Clancy and one other person in the room were aware of the contingencies that had been put in place. Tim nodded and did his best, but failed, to generate the air of indifferent nonchalance that he craved at the moment when eyes were upon him. As her perceptive vision held him for that instant, the only emotions she could detect on his face were anxiety and panic.

She continued to talk, being aware of, but ignoring, a slight ripple of surprise and disquiet in the room. Every time she paused, more took the opportunity to look at the new kid on the block – the rookie agent. Many were worried by what they saw and wondered what would the casualty rate be if he fluffed it.

"Rehearsals all day tomorrow, please, and we fly out overnight so, as you all know by now what I am going to say next – get some sleep. Toby is out there as we speak. I should hear tonight but assume take off is at 5 am Wednesday unless you are notified to the contrary. Please, all of you, make sure your jabs are up to date and, if in doubt, phone admin today so we can get them done at short notice. This applies to you especially, Tim, as you'll need jabs for Yellow Fever and all sorts of other nasties."

The team arrived at the airport some time after 4 am at a remote part of the airfield usually reserved for freight operations. Both the personnel and their equipment were soon loaded. They waited with more nervousness than usual. Very few had been able to comprehend why Tim had been chosen. More significantly, they worried what fate awaited them with an inexperienced agent in a key role, whom they were then expected to support come what may. It cast a pall of gloom over their collective mood and the mission as a whole. Lack of sleep for nearly all of them did nothing to improve their outlook. They could only hope that Clancy knew something that they didn't. In truth, she was rarely wrong. Perhaps there was a first time for everything. The aeroplane taxied until their clearance to depart came from the air traffic controllers. A few minutes later the special charter, with the entire team on-board, took off from Manchester, as planned, at 5 am. The Boeing 757-200, sprayed in an anonymous sky-blue, featured Rolls-Royce engines and winglets, which would extend the efficiency of the plane and thus its range, to a maximum.

Toby had supplied video surveillance footage; also a last-minute update, reflecting weather conditions and the terrain they would encounter. Plans were re-worked accordingly. Tim's central role was not altered. One or two members of the team continued to look at him, and also Clancy, suspiciously. Her expression remained focussed, business-like and impassive at each of those glances. She caught Tim observing her on one occasion. Clancy had known all along that he'd accepted her card and acted on it because he liked what he saw. She could only hope, however, that such considerations were of little moment compared to the more powerful thoughts where he decided to do something with his life and what sort of person he wanted to become. She'd said as much to him during their drive back to his apartment. It was time to see, and no doubt it would be apparent to all, including him, very soon, if he could make that leap from playboy to covert agent. His quiet demeanour, as he sat by himself, perhaps reflected the changes that he was putting in place within. She wondered, objectively, what thoughts were progressing through his head and also whether he would step up or fail. She understood that by the end of the day she and he, as well as everyone else, would know.

"Any questions for me, Tim?" she eventually said after she caught him looking once again.

"No, Miss Clancy, thank you," he returned with nervousness on his face that was as nought to that existing within. She sat back in her seat and pretended to be asleep, though her active and resourceful mind ran thousands of scenarios and a million thoughts as she did so.

The plane flew throughout the morning, covering the four thousand miles to Katsina airport, Nigeria, which was the closest airport to their target: one that would not only be able to accommodate their transport plane, but would also arouse no more than minimal suspicion.

Upon landing, the team disembarked and retrieved their equipment from the aircraft hold. They got into waiting transport. True to his word, Mr Nukumobo had made sure that transport was waiting for them as soon as they set foot on African soil. The plane was immediately re-fuelled and turned round in preparation, should the situation demand, for a rapid departure. As soon as their equipment was loaded, they crossed the border into Niger for the drive north.

At this time of year the weather was fairly temperate. Being not far from the equator the length of the days varied very little. However, the dry dusty conditions and the thinning vegetation meant that their convoy could be readily spotted. As they left the more ideal deciduous forest and woodland savannah of Nigeria behind, the conditions soon began to thin into less-useful brush-grass, but an environment that still supported at least some vegetation and crops. As they went even further north, vegetation thinned out still more to a mix of grass brush and thicket. Had they continued to travel north semi-desert would have soon taken over and then, in turn, the great Sahara desert. Following the river gave them some more protection and they were able to use its route as a guide and also to reduce the dust cloud their convoy gave rise to. Just over an hour later they met up with Toby and Stevens at the rendezvous point just to the north west of the city of Maradi.

They decided to avoid the town centre so as not to draw attention to themselves. While the team assembled and set up, Toby joined Clancy in the Range Rover. He closed the door. Uncharacteristic worry was etched to his face, as he struggled with his inner thoughts.

"Is it true you've asked Tim to be the one who protects and recovers the target? It's a pretty important role. Do you think he's ready for that?"

She chose her words with care, her speech somewhat slower than usual, "Some would say possibly not, though I believe otherwise. I think now is a good time to find out."

"Is that wise? If he messes up, it could affect the entire mission."

"I'm of the view that he will come through. He is filled with such negativity and lack of self-belief. The others sense that he is a bit of a starry-eyed dreamer. I am hoping there's more to him than that: he needs to discover this, too. I suspect that the way to get the best out of him, while at the same time give him some confidence, is to place him in a central role and trust him to succeed. Once he's done that, then I'm sure he won't look back."

"Clancy, what if he *fails?*" a little desperation now modulating his voice. "And this is a tricky operation, a long way from home. Could you not have let him in more gently? Were there not easier missions you could have immersed him in?"

She nodded, as if accepting his point, or at least acknowledging that she'd thought of doing precisely that, but had rejected such a plan.

"No, I think it has to be something now and it has to be a substantial role. The team are too restless and he is undermining his own skills with negative thoughts. It has to be him and it has to be done quickly. They are all on a bit of a knife-edge. I think he will come good for me. Furthermore, if we are to get him on the right track from the outset, we have to place some responsibility on his shoulders. My assessment of him is that this is what he has

been lacking all his life. I think the others see him as some feckless playboy who dreams of a more exciting hobby, perhaps. I, however, think he is ready to make the leap to *be* the serious and competent agent who can be depended on."
He listened, but all the non-verbal clues on his expression gave off nothing but incredulity. She knew that she'd have to challenge him and that now was the time. "Look, Toby, you don't usually question my judgment in this way."

"Maybe he has lacked a responsible role because he *buckles*? I'm sorry; it's just that I see the way he looks at you. Others do too. Are you trying to prove something?" he asked, with further anxiety creeping into his voice.

"And what might that be?"

"That you are strong and dispassionate, that personal feelings have not got in the way, here."

"I am!" she offered and, looking offended, "and they haven't." as he continued,

"and that you always commit the best person for a given role, based on objectivity."

"Exactly, I do! And it is."

"What! Are you certain that you are not a little confused? But you see the way he looks at you? You were the one who wanted to give him the card. What will the others think?"

"The others will *trust* me," she bit her tongue quickly, to prevent the words that might then have followed 'unlike you'. Feeling the anger rise within, she knew that it was neither the time nor place to reveal to him the depth of resentment she felt. She would, however, revisit it and soon. "Look, Toby, it's about him, his development. We don't want some quitter, just a spectator, simply drifting on. Yes, I gave him the card and he took it. He is ready to step up and *be* the hero. We want someone who can act decisively and assume responsibility. Now is the time to find out if he *is* that person."

"I can't help but feel it's too soon, and you are *wrong*. What happens if the mission goes pear-shaped and one of the girls, or our main target, gets shot or injured?"

"This is the best way; my assessment of him is that he will come through for us and deliver what we hope, and what *I* expect. There isn't any other agenda. Are you implying otherwise?"

She stopped and studied him more carefully. It wasn't like Toby to doubt her in this way. Her instinct about Tim's unprofessional behaviour had been correct. He was already having a damaging effect on the morale of the whole force. This is why she had placed him in a vital role. This was the time to expunge doubts about him, and reassure those who thought he was simply so much baggage: whose personal feelings had long got in the way of his effectiveness and usefulness within the team. She continued to look keenly at Toby. She knew that he could overrule her; this had not happened before, although he had pushed for the operation involving Alexis; going against her advice. She knew at that time that it was something – that she was *someone* – he hungered for. Clancy just had to go along with it. To do anything else, given what she'd gleaned, would have been unwise as well as cruel. Moreover, he still had not discovered all the things that she'd had to do to get that mission back on track. She had decided never to reveal any details of what that had involved. Curiously, of all the agents, only Tim had guessed exactly what the mission, with regard to Alexis, had come down to. This is why he had assumed that she was in love with Toby: for, surely, only someone who loved him could have risked everything in the way that she had.

Nor did she choose to reassure Toby that she had assigned Brady to shadow Tim and take over if the need arose, even if he were killed or captured. This was the penalty she chose to impose on him for not trusting her. Ultimately, he was either going to have faith in her or countermand her. He chose the former, looking away from her steady gaze, while hoping she would not guess how close a decision it was. When all was said and done, not showing allegiance to her would mean the end of Horizon; he knew this, and he knew that she did, too.

"Yes, yes Clancy, forgive me, I am just a bit nervous so far from home in a covert operation of this kind. So many things could go wrong. You are right, we have to put him in the line of fire, if he is ever to be of use to us, and the others have to see that too. I just didn't want personal feelings to obscure things." Although he spoke the words, it was only his confidence in Clancy that carried them. His private thoughts on Tim were very different and he couldn't prevent some of them from surfacing in that moment.

"Do you think we've been hasty taking him on? Were *we* wrong to offer him the card? He seems so, so, awestruck...." Toby began, but thought better of crystallising his words in more detail.

"No I don't. I think he'll be fine. I have had a good talk with him and he understands. Besides, you agreed, as I recall, that I could give him the card?"

"I just worry that he can't help himself," he suggested, gravely.

Her eyes at their deepest, deliberative shade continued to hold him. "We shall see, and we shall do so today."

She nodded and smiled disarmingly. He'd reminded her; perhaps unintentionally, perhaps not, of the favours she'd called in from him as regards Tim. Ultimately, it came down to something simple and yet obscure; Toby could not understand why she'd taken such a stance on Tim – the Johnny-come-lately. He wondered for a second or two whether she had gone soft on him. It was widely held that she could have any man she wanted, with just a flash of the stunning smile. He had seen, on many occasions, how she could manipulate them, any of them, whenever she chose, like putty in her hands. He couldn't think there was a romantic interest in Tim and this is why she'd put him forward in this way. Perhaps she was simply putting him forward now *because* there was no love interest there and she needed to demonstrate this both to others and to herself. Indeed, if there were, it would be bad news for the whole organisation, especially if such feelings were now clouding her judgement. In any event, ultimately it came down to one simple thing amidst all the potential motives that one might have as regards the other – he had to trust her judgement and anything else was a secondary argument.

Her next words broke his train of thought. "If I might change the subject, then. We have a little job to do here today. Are you staying here with me?" He nodded his agreement. "Very well then, could you help me to set up over there? We could do with a bit more covering fire. We are to provide sniper support just before our team go in. I take it you are sure of Santhi's whereabouts?"

"Yes, exactly where I reported. Our information says they are all being held in a groundnut warehouse just east of the village over there. Sources say they have all been there for some days, including Santhi. They are waiting for transport to be brought up."

The main force had gone on to be in close proximity to their target. Stevens had joined them. They'd hidden their 4x4 transports by parking them out of the way, behind a small clump of trees. Camouflage netting, thrown over the vehicles, had also helped to reduce their visibility.

Clancy was planning to use a similar group of trees to set up. She could see the warehouse through her binoculars. She got out of the Range Rover and removed a large oblong case in matt dark-green from the boot. It had stencilled letters on the front that simply said "Clancy". This contained her Accuracy International L115A1, thought to be the best sniper rifle in the modern world. Hers had been specially modified; the folding stock had been re-crafted in extremely light materials, which had reduced the all-up weight to just over 6Kgs. The 27 inch barrel had been bored out, with a five-groove spiral, to one in nine, so that the bullet was made to spin more vigorously as it travelled, before being ejected, bound for its target. This meant that every nine inches the round would be spun, by such rifling, rather than the more typical every ten or more. This was said to give the bullet more stability on its trajectory. She used hand-finished Lapua Magnum rimless cartridges of calibre 0.338 inches. These are cartridges designed by a Finnish rifle manufacturer specifically for the AI rifle, comprising a rimless, bottlenecked centrefire cartridge. Centrefire cartridges have their propellant triggered in the middle of the base of the cartridge and are more robust in handling as well as giving higher pressure, leading to longer range and greater energy in the projectile. Today, Clancy was using standard ones, but had also been known to use specially modified, *wildcat* cartridges and overpressure ones on certain missions.

He watched as she set up her rifle, making sure that the support rest was on stable ground and that she still had a vantage point. She'd already estimated the windage, which was the likely effect of the wind on the bullet as it travelled the two seconds to its target over the distance. Then there was the fall of the shot as it progressed. This, too, she'd already calculated. He selected his own rifle, which was similar but unmodified. He'd accepted that he didn't have the same skills as Clancy and thus modifying the weapon would produce no further gains.

She lay prone next to him. He looked over at her. This was her element, as a dolphin born into water; the field before her of miniscule targets, of pinpoint precision, was her domain. Moreover, it was but one among many in which she excelled. She was the core of Horizon and just about all both respected and looked up to her; as she had shown herself to be capable of out-shooting and out-fighting so many of her male contemporaries. She could also outrun them and, if the need arose on occasion, out-drink them. Without doubt, she had earned every ounce of praise that in quieter and confidential moments they heaped upon her. She had guessed, of course. Toby had recognised long ago; the way they looked at her, the way they hung on every word when she spoke and the way they followed her every instruction. Notwithstanding this, even her perceptive streak, which was a wide one, had failed to pick up the absolute awe in which she was widely held. Perhaps nobody could blame Tim for being so spellbound by her. The difference was that none of the other agents would ever permit even a hint of this to be displayed or voiced, whilst the new chap demonstrated it with each breath he took; and seemed to be awestruck by it all.

"Are you all set?" she asked Toby.

"I am, Clancy, though don't expect me to be hitting targets just next to yours?"

She nodded, "Very well then, perhaps a bit of covering fire would be nice, but don't shoot our hostage or any of the other girls now, will you? One or two near misses will help to stir the captors up a bit, but killing the hostage is not a good idea." She feigned seriousness, but then couldn't halt the smile from appearing on her face. She was always at her best at the start of a mission; when others were at their most nervous. He laughed. Looking at the range, which was a little on the optimistic side for him, he knew that he had better concentrate so as to not let her down.

As they waited, the other members of the team walked slowly towards their target, having left their transport a little way back and out of sight. Ground cover here was more scarce, but one or two low earthen hills were used to mask their approach and provide cover for them, once in position. The entire force waited in the dry dusty conditions and in the unwavering intense sunshine that provided not only illumination, but also uncomfortable heat. They had brought charges to blow the doors; in addition, smoke and stun grenades to toss into the warehouse as soon as an opportune moment presented. Before such a strategy was put in place, however, Toby's earpiece crackled into life.

"Okay, 'Rear End', this is 'Pathfinder', I can see some old army trucks approaching. It must be that they are on their way here. Hopefully, we should see some action soon."

"Understood," came the reply from Toby, as he then wondered aloud who suggested that he and Clancy, providing covering fire, should be called 'Rear End'?"

"Oh, I think it was Tim who suggested that," came from the Pathfinder unit, assigned the role of monitoring the warehouse and surrounding area.

Clancy chambered the first round from the five shot magazine. "Come on then, 'Rear End', time to see if these chaps have any steel about them, or if they are simply abusive bullies," she said, with full-blown excitement written to her face. "It's time to take the fight to them," she concluded, with glee.

Two 6x6 trucks appeared, featuring fading army camouflage, which seemed quite superfluous on the dry dusty expanse of the centre of Niger. The three live axles dipped and wallowed in the rough terrain as they made haphazard progress. She inserted the earplugs into her ears and Toby did the same. Eye protection, which he then passed to her, was provided by special goggles, which offered a slight filter against the glare of the sun. Clancy was in position and ready. She looked through the Schmidt and Bender PMII sight, relaxing as she gently bonded with the weapon that she knew would allow her control of the battle, provided each person of the team behaved in the way that their rehearsals had advised. She set the fin dot reticule of the sniper sight on to the warehouse door and knew, unequivocally, that no target could escape her.

So many parts of Africa seemed to be in a state of perpetual conflict. Bad men had exploited this for their own benefit and prosperity. To their mind all life was cheap in Africa. They didn't care who suffered or to what degree they did so, in the process. Three men got out of each of the trucks. They were dishevelled and unkempt. Some sported old army fatigues that they'd been given in some long-forgotten military campaign or other. Each carried a Russian-made assault rifle. Walking straight to the warehouse door, they were totally unaware of the team that had formed a cordon around the entire front of the warehouse: a covert force that was now carefully watching their every move.

One of the men banged on the green door with the butt of his rifle. After an exchange of words, the hinged wooden door was eventually opened. A few moments later about twenty girls were led out. They walked slowly, with stumbling and uncertain movement; being dehydrated courtesy of neglect; and dazed by events. All did their best to shield their eyes against the sunlight after being kept in a dark and dismal warehouse, with little water and no food. Hunger stalked them in the form of lethargy and weakness. Some of the girls quietly sobbed, but most were so exhausted that they wished only for a swift death, to grant them an exit from unremitting misery.

Four men appeared from the warehouse; their self-assured swagger very much in evidence as they joked. They were neither hungry, nor thirsty. Their clothing and equipment were both newer and in much better condition than that of the others, who'd arrived on the trucks. One ate a large mango from which he took a couple of bites, before throwing it on the floor next to one of the girls, who managed to take possession of it just as several others eyed it desperately. He laughed easily at their discomfiture, as his head came back showing enormous white teeth that seemed to glow even from the distance of a thousand metres, held in Clancy's sniper scope. She resisted the temptation to fire a round off at such an appealing target. Two men were despatched to stand at the back of the girls. A further two were detailed to each side, and the remaining four continued to glare lasciviously at the wretched abductees from the front. One of the men who was also better-dressed and better nourished than the others came forward to address the girls. He sported an array of gold teeth together with, almost matching, gold-framed designer sunglasses, which hid uncaring and unfeeling eyes. He had long ago been encouraged to see their prey as a simple money-making vehicle, rather than as human beings who had loved ones waiting for them who'd continue to do so, until the end of time.

"You are now our property, we will do with you as we please. Those of you who can recite versus from the Qu'ran will be set free." He laughed again; knowing that in the assembled terrified group there were unlikely to be any that could attempt such a thing. "The others will be shipped to Europe for prostitution and sold into slavery. Anyone who attempts to run or to escape will be beaten to death with the butt of my rifle." He made a suitable stabbing action with the appropriate end of the rifle and laughed again as the gold-rimmed sunglasses jumped a little in sympathy while they glinted in the sunshine.

The Horizon team who were hiding at either side of the warehouse were aware of his noticeable Essex accent. The girls remained seated on the ground, forming a rough square; some wept quietly, which seemed only to enhance the men's enjoyment.

"That is after my men have had their fill of you. Now, they will each have their pick."

All of the men carried AK47 Russian assault rifles and wondered who would be allowed to go first while the others stood guard and watched. Some licked their lips and others rubbed their leather belts with eager anticipation.

"You will then be loaded into these trucks and driven south to a port outside Lagos, where our transport awaits. From there, you will be shipped to Western Europe, where your new lives will begin as other men's property. Once they have paid us, they will set you to work in whatever way they see fit. You will be used until you are of no use to them, or you grow too old. This will be the life you will know, one under the control of your masters."

Clancy asked of Toby, "Can you manage one or two at the back?"

"Clancy, it will be my pleasure to despatch one or two of these charming men. In fact, seeing such shining examples of humanity may sharpen my aim."

Several of the men wore bullet-proof vests. Smiling unconcernedly, Clancy knew that at this distance, against the magnum cartridges they had loaded, they would offer scant protection. A round sent on its way at a muzzle velocity of 2,800 feet per second would take rather more than a bit of Kevlar to arrest it. She knew that her rifle, with the cartridges she had selected, would pierce better than military-grade body armour at up to a thousand metres. Moreover, fragments from the vest as it was pierced would add to the damage caused to the victim. Clancy also had several imaginative shots lined up for these men. It was time to see how deep their resolve and commitment to their cause, such as it was, ran.

The recovery team were to advance at the first two shots from either Clancy or Toby. All knew, without doubt, that it would be Clancy's round, and that it would be delivered with unwavering accuracy.

The leader of the men continued to posture in front of the group of terrified girls. Clancy watched him via her sniper scope. She hoped that this was all he would do. Unfortunately she was to be disappointed. The leader looked over the top of his gold-rimmed glasses, making what seemed like an arbitrary choice but which probably revolved around weeding out one of those so emaciated and unfit that she'd never make any sort of price. He pointed to one of the youngest girls, one who was not only starving but also continuing to shake with fear.

"You, you will be the first. Stand and begin your quotations."

Others looked at the hapless girl. They felt not only unabridged terror on her behalf, but also the realisation that they could be next. The poor girl continued to tremble, fear held her like an invisible vice. The leader gesticulated to two of the men who then approached and lifted her up and on to her feet.

She wailed plaintively. Clancy estimated she was about twelve, maybe even thirteen. It was this last thought that sent Clancy into her most dangerous and destructive pattern of thought: one that was feared not only by all who knew her but also by Clancy herself. Unfortunately, the girls' captors had long since stopped seeing the people, the young lives and the innocent young women. They saw only a business opportunity and a way of pleasing their boss, whose wrath was worse than any descent into inhumanity and depravity. Moreover, their influence over the poor, wretched girls was one based on fear, humiliation and abject cruelty; and each of these things was to be established by example.

The leader approached, now making ready his rifle butt. He smiled as he barked out more orders.

"Strip her!"

The men either side ripped her pale cotton skirt and cotton shirt from her tortured frame.

His gold teeth seemed to become more prominent as he shouted at her "I am waiting, begin at once."

The poor girl mumbled something, but it was never going to be enough, as she stood there naked, emaciated and shivering with exhaustion and terror in front of all those people. The other men leered, enjoying the spectacle, which was about to become even more depraved.

The leader's patience had evidently run out. In what appeared as a running attack, he began with a blood-curdling cry that could have only been issued by someone full of hatred and anger. He smashed the rifle butt into the middle of her chest. Those nearby could hear the sound of her sternum and ribs breaking like a few dry twigs of kindling being readied for a fire. Observers could see his eyes bulging despite the sunglasses. More than this, it was almost as though he was trying to beat her very soul from her fragile frame using unremitting hatred as the vehicle. She fell to the ground; her bony knees hit the dry mud with a sickening thud. Even her cries and screams were muted by her state of emaciation and her acceptance that she was to die that day. The leader continued his work with the butt of the rifle until the blood flowed and the screaming stopped.

Long before this low point in human behaviour was reached Clancy was ready to despatch him with a single kill shot. Just as she was about to fire an urgent message came in.

"It's Pathfinder here, there are some army trucks full of soldiers heading your way. These look like the real thing. If they hear shots they will investigate. We won't know how they will behave if they see the girls and where their allegiance lies. Please stand down pending further instructions."

If Clancy had been any nearer she would have used the knife she carried with her. She had also brought her suppressor but she knew at this range the cartridges would be significantly compromised and would either fall short or be off target. In any event she had decided that this man, the one she was desperate to shoot, would have his reckoning and soon. Toby looked over at her, he could see her struggling with her emotions and also with the one that had beaten her on many occasions in the past with disastrous consequences for all concerned – anger.

"Clancy, are you all right? The others must be feeling it too, Clancy, it will be a few minutes longer, we'll know where the troops are headed by then."

Clancy could feel her grip tighten, her respiration sped up and her hands began to shake. Normally-dry skin began to perspire profusely, which affected her grip and even her vision. Her whole body now began to tremble with unabridged rage. As the years had passed she had done so well to defeat the anger that had marred her progress and set her development back time and time again. In truth this was the only thing that could defeat her so convincingly – herself. She had tried on so many occasions to master it and failed at each turn. It was only eventually by harnessing her anger to drive herself along more positive lines in hand-to-

hand combat, in shooting and in physical exercise that she
had gained some traction. Clancy understood why Toby was
concerned, even this did not abort it: there would still be
times, like now, when it would defeat her and would dictate
an unwise or precipitate act upon her with disastrous
consequences for all concerned.

Toby knew they would perhaps have seconds left
before Clancy would open fire anyway and if need-be would
engage the army trucks, too, without thinking of the
consequences.

The two men dragged the body of the young girl to one
side. Her heart-rending cries had gone on for some minutes
but there were only so many physical insults that any human
body, let alone a young and starving one, could handle.
Sadly, the passing of her suffering also meant the passing of
her life, which had been beaten out of her in the most brutal
fashion. The leader then took off his sunglasses and began
to wipe them of the spattered blood as if he were relaxing by
a pool somewhere and was cleaning the smears of sun
cream.

Toby continued to look at Clancy; he could see the long
fingers going through the rehearsal of squeezing the trigger.
He knew very soon she'd begin firing and would engage
everyone if she had to until calm was restored to her.

The leader replaced his sunglasses. He then pointed to
another girl. Clancy saw with horror that this was Santhi.
She knew that Tim would be able to see this too. Ultimately,
it was worries over him that saved them all that day; her
thoughts diverted from intense anger to worry about
whether he would hold his nerve. Clancy swung her rifle
round to view his position.

Toby looked deeply concerned, he continued to stare at her and called to her. "Clancy are you okay? Clancy, more information will be through in a minute. Hold fire, I'm begging you."

Santhi stood. She wasn't going to moan and she wasn't going to beg. Moreover, she was going to look her depraved attackers in the eye. Nor was she going to give them the satisfaction of seeing her scared. Clancy wondered at that juncture if she thought about her parents and the love they undoubtedly held for her. She wondered, too, if Santhi would ever know of the operation that had been built around her, with the sole purpose of freeing her and as many others as possible.

In that moment her earpiece came to life. "It's Pathfinder here, the trucks have turned off and are heading north most likely to Agadez. Mission is go. Repeat mission is safe to proceed."

Clancy did not fire immediately. She knew that her body was too tense in order to fire accurately.

Once again, Toby looked over anxiously at her as he wasn't sure he could make the shot that was needed. He saw his colleague taking deep breaths, which she gradually deepened and slowed. At the end of one of these the trigger was squeezed and the shell was on its way.

Ultimately, she'd decided not to kill the leader, at least not yet. However, he fell almost immediately; the further speech he had planned, before he'd begun to butcher Santhi was cut well short of the words he'd intended; being replaced with agonising cries and howls of pain, as he went down like a skittle upon impact from a bowling ball. The cartridge penetrated the armoured vest and continued into his right lung cavity, which caused a massive pneumothorax as the lung deflated catastrophically, but also grazed the uppermost part of the liver, causing significant, but not at this stage lethal, bleeding.

Even before he had hit the ground, Clancy had chambered the second round and this was despatched as the report came in a split second later. Meanwhile, Toby had started shooting at the two guards at the back, those nearest their position.

The girls were in panic as their tormentors started to fall. The Horizon team, right on cue encroached from either side. Remaining hidden, for the time being, they crawled forwards, utilising whatever cover was available as they did so. Clancy's second round was aimed through the knee of the person standing next to the leader. The bullet pierced the popliteal artery as it shattered his knee; also causing him to fall and to bleed profusely. Both men wailed in complete agony and the second one to be shot, in particular, made intrusive levels of noise as he screamed, writhing like a tortured worm on the ground, completely distracting and demoralising his comrades. They kept looking at him when they should have been looking for their nemesis – the sniper.

The other guards reacted quickly, but could not identify the location of their attacker. This was the overriding advantage of the long-range shooter. Men would start to fall and it was often impossible to gauge where the assailant was located – provided that he or she had the skills to shoot out to such a range, and, vitally, had chosen a secure location. Clancy was the master of such skills, employing such with effortless ease, bordering on the instinctive. She knew, too, that snipers who chose to climb trees, to afford themselves good visibility, could be especially vulnerable, once discovered.

At this point, the Horizon team rushed in from either side. Tim was the first to leave his position, being aware of the danger the subject was now in. The poor girl remained frozen to the spot as the guards began to fall. Clancy had chosen almost surgical disabling shots. As soon as they'd begun to experience the agony that such well-directed shots visited upon them, any thought of picking up a gun and shooting straight seemed to be unlikely. One of the agents carried a megaphone to tell the girls to remain as low as possible; they did not need much persuading. Most hugged the dirt for dear life. Despite recognising that help was at hand, unabridged terror stalked them. Their screaming closely matched that given off by their captors as they were neutralised one by one with precise shots, designed to cause most pain and disability and yet, not kill them.

One of the guards saw Tim running in and prepared his assault rifle ready to shoot him. Clancy fired immediately. A second later the bullet passed through the stock of the rifle he was about to present and carried on into his abdominal cavity. Tim saw him fall, but did not waver and continued to make progress straight for his assigned target. Having reached the young woman, he immediately pulled her down to provide her with more cover. He crouched by her side, speaking quickly but clearly. He carried a spare bullet-proof vest for her. "Miss Nukumobo? I have come for you; your father has sent us in to rescue you, and the others. Put this on quickly, please, and then, if you'd run ahead of me this way?"

She stood up as he did. One of her kidnappers aimed an AK47 and prepared to shoot her in the back. Clancy had sight on him and within the central reticule of her sniper scope. Having chambered it, she made ready to despatch another round.

Before she could do so, however, Tim reacted without hesitation. With his right hand he reached for the 9mm Glock, tucked into his rear waistband. At the same time he stretched forwards with his left hand and pulled the startled girl towards him with as much force as he could muster. Her cheek came to rest on his left shoulder as he did so, winding her with the rapidity of movement. Placing his left arm around her waist, he presented the Glock with his right hand, so that it extended past her left side, and fired. It seemed that a neat one-centimetre entry wound appeared almost instantaneously in the middle of the guard's forehead. A slightly startled expression appeared on his face for a millisecond, but this would be the last emotion he would feel. A somewhat larger exit wound appeared at the back of his head and he fell where he stood.

Brady had gone in behind Tim. He looked for a second towards Clancy's firing position. He knew that she would have sights on him. The careful nod he sent in her direction spoke volumes. One or two of the captors tried to run. All were shot with a variety of disabling, but intensely painful, leg shots. As soon as they had all been brought down, their weapons were removed and they were herded or dragged against the wall of the groundnut warehouse. A variety of moans and shrieks were given off by the men depending on their resistance to pain and the degree of injury they'd received. One or two wept and cried out for unseen others who must have been a long way away in every sense of the word. The dead kidnapper was placed inside the warehouse.

Toby pulled away from his optical sight. A mixture of relief and sheer delight lit up his face.

"Wow! Good moves from Tim. Did you see that, Clancy? The kid is a natural. He handled himself very well. It seems we have ourselves another agent."

Clancy smiled back; she knew that instinct rather than a cool assessment had led her to this decision and, for now, it had paid off. She succeeded in mastering the relief that was about to form on her expression and managed a magnanimous smile instead. "You owe me a G and T, I think. Not bad for his first armed outing, eh Toby?"

"Even the kill shot was perfectly appropriate and timed to perfection." Toby adjudged.

As she had been hoping, Tim had not only acted quickly but had used good judgment. More importantly than all these things, the others had seen how quickly and unequivocally he'd taken action.

"Yes, he only had time for the one shot or the other chap might have got a few rounds away," she thought aloud.

Clancy would never know whether she had hesitated deliberately in felling the guard who was about to shoot the hostage, in the hope that Tim would come through. She recognised that it was a dangerous and finely-balanced decision to make. Mercifully, it had worked out for the best – on this occasion. Relief fell across her face, as she stood up and looked away from Toby. The female sniper walked forwards from their position. Toby started packing away the guns. While he did so, he looked after the Clancy. She had delivered yet another surprise and his opinion of her, as always, of the highest order. Unfortunately, a flaw that he thought she'd mastered some time ago had reared its head once again: her ability to contain her own depths of anger.

Approaching the warehouse, she was deep in thought. She heard Tim say, "You are safe now, Miss Nukumobo. We will have you out of here shortly, and you will be on your way to meet up with your Mum and Dad. They are waiting for you. I will notify them immediately that we have you and you can, perhaps, speak with them directly. We wondered if you'd like to ride in the Range Rover; you will be more comfortable there. We have some food and some water for you and for the rest of the girls."

Most of the time she wept, being acutely aware that, until these people had appeared, the outcome was going to be very different.

Clancy thought contemplatively, "couldn't have put it better myself".

Introducing herself and then Toby, she hugged the distraught girl as Tim went to find some food and water for her from the Land Rovers that had quickly been brought up.

Many of the girls were in a poor state, having been kept in the warehouse for several days without any food and only fetid water to drink. As soon as they were more settled, each of them would be allocated places in the transport and driven south, back to their own families and freedom. For now they drank and ate, for the first time in days. A little convoy was assembled and some of the agents had been detailed to drive them away from the distressing scene and out of captivity, as soon as they'd had some refreshments and were able to travel.

"Well done, Tim, great work. You handled yourself and any unexpected developments like a pro. Absolutely brilliant."

"Thank you, Miss Clancy, and thank you for showing faith in me."

"Don't even mention it, Tim."

He remained a little fazed by the whole experience and the rapidity of events. It took him a little while to calm his pulsating thoughts and he then returned to the practice of which he would never tire – asking her questions.

"May I ask? I was going to ask you about the kill shot. I see that you and Toby used mainly disabling shots?"

"Yes, Tim, correct. These men for the most part will survive. Not to say that the course of action you chose – the definitive kill shot, however, wasn't perfect. The limited time and the fact that your opponent would have killed the hostage if he could, meant this was the only shot you could have attempted and certainly the one I would have chosen, had I been in that situation."

"Thank you, Miss Clancy. Is there a reason why you choose the wounding shot, with these horrible people?"

"Yes, we only use kill shots when we have to. For most of the untrained opponents we come across, a really painful shot, especially one that causes a bit of bleeding is a good choice. You'd be amazed what a bit, actually quite a bit, of pain and more than a little bleeding does for some of these fanatics. It does tend to focus their minds pretty sharpish. And suddenly, exhorting others to commit unspeakable acts in the name of their perverted cause becomes less appetising when it's their foot that is gushing blood. They soon forget about world domination when their femoral artery needs clamping off, or they can no longer stand up. The other point is that disabling someone in this way drains the resources of their organisation much more than a clean kill. Sadly, I'm sure that many, if not all, of the wounded are quietly disposed of by their employers. That is then on their shoulders, not ours. It also has to be said that in this part of the world, there is a steady stream of new recruits ready to step up and wield the Kalashnikov; a disabled chap is going to be quite a liability. Furthermore, patching them up will be a time-consuming and costly exercise as well as diverting resources from the able-bodied."

"So, should we take them with us?"

"I think it's a nice thought but please remember, at all times, the mission priorities. Would you have wanted to leave some of the girls behind so we could transport a few wounded thugs back to town? It's up to their warlord employers to look out for them, recover them and make sure they get medical attention. Not looking after them, leaving them to rot or promptly shooting them in front of their peers will be a powerful disincentive for new recruits. They'll be okay in that warehouse for a few days, I expect."

While Clancy was talking to Tim the former guards and abductors were being dragged and propped up against a low wall by the warehouse. One man remained where he'd fallen and Miss Clancy walked over.

"Ah yes, my friend. You're from England if I am not mistaken? What happened, they took your sickness benefit off you and you decided to up your game by murdering young girls? Let's see now, I am going to quote from the Qu'ran and you are to follow. Let's give you a taste of your own medicine. If you fail then, perhaps I will show you as much mercy as that poor kid over there.

Shall I begin?

'And the Lord has decreed that you worship none but Him. And that you be dutiful to your parents.'

Now your turn -

Silence – now there's a surprise." She pulled at his dog tags around his neck, dropping them with disgust as if it were not a man she was talking to. "Jerome here, from Brixton doesn't know much about the teachings of the Prophet after all.

"How about 'And walk not on the earth with conceit and arrogance'? That's one of my favourites.

"Any takers, anyone care to try their hand here, from you fine upstanding gentlemen?" she said, to the few of his accomplices that were still able to take an interest in the proceedings.

Clancy now produced a large knife. At this point the leader of the men started squealing and begging for his life.

This went on for some time until Clancy became tired of the number of ways he was able to find to beg and scrape to plead for his pitiful life.

"You see Jerome, I'm thinking that you aren't a Muslim at all. I think you are just a debased murderer who has invented a cause to try to justify his brutality." She took out her mobile phone and took his picture. "I'm certain there will be a file on you somewhere and that it contains some pretty depraved stuff. You are a monster Jerome. I'm thinking that killing you is too good for you. I'm rather hoping that that nice abdominal wound will finish you off after a few agonising days in that warehouse, with that stinking green water you deigned to let those girls have. That's if your leader doesn't do the job for me. I suspect medical help will be too expensive for him to lavish on you and you'll be left to die in some dark corner somewhere. That's the thing about depraved perverts like you, even your boss won't fancy having you around when he is entertaining his real friends. You'll be a bit of an embarrassment to him. I suspect it'll be easier for him just to put a bullet to you. I think killing you would be a kindness to you and to be truthful I am not feeling kindly towards you just now.

"Of course I know, Jerome, it's not your fault is it? You were just looking for warmth; a little love at the end of the day. You never meant for it to go that far. Your wife didn't understand you, so you looked elsewhere. There would be no harm in it. Nobody ever need know."

Those observing detected that Clancy's hands were shaking with rage. The most observant like Toby and Tim recognised that she'd gone back to a very different time and place and was re-living something far more personal. The wild, unstable look she held in her eyes made her captive even more frightened. He now started whimpering like a whipped puppy. Suddenly, she moved on.

"Yes, that's it. Your mum brought lots of men home, didn't she Jerome? None of whom was your Daddy. You hated her for it and then one day she didn't come home at all. Your Daddy never forgave her and so was created our little women-hater, here." The sharpened blade glinted in the sunshine; it looked even larger as she moved it towards him.

"As you are not frightened of exposing a bit of flesh, it's time for us to find out if you are a good Muslim or not and there's an easy way to tell." She started hacking with the blade at his army fatigues exposing his underwear.

"Ooh Calvin Klein, nothing but the best for you eh, Jerome? Now let's see what have we here?"

She cut his underwear from him.

He shrieked with fear and continued to plead.

"Just as I thought, and what a fine member you have. Perhaps it's a bit too long? And your luck is in today, Jerome, because I'm rather good at this operation. I can never remember, though, whether I should cut one inch or two. Some tell me that I cut a bit too much off – I reckon just an inch from the end should do – you'll still have quite a bit left."

His piercing cries and his pleading rose to a crescendo. Tim thought he was going to faint. Jerome desperately tried to get away from Clancy but she was not about to let him avoid what she felt was coming to him. Toby did not try to interfere; all the team reckoned that whatever punishment Miss Clancy had decided on would be perfectly appropriate.

She raised the knife and Jerome shut his eyes, the pleading suddenly stopping. Justice, at least the only kind he knew, was about to be administered.

She stared at him with a mixture of hatred and disgust in her eyes. Without looking at the gruesome blade she brought it down violently like a guillotine. It plunged into his left thigh like a dart into warm wax. It only came to a halt when both he and she felt it graze the femur with agonising consequences.

Twisting the knife round a little before she withdrew it she wiped the blade carefully, almost tenderly, on his tunic. He continued to bellow with pain and sobbed for mercy. She stood up looking a little calmer; the violence had, not for the first time, cleansed her of anger.

"Ok, please put this filth among men in the warehouse with all the others and lock the door. I don't think the dead chap is going to smell too nice by this evening, so it should perhaps focus their minds a little on the risks of the type of work they've chosen."

She walked away and didn't look again at him as he continued to sob. His pleas for mercy that he'd denied to others still ringing in her ears like a smell of something rotten that she could not evade.

Other agents had fanned out either side of the warehouse to make sure that the perimeter was secure and that other terrorists had not surreptitiously moved up to attack their positions. A short time later, having had something to eat and drink, all the girls were invited to get into the vehicles that made up the small convoy. The team had brought five body bags with them and one of these was used for the poor young girl whose parents' grief for their missing daughter had only just begun. They covered her body. A few respectful words were offered by Toby as the team formed up around the body before she was zipped inside. Her thin emaciated form hinting at all the things in life that had been and now would be forever denied to her.

While Clancy was walking round one of the trucks with Tim she heard two members of the team, Griff and Tracy, discussing things while they were seated in one of the soft-skinned vehicles with some of their escorts.

"Good old Clancy, she came through again, what wonderful shooting," Tracy began.

Griff, however, was very keen to talk of other things. "Yes, I really thought she was going to chop off that chap's nadgers."

"Only got what was coming to him. I hope he has a slow and painful death stuck in that warehouse. I wouldn't waste a bullet on him, either." Tracy now nodded to him as she expressed her views on the episode.

Griff's eyes widened as he relived events. "Did you see the way she looked at him, and the sheer terror on his face when she got her big knife out?"

Tracy was in full agreement. "Oooh, yes I loved it when she started cutting his clothes off him. Did you see how angry she got?" Griff then continued, "Yes, nobody wants to see her get angry. We all have to keep our heads down when that happens, as things can get pretty wild; it's like a blind rage that cannot be controlled. Hasn't been seen for a while, so I'm told. Apparently the last time it happened the mission went badly wrong."

The two agents quickly went quiet when they heard Tim ask Clancy a question and realised that their voices could be heard.

The mood of the team on the return journey was much brighter, despite the loss of one of the girls. Agents, who'd been assigned to transport the others south so that they could be reunited with their families, started the trucks. Some members of the force were assigned armed escort duties to support those driving, to ensure that they reached their destination without incident. The remainder of the team went straight to the airport and waited until those on transport duties had released the prisoners, either to their families, or at least in friendly territory. Santhi accompanied Tim in one of the Range Rovers and an emotional reunion took place at the airport between Santhi and her parents. Mr Nukumobo spent a lot of time talking with Toby and after an hour or two the rest of the agents arrived. Within minutes of them doing so, any remaining equipment was loaded and the transport took off, bound for Manchester.

Clancy noted that Tim remained quiet. The expression that existed on his face, however, now very different from the one that had been in evidence only a few short hours ago. Just as significant were the looks that the rest of the team gave him. One or two looked at her. The slight nods that came her way were almost those that a victorious general would attract from his grateful troops, who once again had been given a demonstration of unassailable skill in battle. Most of the emotions on the agents' faces, however, were those of curiosity and were unequivocally aimed at Tim. More important than all these things was the fact that they all seemed much happier. They had detected, too, that Tim had come through; he'd shown himself to be the equal of the responsibilities that had been assigned to him. One or two of the more astute ones guessed that he had passed the test that Clancy had set for him. Toby noted the more optimistic and settled mood. He also understood that both he and Tim had been set tests; he could only wonder if he had failed his. As the aircraft banked north, homeward bound, he looked at Clancy. "Well done, Clancy, what a brilliant operation. You said there was something you wanted to say to me?"

"Yes, Toby, but not here." She looked around the plane; everyone sat in close proximity and even quiet voices could be heard when there was something worth hearing. "It'll wait a bit longer, Toby."

Out of the corner of her eye, she saw that Brady had gone up to Tim, shaken his hand and patted him on the back. She could see the slight glow of satisfaction and pride that existed on his face. A few moments later, she saw that Tim glanced in her direction. She moved so quickly, however, that it looked as though she was in animated conversation with Toby. The aeroplane continued to ply its way north and would land in Manchester some hours later.

CHAPTER IV

Retribution

A few days later, Clancy was leading the debrief meeting at Horizon HQ at Salford Quays.

"Well done team, all the prisoners were recovered safe and sound, unfortunately with the exception of one casualty. Our primary objective, Santhi Nukumobo was reunited with her parents, as you saw, at the airport. In addition, we freed all the other surviving captives and removed every single last one of them to safe refuges. I realise it's the tip of the iceberg but, for now at least, we achieved our mission objectives, and also earned significant bonuses. More important still is that we struck against some really objectionable people: more of this later. Firstly, I would just like to go through the mission surveillance. As routine, we sent up a drone with surveillance cameras and also set up our customary ground-based surveillance. So many of you performed really well and even Toby managed some accurate fire, shooting out at nearly a thousand metres. I don't think he missed a target, unless of course he's keeping quiet." Toby just smiled as eyes turned towards him, but otherwise said nothing. Some of the team cheered and whooped in delight as his skill with a rifle was not regarded as one of his strong points.

"Special mention must go, too, to Tim. As you all know this was his first live 'armed' field mission, and I would like to congratulate you, Tim. Those of you who have been with us for some time know that we sometimes offer a 'golden gun' award for excellence in the field. Most notably, it applies to those who showed initiative and bravery or who just did the right thing at the right time. All those involved with a mission are asked to nominate the person who, in their view, is the agent who has stood out the most among his or her colleagues. I am pleased to say that by unanimous opinion, you feel that such an award is warranted now. Without further ado, I can say that the award goes to you, Tim. If I could ask you to step up and collect this fine trophy."

Tim stood up and Clancy offered him the award, which was a golden revolver mounted on a base, taking inspiration from an Oscar. His peers clapped as he stood in a state of shock and surprise. He came forward somewhat nervously and hesitantly. The room, however, erupted with genuine pleasure and delight. They all recognised that, although he was a new recruit, they had found a colleague who could be relied upon. All attendees were keen to demonstrate that this was a two-way sentiment. Clancy shook his hand and then kissed him, while the room voiced its delight, with one or two lewd whistles adding to the atmosphere. A very embarrassed and blushing agent sat down moments later. He looked at the golden trophy. In his entire life of some twenty-eight years he had neither won, nor earned, anything. Not once had he, by the sweat of his brow or by his own initiative, secured anything that was in any way meaningful

– until now, among these people who'd all been strangers until a few weeks ago. He wanted to go up to Clancy and thank her for coming to find him in that gambling den after his having racked up massive losses. At a stroke, she'd removed him and cancelled his debts that would have fallen on his father's shoulders. He knew, however, that he could not trust himself to deliver such thanks and still contain his emotions appropriately. Without doubt, this was something he would work tirelessly on, too.

Clancy spent a further hour going through some of the mission details, and used footage that had been captured by their drone. To this footage, she added that from the ground-based camera. This was an automatic camera inserted into the ground, which took repeated panoramic shots of the scene, either until it was switched off, or its memory card was full. She used images from the camera to give examples as to what had gone well with the mission and also to identify what could have been done differently. As was her wont, she spoke in general terms when discussing areas that needed improvement and never identified specific agents whose performance had been lacking. This she would always do one-to-one and never in front of others. However, much to his embarrassment, she highlighted Toby's long-range shots and even produced some statistics and graphs showing the distances he'd fired out to successfully. She also showed footage of Tim's rush to engage with and protect the main target. Replay of the images caused still further blushing from Tim. Somehow, she'd managed to exclude the role played by Brady who, known only to him and Clancy, who'd been sworn to eternal secrecy, had been following closely behind. Most notably, she did not mention anything of her own performance. The covering fire she laid down had protected and supported all the agents. Put simply, the success of the mission, not for the first time, was largely due to her efforts. Moreover, the precision shots she made at distances in excess of a thousand metres, not just once, but consistently, displayed marksmanship that few could ever hope to attain. Clancy, typically, was content to sit on the side-lines, while others were highlighted and shown to be good examples to the rest of the team.

"Now, I'd like to hand over to Toby, who has some more information."

"Yes, thanks Clancy. I have a communication from Mitral Nukumobo, who is overjoyed by the success of the mission and, not surprisingly, by the safe return of his daughter." Toby read out the communication that had been received from the steel magnate.

Everyone in the meeting was delighted to have such positive feedback and a short time later the group broke up. Before they left, Toby reminded everyone to be punctual the following day, because they were about to embark on new operations, which would need to be discussed and then planned for. For now, a party atmosphere prevailed, and they broke from the meeting with the intention of celebrating with their colleagues or loved ones. Just before leaving, Tim held the 'Golden Gun' trophy, rubbing it carefully, not quite able to believe it was real, before looking up to catch Clancy glancing in his direction.

Sadly, the bright mood did not last long. Rather than talk about some of the operations that had been scheduled, Toby called them all in much earlier than planned the following day. He stood in front of one of the large screens, as he brought up grainy images of a bomb blast.

"I have to tell you that Mr Nukumobo's wife and daughter were killed, along with two of their security guards, yesterday. Their vehicle had been booby-trapped, wired for explosives, and though it had some armour protection, this was mainly proof against sniper fire. The attack took place in Lagos. As you all know, it's an absolutely huge city, but Mitral Nukumobo is under no doubt that this is a reprisal attack from our friends in Niger for the successful recovery of his daughter. A massive amount of C4 was used underneath their car and went off as soon as the ignition was activated. Very few vehicles, armoured or otherwise, could have withstood such a blast. Many bystanders were killed and the adjacent office block was badly damaged and will have to be pulled down.

"Mr Nukumobo, as you might guess, is distraught at the death of his wife and only child. Rather than take all this lying down, he has suggested another mission. I think, moreover, he is hoping that others do not go through the torment that he is now experiencing and has asked us to act decisively against this abduction and prostitution low-life. To this litany of deplorable acts, I am sure no one is surprised that we now add cold-blooded murder of two innocent women. I am also told that ten others were killed, who just happened to be close to the car when it went up.

"Our client is very keen for us to extend our work and shut these criminals down for good. To this end, he has asked us to go after the man, Mr Mdombku, who is at the head of this particular band of unsavoury traffickers, terrorists and murderers. Our aim will be to bring him to justice, so that he might face his accusers. He has a lot of fingers in a lot of pies. It seems he is a very difficult person to get to, having a virtual army of men at his palatial estate in remote Niger. There, he is untouched and untouchable. However, I am informed that he will be attending the Pan-African Congress in South Africa at the end of this month. This will give us a good chance of seizing him and extracting him to the authorities in Western Europe who would like to put him on trial for a good many crimes and atrocities. Apparently people-trafficking is just one of his many illegal and reprehensible activities and Mr Nukumobo wonders if we are the team to take him down and bring him to justice. A European arrest warrant was served some twelve months ago. No one had the resources, or the stomach, to go out there and serve this despot with it. Now, however, we feel it's high time; therefore, we are going to assemble a team to do just that. Mr Nukumobo is prepared to underwrite our mission.

"You realise, of course, that we will be acting without external backup or support. If any agents are caught, nobody will be keen to rescue us. For this reason we need a small, stripped-down force that can get in and get out, hopefully with our scum-bag warlord locked in a boot and bound for Amsterdam, before anyone realises he is missing. He is more or less untouchable on the African subcontinent. Nobody in Niger has any interest whatsoever in taking action against him and to do so would be very costly in every sense. He can travel within Africa with impunity as no one there has the wherewithal to arrest him. Even the Americans haven't got the stomach for it. Without doubt, his money and his power have also bought many friends. Once he is extracted to Europe, however, a lot of his support will melt away. The authorities in the Hague feel they have a good human-rights case against him, quite apart from the people trafficking. Extradition is also a non-starter. Any law enforcement, judiciary and other officials are either promptly killed or paid off. Who can blame anyone for not wanting to take a stand and end up never being seen again, or have his wife or family killed? They may as well take the money and turn a blind eye. If I am honest, I have some sympathy for that approach. This means, though, that the reprehensible activities continue and this man grows in confidence and audacity. *We,* however, have a chance to strike and Mr Nukumobo is prepared to finance our operation in order to bring it about.

"I've asked Clancy to go through some of the detail as soon as we can get more information. If we can reconvene here, please, this afternoon, so that we can start to look at the bare bones of the mission we have in mind. We can then run some probability figures and go through some rehearsals. Please note we will be restricted as to numbers. The only comfort is that for similar reasons our target will also be limited in the people he can take with him. I am hoping that the odds will be more or less even. I will take any questions now, and then we will see the agents on this list, early afternoon please, for further work up."

A list of names appeared on one of the display panels. Tim saw his name and by his assigned role was simply 'backup, driver'. It seemed that, for now, he had made a good start and all his peers knew that he had earned his place in the organisation and on the team and, most notably, their respect.

CHAPTER V

Suicide Mission

A week later, some members of the Horizon team were in Cape Town, South Africa. The cadre had flown six thousand miles in pursuit of one man. Having a final meeting in a large hotel room, they'd swept it for bugs and also posted a member outside the door as a precaution.

Clancy went through some of the final mission rehearsals, using a projector and her laptop.

"Though far from ideal, given the need for discretion and the number of friends this man has, a small tight operation, here in South Africa, is most likely to succeed. We are hoping to stay under the radar. The cover story is that we are a trade delegation hoping to purchase and import dried fruits; Mebos and Biltong from South Africa to England," Clancy began.

"Forgive me, but what are Mebos and Biltong? Can't say that I have ever had either of those," Tim queried.

"Well, Tim, should you get asked, while you are waiting to transport our target for extraction, I can tell you that Biltong is dried and cured meat. I hope you have strong teeth if you get offered some. She smiled at this point, displaying her even teeth, which were framed by the pink, shimmering lips. Mebos is like dried fruit made out of apricots, usually. Both are typical South African delicacies and widely available here. So, Tim, if I may continue?"

"Oh yes sorry, Miss Clancy, just had to ask."

"Our force, we are hoping, is small enough not to draw attention to ourselves and yet be effective enough to grab him. The surveillance team has been following him discreetly for a few days, so we are aware of the minders who have accompanied him. He has a suite at the top of the Westin hotel, from where we are planning to abduct him. There are occasions when he is vulnerable, or he behaves carelessly, especially when there are women about. At these times he has fewer minders following him. We watch, we wait: then we strike."

"You mean, we are just going to bang on the door and grab him?" Tim asked.

"Yes, that's just about it. Even he cannot be watched by his limited contingent of thugs and reprobates all the time. There are vulnerable, less well-manned points in his schedule. We will use one of these in order to take action. And, once we have him, we'll transfer him to Port Elizabeth in a jiffy."

Tim raised his hand, "A jiffy?"

"Yes, Tim," she clarified, "you know, in a short time, a trice."

"Ah, yes, sorry, Miss Clancy," he nodded.

"Now, if I may continue, again? We have arranged for transport directly from Port Elizabeth and next stop for our brutal abuser of people, and young girls especially, will be justice. Once airborne, we can then drop him off, not literally, of course, though it is tempting, in the Hague and they can deal with him as they see fit from there."

She moved on by presenting remote surveillance footage and also discussed the schedules of the guards that had accompanied him.

There then began a waiting game where they readied themselves to intervene, when his security guards were otherwise distracted or thin on the ground, or the Horizon team's intervention was going to be noticed by as few observers as possible. Eventually, all these factors combined.

Clancy and Brady took the private lift to the top floor. They knew that this was where Mr Mdombku's suite of rooms was situated. It was reserved solely for his use. There, they waited. A short time later, he approached with four minders and two young girls, who were sporting very short and figure-hugging clothing that was also low-cut. Tottering precariously on really high heels, they giggled under the influence of the large amount of alcohol they had been plied with. Clancy wondered how old these girls were. Two of the guards went ahead in order to open his room. Mr Mdombku walked behind them, linking the girls either side, without a care in the world. Bringing up the rear were the two other security guards.

Clancy spoke just as the first two minders were about to open his room.

"Mr Mdombku?"

He did not even look at Clancy, preferring to speak to his guards.

"Tell this bitch to leave me alone. She should not be allowed up here. The hotel promised me exclusivity. Whatever she is selling, I do not require. Unless, of course, it's her body, which I might just have a use for, once my friends here have entertained me for an hour or two. Tell her to come back later, and I shall see what she can do for me."

Clancy spoke to the two girls, ignoring the warlord completely. "If I were you, I would leave. Leave, and leave now, before it starts to get nasty. Go home. Go home to your Mums and Dads. Leave this paedophile to me."

He laughed and the guards, looking a little more uncertain, also laughed. Steady, unwavering eyes now looked at him, like purified copper that had been smelted and poured into ingots to cool. "I'm not here to sell you anything, Mr Mdombku. And what I do with my body is up to me. I have a present for you, though, of an arrest warrant that was issued some time ago by the European Court of Human Rights, and which I am now serving on you.

"I represent more than a few important and concerned people, who wish to question you about some reprehensible practices on your part. It seems *your* body is wanted after all, Mr Mdombku." Although she couldn't quite defeat the smile that formed for an instant, she still managed to impart something of menace on her expression that she wanted him to witness. She now said, almost nonchalantly, "I'm simply here to deliver you to them. I do hope you have a change of underclothes because, I'm afraid, you'll need them; maybe about twenty years' worth, if you are lucky. I'm sure they'll have a nice prison cell lined up for you somewhere, where you can satisfy your own, or more likely someone else's, sexual proclivities." Clancy struggled with the anger and distaste she felt for this monster. There was also something more complex at work: something buried in her past, but never far from the surface. In any event, it had been unequivocally awakened, and was in full flight now.

He laughed no more. His facial expression became more concerned, displacing his indignation. His skin appeared shiny as he started to sweat. Pointing to two of his men, he barked out orders.

"Hit her, and hit her very hard. Now! Smash this disrespecting bitch, who dares to speak to me this way!"

One approached Clancy unconcernedly. He had no qualms about hitting a woman. Intending to do as his boss commanded, he looked at the thin woman who didn't have much meat on her. No doubt, she would be screaming soon, and he decided that a quick blow to her face would suffice. Brady came forward, as the other approached. Two of the guards, by the room, held back, thinking it would be unlikely that they would be needed and that very soon they would see a little sport. The young girls looked terrified.

As the guard approached, Clancy turned to her left using a twisting motion from her waist. The guard saw this as his opportunity to attack. Rushing forwards, he showed little caution; always a mistake when Clancy was one's adversary. He looked at her face while deciding where to land his first blow. Her right arm came up and she kept it very high as she bent it at the elbow. The minder thought she was simply protecting her face from the blow that he expected to deliver momentarily. Continuing to bring her arm up as he came closer, she brought this across her torso, which was still turning to the left. Holding her arm at a right angle, she held it aloft, now poised like a trigger. At the precise moment when he had committed himself and could no longer recover, she swept her elbow, still held at ninety degrees, back the way it had come, using it as one would a club. The movement, so typical of Clancy, was exact and perfectly timed. She caught the right-hand side of his jaw with the rotational thrust. The lateral force, so applied, was pitched just at its weakest point. His jaw joint could be heard cracking with the violent, but accurate, blow thereby both fracturing and dislocating it. Intense pain wracked him. His instinct under such pain was to bend forwards and reach up with both hands to clutch at his chin, which was now lying at an odd angle. Accompanying the agony was also the fact that it interfered with his breathing, just at the point when he needed deep unobstructed breaths.

Clancy continued the clockwise rotation of her torso, back the way she had come. Keeping up the momentum, she brought up her left knee, while her right leg supported her entire body weight, allowing the next blow. As her knee swung back towards her right, she held it in flexion. Using the same turning force that had broken his jaw, she harnessed the rotation and the weight of her flexed left knee, now applying it against his right knee in order to sweep it sideways. The force so unleashed pushed it in a medial direction, in which it was not designed to travel. It quickly gave way as an entirely new agonising pain both wracked and destabilised him.

He tottered forwards, while his right leg collapsed beneath him. Clancy retreated just a little, using her left leg to bring her whole body away from him, but coiled, ready to strike.

Her left hand came up, the palm fully open, almost to face height, ready to stabilise him, if need be, to commence the next blow she had prepared. She opened her right palm to its fullest extent and also extended her wrist fully, so that it was positioned at a right angle to her forearm. Her long arms having the appearance of a preying mantis poised to strike. She retracted her right arm, like a piston, but kept the palm in hard extension against it as she drew it back. At the same time, she rocked backwards on to her left leg, having suspended the rotation. She then brought the whole arm forward with a violent thrusting stroke whilst using the left leg to also propel her entire torso back towards him. The lowest edge of her right palm caught his nasal bones, just at the correct angle, driving them upwards towards his skull, as they pierced the cribriform plate.

Having received three devastating injuries in the space of as many minutes the giant of a man collapsed in agony at her feet. She allowed him to fall; any resistance from him had long since disappeared. His wails of agony being affected by the jaw that left him choking on the blood that gushed down his nose mixed with cerebro-spinal fluid, caused by Clancy's last blow.

It took Brady a little longer to subdue his opponent, having caught one or two blows that he'd failed to entirely avoid. She smiled as she caught his gaze.

"Heavy weather, Brady?"

"Sorry, Clancy, I'll have him in a moment."

At this, Brady projected forth an enormous blow to his opponent's stomach, which caused him to double up. The Horizon agent then grabbed behind his head and pulled him forwards on to his right knee, which then came up with violent hyperextension from his thigh, whilst keeping the knee flexed to meet his opponent with devastating force in the middle of his face. He, too, collapsed in agony at Brady's feet. Both agents stepped forward, their quarry now directly in front of them.

For the first time, Mr Mdombku's face registered fear. He looked at the two remaining guards, their expression not showing any enthusiasm for joining their contemporaries, who were groaning and gasping for air on the floor.

"Shoot the bitch. Shoot her now! Shoot her in the face."

The minder moved to find his revolver on his left side, under the suit jacket.

The two girls screamed and ran past Brady and Clancy, towards the lift. Just at this point, the lift doors opened and a further two Horizon agents came forwards.

Clancy grabbed her Glock, which she'd placed in her rear waistband. She pointed it at the two guards.

"The first one to draw his gun shall be the first to die," she advised, in a study of calmness and control. The men looked at each other, knowing that she had no need to rely on the artifice of exaggeration in order to convince them of the danger they were in. She then used her left hand to withdraw some restraints from her pocket. She dangled them in front of the warlord. Her voice had become clinical, "Time for you to face your accusers, I believe. I suspect there will be more than a few of them. I'm told that you'll be given a fair trial. This is more than you afford for those you abduct, sell, intimidate and execute. In short, you will be shown all those things you deny others. It's the end of the line for you. Now, are you going to come quietly or are others going to get hurt? You wouldn't want to see me get angry would you, as this would not be advised?"

Having seen what she could do, whilst remaining relatively calm, none of the men there present wanted to see what losing her temper would entail. Brady couldn't resist a fleeting, but wicked, smile. The three men froze, suspecting that nothing could save them now. This woman, who had appeared from nowhere, seemed to be master of every skill she was called upon to display and at all times remained very firmly in charge of the situation.

Mr Mdombku swallowed very hard. Surely, only a miracle could change the outcome, while he pictured that stark concrete cell: and worse. Sweat broke out on in force on his wide visage. Just then, a door opened from the service elevator, behind Mr Mdombku. A waitress, in a black dress and white apron came out of the lift, singing a cheery song as she did so. She seemed oblivious to the group that were in the corridor. Stepping forwards, she pushed her trolley laden with several covered plates and a magnum of champagne in a large bucket of ice. Having completely vacated the rickety old lift, she walked towards the group, not detecting the danger she was exposed to. The hotel managers had instructed her that she was to turn a blind eye to anything she saw, and encountered, while she was attending Mr Mdombku's suite of rooms. She reflected later that surely they couldn't have been referring to the situation in which she now found herself immersed.

Clancy acted immediately. She held up a flat palm to the woman who remained oblivious to the scene in front of her. She shouted, "Please go back and return to the lift; don't come any further forwards."

As is the way with such things, Clancy's warning gave Rueben, one of the minders, inspiration. Fortuitously, he could see how the innocent woman could be used to protect his boss and had even provided the route.

He called to his associate in a deep rich voice. "Victor, hold that lift before the door closes."

As soon as Victor made for the lift, Rueben grabbed the maid who, suddenly, could not only see the peril she was in, but also displayed a level of terror to match. She began to scream with a high-pitched wail. The guard stepped behind her and then used her, as she still clung on to the trolley, as a battering ram to push towards Clancy and Brady. Rushing forwards, he applied as much force as he could muster to both woman and trolley. As he did so he called out.

"Excellency, the lift, please!"

For a moment the despot was granted relief from his paralysis and fear. His bloated bulk moved as quickly as his legs would carry him, towards the lift, while Victor held the sliding doors open.

Clancy acted still more quickly; she extended her arms forwards while preparing to side-step the trolley and the waitress. Holding her body flush against the wall, she grabbed the trolley with both her arms at full extension and then accelerated the progress of both, making sure that they moved safely around and past her. Brady had the presence of mind to also hug the opposite wall of the corridor. The young woman, who continued to wail loudly, could think of nothing else, other than to hang on to the trolley as best she could. As Clancy spun both around her in a shallow arc: they were, in that moment, moving faster than either had ever done before. She grabbed the magnum of Champagne as it flew past. Although both continued down the corridor for a short distance, the trolley soon overturned as it struck one of the guards still groaning on the floor; and the terrified maid, half a second later, followed suit. The two agents who had recently arrived managed to get out of the way of the trolley and stepped over the guards, while doing their best to catch the panicking waitress as she fell.

As Clancy and Brady approached, Rueben sensed that they were running out of time.

"Quickly Excellency, in to the lift," he shouted, the desperation readily apparent. Upon hearing that his boss had entered the lift, he quickly retreated while Brady and Clancy advanced. Clancy held the bottle of Champagne by its neck and flung it in the direction of the open lift. It passed through the doors, which were beginning to close, and shattered within, drenching both Victor and the despot in Champagne. Sadly, it failed. Clancy had hoped to obstruct the doors as they closed, thereby causing them to open again, and allow her to get to the warlord.

In the last second, the remaining guard made a desperate run for the lift. Managing to insert his hand between the doors, he knew that they would open any second.

Mr Mdombku, however, had other ideas. He slapped Rueben's exposed hand firmly, causing him to withdraw it; leaving the person whose quick thinking had saved him to the mercy of the Horizon agents, as the door closed. Without any further hesitation, the lift descended.

Turning with some fear and trepidation, the guard managed to draw his gun. Clancy had dropped hers as the trolley had come forwards. Seeing it on the carpeted floor just in front of her, she knew that she did not have time to retrieve it. Using her left hand she threw the metal restraints directly at the guard's face, causing his aim to be deflected and also considerable pain as the weighty metal rim hit his nose. She rushed forwards, using the few seconds that her intervention had bought. Before he could fire, she quickly brought up her right leg, keeping it perfectly straight as she did so; kicking the hand that was holding the gun, so that it fired harmlessly into the ceiling. Brady then came forwards to subdue Rueben before he could prepare another shot. He turned quickly, presenting his back to the guard. He pushed back into the stunned man and then restrained his right arm that was still holding the gun. Grabbing the weapon with both hands, keeping the guard's right arm on his right hand side, he now backed forcefully into the bewildered man and snapped his head backwards into his forehead. The pain and shock caused Rueben to drop the gun. At this point, still with his back to him, Brady then brought his left arm up flexing it at the elbow in order to deliver another blow into his cheek from the left hand side.

Clancy used the time that her colleague had bought her to rush to the lift, but she was too late. She smacked the lift door with her clenched fist. The metal panel buckled and clattered under the impact. She guessed, presciently, that their chances were moving away from them. She looked at the indicator, which showed tauntingly that it continued downwards. Knowing that the parking garage was in the basement, she guessed that this would be the despot's destination.

Without wasting any more time, Clancy moved back from the lift doors.

"Stairs, now! Everyone," she advised, somewhat redundantly.

They raced down the stairwell, leaving the three disabled guards and the maid, all thinking that they were lucky to be alive. They found the flight of concrete stairs, in the minimum of time and jumped down them several at once. Inevitably, the elevator dropped more quickly than they, as well as having a head start on them. It soon reached the basement and the underground parking.

Mr Mdombku's driver was playing cards with one of the minders when the lift doors opened. An agitated Victor approached, followed, breathlessly, by an even more agitated warlord. Both were covered in expensive champagne and shards of glass.

"Straight to the airport. Now! Go now, faster than the wind. Your life depends on it!" came from the tyrant. The driver didn't need any clarification, nor did he hesitate. Having seen, first hand, how violent his boss could get when impatient, he assumed, not unreasonably, that the degree of fear written to his face could only render his outbursts even more treacherous.

They clambered into the black 4x4 and within seconds they were underway, bound for the airport. They hurtled up the exit ramp, the suspension bouncing violently as they did so. The driver steered directly for the freeway, Nelson Mandela Boulevard, which in turn led to Settlers Way and then directly to the airport, and Mr Mdombku's private jet.

He telephoned his pilot. "Get the jet ready for immediate take off. Start the engines and be prepared to leave as soon as I get there."

Although the pilot had, as instructed, remained at the airport, he had used his free time to get hold of drink, which he had shared with the air stewardess. Both had consumed more than was wise and he wondered about, somehow, getting the plane aloft. To refuse to do so would go very badly for him and he prayed that he had time for a strong coffee.

Tim and another agent, Scott, were parked in front of the hotel. Tim was attempting, without much success, to chew on a hard strip of Turkey biltong. A hungry dog watched him with a keen interest, its mouth watering profusely. The agent saw the 4x4 leave with indecent haste. Realising, at once, who was in the SUV, he started his engine, throwing the strip of biltong towards the dog, mid-chew, through his open window.

At that moment, Clancy's voice appeared in his earpiece. "Tim, bad tyrant, pervy guy, coming your way. Most likely, he will run for the airport. Intercept him if you can? He has left three of his guards behind, so there can't be too many in his transport. Do whatever you have to in order to stop him or slow him."

He spoke into his communicator, "Understood, Miss Clancy, I guess this chap is in the black SUV and, yes, it looks like he's heading for the airport. We are in pursuit. I won't let him get away," called Tim. "I'll ram him, if I have to. Scott is here with me; firstly, we'll see if we can shoot out his tyres." Within a couple of seconds he'd set off and tore after the rapidly fleeing SUV.

"You should be able to track my signal, by GPS, so I'll report back with more information," offered Scott.

"Yes, he's heading for the freeway, which leads to the airport," he then confirmed.

The speed picked up and Tim knew that at this time of night the roads were clear. If they took a direct route to the airport, it would be unlikely they would evade him. For now, all he had to do was keep up with them. Scott reached behind and retrieved a Sig-Sauer MPX semi-automatic from the back seat. He checked the magazine and made it ready to fire. He screwed a silencer in the end of the barrel to reduce the noise and flash and so also protect his ears. Just before he powered down his window, he said "Tim, get as close as you can, then move across them; I will fire a burst in an attempt to rake their tyres. That thing will soon slow down, if I can take out a couple of tyres."

Tim nodded, as the car continued its progress in the balmy summer's evening. Closing the gap, he pressed the pedal, revving the power unit until it screamed in one of the lower gears, as the kick down provided as much acceleration as the engine would allow. The distance closed steadily. All Tim had to do next was to drive diagonally behind them, moving at a slight oblique angle, thus opening Scott's arc of fire so that he could then destroy the tyres with a burst of bullets. Scott moved to lean out of the window. He knew that Tim would have the car within the angle and range of fire within a second or two. In that moment, however, a rear door in the black SUV opened.

When asked later, Tim would not be able to say why he acted the way in which he did. He would not be able to recall any particular gift of prescient vision or even of suspicion about the car in front. In any event, his reflex and prompt actions saved not only his own life, but also that of his fellow agent. The moment he saw the door open, Tim eased off from the accelerator and instinctively braked. Scott had released his seatbelt, so as to be able to lean further out of the window. He screamed at him, "Scott click in your seatbelt, now! And hang on, I have a bad feeling about all of this." Scott did as he asked and sat back firmly into the front seat, abandoning his burst of fire for now.

As soon as the seatbelt had clicked home, the pursuing agents saw a large bundle being ejected through the rear door. At first, Tim thought it was, perhaps, a bale of rags or even a large bin bag. A second or two later they both realised, with horror, that it was one of the security guards who'd been pushed through the opening, having been deliberately jettisoned from the car. Courtesy of the open window, they heard the man scream. The single mercy was that his unabridged terror would only last for a moment or two. Tim rammed on the brakes as hard as his strength allowed. The anti-lock system pulsated quickly in an attempt to maximise the braking effect. Their SUV slewed across the road. Ventilation on the four discs attempted to cool what had now become very hot. Although Tim had slowed their car, he was still far too close and would thus be unable to avoid him.

The poor man thudded on to the tarmac. Any injuries he'd receive as a result of hitting the highway, in this way, were as nought compared to the impact that was about to be visited upon him. Tim continued to stand on the brakes. Smoke billowed relentlessly from the large tyres, as they struggled to stop the unstoppable. He knew that he was far too close to either halt in time or swerve in order to go around the unfortunate chap; who, it had been decided, would be sacrificed in order to save one detestable man. The agents felt the front of their bulky SUV dip as the brakes exerted their maximal effect. A moment later, the seatbelt pre-tensioners came in, just as they hit him.

The massive and weighty pursuing SUV appeared to dip at the front end. At the same time the rear seemed to jump upwards. Accompanying this, there was a rapid slowing of the vehicle. Before any of these things, however, all the airbags went off with an explosive thudding noise, which rippled around the car's cabin. The poor man died instantly but, as he did so, he destroyed the front end of the car. The entire engine dropped out of its mountings in order to save the occupants. The car swerved across the road before coming to a complete stop after some distance.

"Are you okay, Scott?" the driver asked his colleague.

"I am, thanks to you. Nice one, Tim, well done. If you hadn't braked when you did, I'd have been hanging out of the window and, no doubt, would have ended up with our friend back there, and in a similar state." He swallowed hard and glanced back at the terrible devastation that had been wrought. "I owe you, Tim, thank you!"

Scott then spoke to Clancy, his voice shaking a little with thoughts of his close shave. "Sorry, Clancy, they've got away. They threw out one of their own men right in front of our SUV. Tim did so well to stop, or we'd have been killed, too. He must have died instantly, but it's a terrible mess here and the car's been totalled."

Clancy did her best to hide the disappointment in her voice, though she recognised that the mission was over and their prey had escaped. "Okay, you did your best, we are on our way. We'll head straight for the airport, but I'll send Brady to pick you two up."

Clancy got to the airport. Her frustration increased tenfold by her getting there just in time to see the despot's private jet take off. Had she had her rifle, she would have dearly liked to try a couple of shots to see if she could take out an engine with armour piercing rounds. This would have forced the plane down immediately. She knew her hand-gun would not be able to get even close. The perimeter fence had been breached by the black SUV being driven straight through. It had continued for a short distance towards the waiting aeroplane, before being hastily abandoned, with the doors remaining open, as the occupants had fled in total panic.

Mr Mdombku dabbed at his sweaty forehead. His hand was shaking visibly, as he tried to apply his handkerchief, but the readily apparent tremor paled into insignificance beside the turmoil that existed within. He didn't like to show weakness or fallibility to his men, because it undermined his authority. This, in turn, made him even more testy than usual. It took him some time to calm down; he waited until his racing heart had slowed and he could collect his thoughts. By supreme effort alone, he managed to stop himself from taking gulps of air against the panic that rested within.

"Who was that woman? Was she the same one who attacked our warehouse?"

Two of his security guards hesitated; they knew he was not one to impart bad news to at the best of times and they wondered how he would receive such information in his present state. They each reflected quietly on the fate of their colleague who had been sacrificed on the insistence of their boss, in order to save his own skin. It was only when the guards saw his anger rising with the delay in their replies that one of them spoke. "I think your Excellency is correct. It was the same girl we saw on the CCTV at the groundnut storage warehouse. She is the one who came with the others to free the consignment of women."

Out of his fear came anger and, with it, the need for revenge. "It's time that we dealt with her and her fellows. We need to teach her a lesson in what happens to those who try to interfere with my business. How dare the bitch think she can accost me in this way?"

He continued to rant for some time, his voice becoming ever louder. It was only when tiredness set in that he calmed down. During this time, all the two remaining guards could do was to nod at him and hope that his penchant for throwing people through doors was not about to be repeated at 25,000 feet while they flew north. After some time, a calmer and more deliberative frame of mind had come to him, but still flowed with the need for revenge. The whisky that he'd been downing in copious quantity had slowed him somewhat, but not really dulled his vituperative edge. Continuing to rant, his words increasingly slurred, he affirmed as to what he was going to do with 'that whore of a woman' who had the effrontery to think she could arrest him. Eventually, a single moment of clarity came to him.

"Very well, I see it's time we dealt with her," he shouted, as the two guards looked nervously at each other, neither wanting to see the girl ever again, let alone go up against her. "We are going to need help at the highest level." The guards nodded enthusiastically, realising that they were now off the hook.

"As soon as we land, we will contact our Russian friends and ask them to help sort this problem for us. They are to teach her a lesson she will live, for a short time, to regret." He laughed.

"They are not too pleased with us losing this month's quota of girls. I hope when I tell them that we have been threatened in this way that they will come to our rescue, especially as we have not missed our quota before."

He continued to think aloud as he formulated his next move. "Most likely we will have to pay compensation for the loss of the girls and also to get help. I will tell them money is no object. They are to use any means necessary to bring about the most terrible revenge on her and her compatriots. I would very much like them all to suffer, a very great deal. Only then, before they meet their deaths, will they regret ever interfering with me."

He continued drinking expensive whisky as if it were cold tea. His staff were all grateful when he lapsed into a fitful sleep. The engines whined dolefully, being pressed harder to make an airport in the south of Niger with all speed.

Clancy and Toby were having a meeting by videoconference. Knowing that things had gone badly, he began by asking her how she was.

"Mm not good, Toby," she looked tired and upset.

"We should have worked it up a bit more. If only we'd had a little more time. The Pan-African Congress was on us too soon. We didn't firm up our plans with the usual vigour and it's cost us – dearly. This man, who gives a new meaning to 'scum', has got away. I'm frightened that it will be ages before we get another shot at him." Sadness and regret continued to weave its unhappy work over her features which, strangely, had the effect of enhancing her beauty. Her eyes darkened to their deepest shade but, paradoxically, seemed to enlarge, becoming clearer and more reflective of the available light. The high cheek bones appeared to stand with more relief against the clear skin and her full lips deepened to become more pinkish, in perfect sympathy. He'd thought before, on many occasions in the distant past, that at such times she was at her most gorgeous, but had never shared this with anyone.

Toby hesitated, being unsure of what to say in order to console the poor girl, before beginning, "You know we had to act when we did; the congress was a once in a lifetime chance to bring him down."

"Yes, and we fluffed it."

"Well, Clancy, at least he knows he cannot operate with impunity any more. Whatever he does now, he'll be looking over his shoulder."

"That's what worries me. He's the sort of man who will do something really stupid and not care about the consequences. Look what he did to Santhi and Mrs Nukumobo. I am frightened as to what he will unleash, until we can get another chance to stop him. If only I'd had my rifle with me, I'm pretty sure I could have hit one of those engines as he took off. Could we get a strike authorised, do you think? I'd volunteer for the mission. I could take him out, something surgical: really long range. I'd use those overpressure cartridges that shoot out to over two thousand metres. I'm sure I'd be able to do that. Nobody would ever know, Toby. I could go in on my own, and just finish the job."

He nearly made the mistake of assuming she was joking, but the disappointment etched to her face held a very different interpretation. He continued, more nervously still, "Clancy, that's not like you. What about bringing him to justice? Besides, it would be a suicide mission."

"Trust me Toby, I know this man is bad news. And, I don't care, it would be a small price to pay."

Toby had learned to have faith in her instincts. It wasn't often that she was wrong. He had just had an emphatic reminder of such a thing with her handling of their new agent. Although it wasn't like Clancy to suggest a cold-blooded execution, it could only mean that this character had generated strong and unpleasant feelings within. Furthermore, he knew that he would be unwise to discount her views now. Toby became even more nervous as a truth he should have known from the outset was visited upon him.

He would be correct not to do so. When ruin later beset them all, he would remember her words, and her advice, with some considerable regret. For now, he was shocked, his thoughts disabled by her willingness to volunteer for what amounted to a suicide mission.

"Very well, Clancy, we will get our surveillance team and our planning team on it and we will mount an operation to *arrest* him as soon as we can. He will be more wary for a few weeks but then, hopefully, he will get lazy. At that point, he will make a mistake and get careless, perhaps. We will be ready and waiting to strike and extract him. As regards the price to be paid – that price will never, ever include *you*. Please don't ever talk like that. Not after how far we've come. How far *you've* come. " His fear and regrets rose deep within.

Clancy was disappointed. She sensed there was something of urgency about the situation.

"I suppose it will have to do for now. I'm sorry I just didn't put one in the middle of his forehead, when I had the chance."

"Wow, Clancy, he has really got to you. I've never heard you speak in this way."

"Oh, I suppose I am just tired. I'm sure I will feel better in the morning," she offered with more hope than expectation. She was compelled to recall some of the more distasteful aspects of this objectionable man, "What sort of bloke throws one of his own men in front of a pursuit vehicle?"

"A desperate one, Clancy."

"Another team at the airport would have sorted it. We could have intercepted him there. More men and more planning would have had him in the bag. My AI rifle on a firm rest would have taken care of that port engine."

"Look, Clancy you know we were too fully stretched to field more agents. There wasn't enough time to recall them and re-commit them. You are tired. As soon as we can, I promise we will take a look at it and review the whole operation. Also, okay then, suppose you'd taken out the engine, just at take off, and the thing had come down in the middle of Cape Town. Even I couldn't get us out of that one. We *will* deal with him, Clancy, I promise. But, it *has to be* when the time is right and it will not involve sacrificing you, or anyone else."

Sensing that she was worrying him, she moved the conversation on, "On a brighter note, Tim once again performed well. His instinct in the pursuit was just about perfect. Reading their reports, he definitely saved Scott's life and probably his own. An eighteen-stone man being dropped in front of your car doing eighty is a tough spot to get out of. Did you see the state of the SUV?"

"You are right, Clancy, he is shaping up very nicely. His pursuit would have carried the day had it not been for the poor chap they threw in front of him. Well done, Clancy, you made the right call as regards him, all along. I was wrong to doubt your judgement. I am so sorry, Clancy. Forgive me?" Such words only made him feel even worse when destruction rained down upon them, but he knew he had to offer them and realised that the full apology, due to her, was also overdue.

"For a moment, I thought I heard a little praise coming my way: maybe, even, an apology? Funny, can't say that I have heard either for ten years or more."

"Yes it is, Clancy, and make the most of it, because it may be another ten before you hear another."

"Don't worry, I won't let it go to my head."

"Now, you know, I am always singing your praises."

"Oh, only teasing, don't let it worry you. I am not about to leave and take up pig farming."

"Now, that would be a waste."

"Really intelligent animals, you know."

"Stop right there before I get insulted, we'll meet up back at base?"

"Very well then, I'll turn in and we can perhaps regroup at the Quays in a few days."

"I have another mission or two to close."

"Very well then, let me know as soon as you can meet me back in Salford."

"I'll be sure to do that, Clancy, nighty, night."

She switched off the link, realising she felt a little better. He knew just what to say to support her, although she detected he'd had to work harder than usual. She showered and changed for bed. Her skin crawled whilst under the near-scalding jets of her shower, as she thought of this monster. If only she'd put a bullet to him.

Toby closed down the link with some relief and yet, inevitably, guilt rose inside. He knew ultimately that she could see through any attempt at subterfuge on his behalf. He realised that his words had failed, failed to repair what could not be repaired. He accepted, unequivocally, that they should have never taken on the mission, for he knew only too well what had stirred Clancy's revulsion to this abuser of young innocent women; something locked within her memory, but never far from the surface. Of great significance was the fact that he could see it had re-awakened within her something that he thought she had gained mastery of. How could he have been so stupid? So stupid as to endanger her in the way that he had; now, not only was it too late, but there was no way back. Even worse, was the fact that he didn't have the courage to raise it with her and confess his mistake – a thoughtless and despicable one. How could he have exposed her in such a way?

The following day more bad news appeared for the team. Mr Nukumobo's body had been discovered near one of his steel plants in Abuja. He had clearly been tortured before death and the white card that Toby had given him was nailed through his forehead.

The same day Mr Mdombku was having a particularly difficult conversation by Skype with his Russian financial backer Dimitry Romanonov who was based in Rostov where the river Don ran down to the Sea of Azov.

The Russian was angry. "You have missed an entire shipment of girls. Do you know how much that has cost me? You told me that you were a reliable person to do business with and now I find myself making excuses for you to others."

"Forgive me, we were attacked by a private security firm, but we are putting measures in place to strike back. We have never missed our quota before."

The Russian glared at him. "And this is the only reason we are still talking. Do you think I have the time to hear your excuses?"

"Please Dimitry, will you not let us have another chance. We know who they are and how to reach them. I may need your help with some specialists."

"Out of the question! I have no interest in associating with lame ducks. I think we had better just terminate your contract with me as soon as you have made reparations, with interest."

"Yes, yes of course I will transfer the funds to your account today without delay."

"That would be wise if you expect to get out of this with your life as well as your incompetence."

"I am sorry, Mr Romanonov; as soon as I have dealt with the one they call Miss Clancy and the team of agents known as Horizon then I hope to prove my worth to you once again in the future."

"Did you say Clancy and Horizon?"

"Yes, this is the private force that has meddled in our affairs."

"Not for the first time have we come across them. They brought down Alexandre Ciesciu some months ago. He was another of our dealmakers, whom we were backing with vast funds. He lost everything including large amounts of our money. We do not take kindly to any of our associates who do not perform or lose money. He has now been jailed by the British. Horizon were instrumental in his downfall. It seems we have a common enemy. It would appear that this is your lucky day. Very well, I will allocate suitable personnel as I can see they have impinged on my business as well as yours. We will give you what you need on condition that this is finished quickly and we will then talk about your long-term future, if any."

"Most kind, you are most, most kind. I look forward to hearing from your agents. Thank you Dimitry."

"I have a great many pleasing characteristics. Suffering fools and showing patience are not on that list, so bear that in mind."

His finger came forward and he dabbed a key on his computer to terminate the link.

CHAPTER VI

Paradigm Shift

A week later, Clancy was holding a meeting in their Salford Quays offices. The large screen glowed and numerous charts, diagrams and workings of probability were displayed for one of their missions. She rubbed her glorious head of hair mainly out of frustration. She stood there with one of their mathematicians, Roger, who was a member of their ancillary team and was not a field agent. They'd been going through some calculations of probability.

"I can't help but agree with you, Roger. The paradigm you've applied does seem to offer a better chance of success. Furthermore, the correlational research you have carried out shows a strong causal relationship between the variables. I can see it, and it mirrors my calculations. And yet, my instinct tells me that doing this will be more effective."

She displayed, using the interactive white board, an alternative approach, not supported by the mathematical analysis.

"You can see I have gone back to our null hypothesis here, but I can't help but feel it will give better results. Is it okay if I ask for a little more participant observation where we monitor the subjects for a little longer before we make a final decision?" Clancy paused, looking expectantly at him.

Roger tried to return her steady gaze. She was a clever and able statistician. He knew that her calculations were usually unimpeachable and he had to be on top form to follow some of the analyses she used. What he found so impressive, however, is when she abandoned what the calculations of probability told her and she decided to go with a different approach. For sure, Clancy was far, very far, from just a pretty face. Her skills in psychological modelling probably exceeded her statistical prowess. Moreover, she seemed to know exactly when to divert from the mathematical probabilities and, more often than not, to go with an altogether more complex assessment – what, some would say, was a gut feeling. He knew, too, that he was here to simply advise and support her. Hers was the final decision and she bore responsibility. What was so impressive about the young woman was that she would always pay high regard to his opinions, and would never ignore his views, or depart from his recommendations without, at least, seeking his agreement first.

Roger nodded and smiled his acquiescence. Accepting that he was putty in her hands, he would agree to anything if she simply sent that smile in his direction, as she did in that moment. He could only hope that she would not notice that his legs were quivering while she looked carefully at him.

Clancy moved back to the interactive white board on which she liked to summarise things.

A couple of the field agents were also in the meeting. Turning to them, she said, "Very well, then, Roger has given the go ahead for a little more monitoring. Please report back, let's say another 72 hours, and we can see what we have?"

Looking through the windows, she saw ropes being thrown down. She was sure that they had been cleaned quite recently and wondered why the abseiling team had been sent back so soon. Dimming the screens quickly, because it was too late to bring the blinds down, she knew that this would be sufficient to hide sensitive information.

Two large men, dressed in black, with matching harnesses, dropped down on the outside of the building. Horizon offices were situated on the top two floors of the office block. She hoped, therefore, that they would be finished before very long.

"Time for a coffee everyone?" she suggested. She watched the men as she drank her coffee.

The abseilers withdrew an elongated sponge from its holster and then swept the window with a slightly foaming, cleaning solution. Then, after replacing the sponge, they used an enormous squeegee to remove the excess water. The squeegee, which was then refreshed with a flick of a wrist to remove the excess water, was let go as it dangled on an elastic cord from their waists. Then, the whole process was repeated.

The two men looked almost identical, having the same frame size and the same physique. Though it was a fairly warm day, they both sported black balaclavas; no doubt, at this height it was colder than at ground level. The other thing she noted was that each man had asymmetrical shoulder development. One was using his right hand and the other his left. She had seen similar development in snipers, especially those using the 0.5 calibre BMG cartridge much-beloved by the Americans, in their M1 sniper rifles. She had used such weapons, but the recoil given off by the large cartridges it was designed for could be quite brutal. Moreover, it promised neither longer range nor greater accuracy than the English weapon of choice. The M1 was also much heavier than an unmodified Accuracy International by some six kilos making it almost twice as heavy as the English product. In using such weapons, several snipers had dislocated their shoulders and one had suffered a detached retina with the violence of the recoil force so liberated. Interestingly, she considered, it did cause asymmetrical muscle development of the shoulder in precisely the same way as demonstrated by the pair of window cleaners. No doubt, using their squeegees whilst being suspended from a harness at such height also created similar development. Continuing to look at the two men, she went on to wonder why they had not swapped sides. This would have allowed them to work to greater advantage, by allowing better use of their dominant arm and, therefore, they could have covered the expanse of glass far more quickly, had they done so. The female agent dismissed such idle thoughts. She'd obviously been watching people, in this way, all her adult life. Sometimes, detailed analysis did not apply, and a window was just a window: an abseiler just an abseiler.

She shrugged her shoulders as she moved on to other thoughts. Within a few minutes, they had gone; she gave the pair no more thought. As soon as they had descended below the level of the meeting room, she restored the level of brightness. Her group resumed their seats, and she continued with the talk.

Chapter VII

Temptation

A clear, but chilly, Friday night lay over London. It was early December and a relaxed party atmosphere prevailed among those seeking a night out. So many workers had, either decided to stay in the city before going home, or had popped out to meet up with friends; or perhaps, to meet new ones. The young woman sat in the packed bar in the West End; somehow, she'd managed not only to find a seat, but to also retain an empty one next to her.

Looking through the glass door, as it swung open, she was hoping that he would look nervous as he approached. Clancy clutched the copy of 'Game of Thrones' and placed it on the bar. Having gleaned much of the information she sought, in one quick glimpse, she glanced away. The long brown hair that shimmered as it used the available light to its advantage, now came forwards to partly cover the pert, well-formed cheek-bones. His apprehension signified that this was a new and unaccustomed event for him. Serial womanisers would always say that their first affair was the hardest. After this, cheating was second nature and, in effect, very easy. Moreover, having got away with it once, or even being excused of it; there was no reason why such rules should not be in force the next time: and the next.

His eyes widened; his heart sped up, running like an express train that he could no longer control. He scanned the gorgeous woman; the beautiful profile, perfect figure and wonderful legs very much in evidence, as she sat there on a bar stool. The seat next to her had evidently been reserved for him. In an agony of expectation, his heart now started skipping beats, almost unable to keep up the pace, as he swallowed hard. He had dared to hope that she'd be attractive. Not for one moment, however, had he considered that she would harbour looks that could stop traffic.

Sitting on the tall stool, her legs projecting forwards, complemented by the most beautiful pair of shoes, she looked like an angel on Earth, walking among frail men. This was paradise, just as he'd dared to hope. This is what he'd been missing. Surely, no one could begrudge or deny him the thoughts that were rampaging through his conscious state. Her diaphanous blouse had been buttoned almost to the top, but its delicate material more than hinted at the full figure contained within.

She turned again as he approached, this being purely for his benefit, knowing that he wouldn't have noticed her first exploratory glance as he'd arrived. He'd been too busy gazing around the room, wondering who was going to meet him that night and what she looked like. Smiling coyly and fashioning a slightly embarrassed look, she lightly touched the book that he'd asked her to bring. Then, she smiled again. This, alone, hit him as if by physical force; like a gust of wind, on a mountain's edge, that took away one's breath.

He should have known she would be the prettiest, most fabulous girl in the whole place. He knew it was time: his time, and here she was. He felt his legs turn to jelly and panic rose from within, but he wasn't going to back out now. He needed this so much. He needed her, or someone very much like her, so much. And tonight, he was going to have what he wanted.

He'd told himself that it was to be only a temporary distraction. For sure, he still loved his wife. It was not unusual for women to put on a little weight in pregnancy. He knew, too, that it was characteristic for them to retain such weight for a while afterwards. Nor was it in any way unheard of for women's sexual urges to diminish at such times. He accepted that it didn't mean that she did not love him. Just as his aching need for him to satisfy inbuilt manly urges did not mean that he didn't love *her*. The poor soul, he reasoned he could never voice to her how desperate he was, for what she could temporarily not provide. It was purely a short-term arrangement and revolved around simple supply and demand. Surely, therefore, it was better to have a quick 'no questions asked' affair. Nobody would get hurt. A quick fling, and, no doubt, she would never know. Finding a willing accomplice to his plans had been easier than he'd thought. In this Internet-driven age, his enquiries had been received, matched and responded to within a few days.

She'd promised discretion. He'd dared to hope that she was not just available and willing, but that she was gorgeous too. Without doubt, his prayers had been answered.

She swung her body round on the stool while he approached, somehow managing to uncross the impossibly long legs in one deft movement as each silky thigh moved over the other. As she did so, the whole progression looked demure, discreet, and yet incredibly sexy – all at the same time. Her long hair was now swept delicately behind her right ear as she looked at him. Clancy smiled again.

He looked at the stool she'd indicated next to her, quite unable to stop staring at the toned figure and those stunning legs. He found himself breathing in deeply, having missed the sweet fragrance given off by a young and vital woman, rather than the baby sick he'd become used to in the past few weeks. Involuntarily, he started leaning forwards towards her in order to catch a little more of the delightful aroma that emanated, it seemed, out of every pore. How he craved for someone just like this.

She was much more confident than he'd assumed. No doubt, she'd done this many times before. He shook his head as if trying to erase the thought that then appeared, while he wondered how many marriages this temptress had single-handedly disrupted. He contemplated now, for the first time, despite his promises to himself that he could contain things, whether his would be next. For how could any man be resistant to the charms of such a beautiful and elegant woman? A little shiver trickled down his spine. He fought to dismiss these damaging deliberations; this was simply a temporary solution to a fleeting problem. His wife would never know. In a way, her readily apparent confidence and experience would make things easier for him. He could simply let her get on with what she, undoubtedly, knew well.

"You must be Peter," she began. The restless array of hair moved forwards, as she glanced away briefly, giving off another waft of the tantalising smell as she swept it back behind the delicate ear, once again.

The full, pink lips sparkled subtly in the available light, seeming to be a perfect frame for the array of white, even teeth, which appeared whenever she spoke and certainly with each smile that appeared in rapid succession.

"Yes, and are you Annabelle?"

"I am and I'm *so* pleased to meet you." She held out a slim, elegant hand with long fingers, which gripped his rather more than he'd expected.

"Thank you for coming and for replying to my discreet overtures."

"And discreet they were, Peter. Would you care for a drink?"

"Is that not supposed to be my line?" he couldn't help but ask. She seemed so self-assured: he so nervous. He realised that he was still standing and shifting awkwardly from foot to foot, like a schoolboy desperately seeking teacher's permission for a bathroom break.

"Sit down, Peter, relax, you'll be fine," she advised; as she gently patted the chair next to her with her long, slim right hand.

She looked at the slightly thinning hairline with the temporal loss, so typical for men of a certain age. Mercifully, he'd kept it short. She'd noted that his after-shave was a little overpowering while she leaned more closely, as if he'd tried a little too hard in this unfamiliar situation. No doubt he'd also scrubbed every inch of his skin until it had become sore as if he were trying to cleanse, in some way, his body with which he was about to betray his marriage; not to mention the woman that he loved.

She smiled again, her eyes glowing almost like gold ingots that had been forged in a furnace and had been set aside to cool with an amber afterglow.

"So, what can I get you?" she enquired.

"I'll have a dark rum and coke," he blurted out, instantly regretting that he'd not requested something that was more fashionable, as drunk by cool, trendy people. He very rarely drank and when he did, he selected an occasional beer of which he could not tell one brand from another.

She seemed to sense his thoughts. "It's okay, then, rum and coke it is. It's not too late to order a 'Porn Star Martini' or a 'Sex on the Beach'. Maybe a 'Bellini', like mine?"

"Pardon?" he said, not quite understanding either what she'd said, or why she'd said it.

"Perhaps we'll stick to the rum and coke?" she concluded, affably.

Turning the elegant neck away from him, just for the moment, she nodded, barely, to the waiter. He responded instantly, promptly ignoring all the others at the bar who'd been struggling to catch his attention and, also, the six orders he already carried in his head.

The rum and coke appeared within a few seconds of her uttering the quiet words, which, somehow, rose above the kerfuffle in the bar, where few voices could be made out clearly. The smile she exchanged in the waiter's direction was more than sufficient a reward, while the long fingers gently clasped the drink that he'd slid over the bar. She passed it to Peter, who looked at it suspiciously as if he'd never seen one in his life, let alone tasted one. He looked around, his nervousness accumulating within, rather than following the relaxed lead she'd taken.

"I've never done this sort of thing before."

"I know," she returned confidently but reassuringly. Sipping gently from her own cocktail, her pretty eyes were focussed, once again, on him.

"Wow, you look amazing," he just had to blurt out. He leant forwards towards her, having become spellbound by the slightest trace of the wonderful smell that he then just had to follow. Stopping abruptly, he realised she was probably aware of him sniffing the air in her vicinity, in this way.

"Why, thank you, Peter," she offered, with a slight emphasis on his name as if she'd been rehearsing it in a play. She looked down, trying to diffuse the weight of his stare.

"Peter isn't my real name," he admitted; looking away quickly, back to his unfamiliar drink.

"I know," she confirmed with an insightful nod.

'Wow,' he thought to himself, 'this girl must be so experienced'.

"So, what happens now?"

"Well, that depends; what would you like to happen now?" Clancy stroked her firm but smooth thigh with her palm, through the short skirt, as a ripple of delicate material ran before it.

"Should we go somewhere else?" he asked, his voice faltering with edginess.

"Is that what you'd like?"

Her eyes seemed a shade or two darker now: her voice, having dipped by a semitone, as she surveyed him carefully. She turned a little more in his direction, swinging her legs round to face him; leaning more towards him as she did so. The hem of her skirt rode up just a little to give him a tantalising glimpse of a smooth thigh; just one of the things that he'd been thirsting after for some weeks. His tremor turned into more of a vigorous shake.

"I'm sorry, I am just so nervous."

"I know; this is all new to you?"

He looked away from her mesmerising eyes that seemed to be able to see straight through him; his view settling on the gorgeous figure and stunning décolletage. His shaking only intensified. She paused, waiting for the conclusions that were steadily coming to fruition in the overworked mind of her tryster.

Then he spoke, his voice steadier for the first time that evening. "I think I might have made a mistake."

"I'm sure you wouldn't be the first to do so, Peter," she suggested, calmly. "The question is do you want to recover now, no more being said, no harm done; or do you really want this?" she wafted her hands in the vague direction over her toned torso. "I'm sure she loves you very much and I believe that you love her. Please correct me if I am wrong, here?"

"You are right. You are correct in just about everything, Annabelle. I have been so foolish."

"*No*," she replied with emphasis and a slight shake of her head, the glorious hair following suit, "I suspect not, I suspect you've been quite wise."

"I think I need to go home now."

"Yes, of course, if that's what you want?"

The most perfect of seraphic smiles was reserved for the last. It was sent, at that juncture, exclusively in his direction. Clancy, as always, the master of managing her expressions, her words and even the non-verbal clues she gave out, showed him, as he stared open-mouthed, an image of genuine delight and something of admiration. Her features seemed even prettier, if such a thing were possible, than those he'd noted when he first set eyes upon her. For a brief period, a feeling of absolute clarity entered his mind: his doubts had been erased; and he knew he'd acted, in this final moment, correctly.

She held out her right hand, his grip as it engaged with hers, now shaky and also quite moist. Moreover, rather than a farewell it was almost by way of congratulation for stepping back from what many men simply would not. She wondered, as he got off the stool, just how many of them could have summoned the strength and self-belief to do the same.

She had seen, on many occasions, the look that men gave when pure sexual desire flowed through every cell in their body. The way the breathing sped up, their eyes dilated to their maximum as they watched, not only out of pure excitement, but also avidly looking for clues as to whether their overtures were likely to be successful or not. They'd often involuntarily lick their lips and a good many would swallow hard; some of them would stammer, others would shake. Some would become flushed and others even perspire in that tumult of anticipation. Clancy had seen the outcome of when that line had been crossed. Several had become friends, or rather more than friends; a small number had become lovers; some had become adulterers and, sadly, one or two had become monsters: for she'd seen, too, those who could not control their urges, even when their overtures were neither sought nor in any way reciprocated.

She considered the number of men who could exert self-control, as Peter had done tonight, to be very thin on the ground. Those who could manage this would perhaps gain enlightenment and self-awareness that would last them for the rest of their days; others might go on to become individuals that one could trust with one's life. At this point, she could only think of one man who had managed this – and that man was Toby.

"It was so nice to have met you, Peter." She leant a little way forwards and kissed him delicately on his cheek. This action was purely for reward rather than any amorous intent on her part. He touched the cheek gently as the light touch electrified him.

"Shall I, shall I pay for the drinks?" he offered more by way of distracting her steady gaze upon him. Moreover, he hadn't quite grasped exactly what had transpired that evening; in the bar, with the prettiest of pretty girls. He was also aware of the weight of stares in his direction from some of the people in the establishment, who'd been witnesses that night. Typically overthinking it, he wondered if, more likely, others were simply getting on with meeting their own friends, having a night out; rather than wondering what the nervous chap was doing with that stunning woman.

"No, Peter, it's been my treat, and also my pleasure. I guess she'll be waiting for you and wondering where you are? Good luck, Peter. Look after yourself, and look after those girls."

His mouth fell open, but his shock precluded any speech. Walking out of the bar, he was still more than a little stunned. So many conflicting thoughts now advanced through his overawed brain. He looked back, just the once, as he made his way through the thick glass door. Ultimately, he accepted that a temporary liberation of his sexual urges would have only led to a lifetime of guilt and regret. He knew, too, that he could simply not do that to someone he loved, regardless of his frustrations. His exit, rather more hurried and poorly co-ordinated than most, even remotely confident, people would have made under the circumstances. He realised that he didn't really remember getting off the stool, or pushing on the heavy glass door in order to leave. He was outside, standing on the pavement, knowing only that he'd walked there. The solitary thing he could remember was that delicate kiss on his cheek.

She looked towards the door through which he'd vacated the premises, staring for a second or two, as she reflected on events. By allowing him latitude to come to his senses and draw his own conclusions, she hoped that he'd learned far more about what was real and what wasn't: what would last a lifetime and what would exist only fleetingly. Turning back to her drink, she saw that her glass was empty. With a simple nod to the barman, accompanied by a delightful smile and a slight touch of her glass, she ordered another Bellini. The most perceptive of those queuing at the bar realised immediately why she had been served so quickly, and before them – as they licked their lips: understanding there and then just a little more of thirst; and of hunger.

Clancy looked again a few moments later to make sure that he'd gone. Sipping on her peach cocktail, she smiled to herself. One or two young men stared at the alluring woman; especially at the empty seat appearing next to her, like a vaccine in the time of cholera. The look she returned, however, more than dissuaded them from making any attempt either to sit there, or to engage her in any conversation whatsoever.

Kicking her lower limbs out in front of her, she looked at the long legs appreciatively and the patent-finish shoes that seemed to extend their length even more. Why was it that in that moment she thought of Tim? Not wishing to reflect on the reasons why this should be so, she reached for the slim, white phone she'd left on the bar and touched it a couple of times.

Placing the phone to her ear, she waited as the call was connected.

"Mandy? He's on his way home."

"You'd have been very proud of him."

"No, Mandy, I wouldn't say that."

"You know, all men feel a bit restless, especially when their wives have just delivered. It's what they do next that counts."

"No, rest assured, I can see that he really loves you and, now, *he* knows that too."

"Believe me, no. I put him under a lot of temptation, just as you requested. If he were going to crack, he would have done so. He soon realised what and who was important, and that's you *and* the twins."

"No, don't think that at all. He came to his senses within seconds."

"No, trust me, he was impervious to my womanly charms, such as they are."

"Only someone who is very much in love could have come through intact. Yes, he did that without question."

"No, don't think like that. Losing his bottle had nothing to do with it. Those who get cold feet, tend to recover and decide they want to stray after all. Those who realise they are already with the love of their life turn and walk, just as he did."

"The account? No, there's absolutely nothing to pay. It was our pleasure. It was my pleasure. He is a lovely man and he'll make a great dad. I am just pleased you found the email when you did, and notified us, to see if we could help you."

"No, I mean it. As I said, there are no charges whatsoever. Toby says that we owe your father for so many favours that he has done for us over the years; it's our pleasure to help in some small way, now. It's the least we could do to help out in a moment of need."

"Just one piece of advice, Mandy. Forget this night ever existed. Never, ever, reveal to him that you suspected anything at all. It goes without saying; don't ever mention me, Toby or Horizon. Just get on, and live your lives."

Clancy permitted herself a sigh of relief that a catastrophe had been averted, as she finished the call.

These simple words were meant to set the seal on their future happiness and confirm that a possible crisis within their marriage had been averted. The Horizon agent was not to know that much worse was about to follow. Nor could she have possibly known that her advice would haunt the poor woman for the rest of her life. Even worse than all these things was the fact that those beautiful twin girls would never know their father. A horror was about to be unleashed upon them against which a potential indiscretion would pale into insignificance.

Chapter VIII

Execution

Peter left the bar. His mind was overflowing, and so, he decided that a short walk, before venturing home, would help him to compose his thoughts. Despite not having actually done anything, he felt guilty. People would always say that an affair began in someone's mind, some time before any physical activity took place. He knew that Mandy would sense that something was wrong and would be able to detect the turmoil and remorse on his face. He realised that he'd have to expunge his guilty thoughts before he got home, or she would see straight through his subterfuge. Walking might help. He therefore decided to remain for a short time in the West End, before getting a taxi.

The streets were very quiet. He thought about his short 'affair' and the person who had offered to make it manifest. Annabelle had seemingly looked directly into his soul. He could have sworn that she had said that he was to look after his girls. How could she possibly know; someone he'd met on the Internet, and a stranger, that his wife had just come through a pregnancy and had delivered twin girls? Perhaps he was mistaken and she had said 'look after your girl' referring to Mandy, his wife. Her words had, nevertheless, unsettled him and he accepted that he would never be able to clarify such a thing. Indeed, it was his best plan now to go home and forget, forever, about the events of that night. His pace quickened a little with his new-found determination.

How utterly foolish he'd been. He realised that he must have looked stupid to Annabelle who was, without doubt, a smart, sophisticated and sassy young woman. He couldn't even decide which drink to order. Why he didn't simply ask for a beer, he'd never know. This was it: it struck to the heart of his failure – trying to be something and someone that he wasn't. Nevertheless, it was better, surely, to learn this lesson now before serious harm had been done. Moreover, he would be a better man: both husband and father, in future.

Continuing along the deserted pavements, he saw some distance ahead of him that a taxi had just stopped and two tall men had exited from it. They were wearing identical black leather jackets. As they approached, he realised that they looked so alike. Without doubt, they must be identical twins. He smiled and nodded to them, as he acknowledged such a thing. The taxi moved off and continued its progress along the road ahead of the men, but then stopped after a short distance; the engine still running. Peter wondered if, perhaps, he should run in order to try to catch it, before it continued on its journey. Feeling for his mobile phone, he realised that he could soon find another. At this time of night several would be in close proximity and looking for a fare. His pace slowed again as he went back to his thoughts.

He looked at his watch. It was surely time for him to see about getting home and perhaps he would call a taxi. It was not quite the last thought that he would ever have. The two men approached, their bulk and their stealthy gait, as they walked side-by-side, occupying much of the pavement. Their hands were hidden behind them. He was just about to step to one side to allow them to pass. As they approached, their black-gloved hands were brought in front of them. One of the men produced a revolver in his right hand and the other man an identical one in his left. Peter may have expressed surprise at such an occurrence but, in any event, the sidearms were fired before he could act on that surprise. The silenced revolvers issued two shots: one went through the middle of his forehead and the second through his heart.

Each of the two men caught the bullet casing as it was ejected from his gun. Both continued to walk, neither feeling the need to adjust their pace in any way, nor to avert their forward-facing gaze. Their only concession to the violence they had committed was having to part temporarily to walk around the body. Both were certain that he had died instantly and, without doubt, well before his corpse hit the pavement, which was within a minute soaked with copious amounts of his blood. As they approached the stationary taxi, they neither looked back, nor thought about the man whose life they had extinguished. Such considerations were simply not within their emotional lexicon; the pair's brains running to a very different tempo that most would find both alien and disturbing. Without fuss or hurry, the two men entered the taxi which, having waited for them, drove off into the night. One or two witnesses came forward later but, in effect, events had occurred so quickly that each person told markedly varying accounts of what really had happened that evening. The police couldn't understand why the incident had had such little impact within their consciousness. Perhaps it had less to do with their powers of observation than with their previously held belief, now shattered, that killing someone would be a momentous event, not something that could be handled with such little impact as buying a cone of ice-cream on a sunny day.

Clancy had taken the 11pm train from Euston and, having fallen asleep, missed the gentle buzzing from her mobile phone, deep in her handbag. Although the journey afforded her only a couple of hours of unbroken sleep, it was to be the longest span of absolute rest that she would enjoy for weeks to come. The first-class carriage held very few fellow travellers, so that she was able to relax, without the weight of the stares of others. Remaining in blissful ignorance, she learned of the horrific events of that night only when Toby met her at Piccadilly in the early hours of the following morning. Experience had taught her that he occasionally appeared in this way, either if there were some really good news, or if something catastrophic had happened. As soon as she saw him, she realised that, sadly, it was to be the latter. They sat in his car for a short time while he conveyed the dreadful news. He then took the M6 south, so that they could meet up with Peter's widow, Mandy.

Clancy was not one for displays of emotion; being the master of her feelings and also the nuances of expression that she allowed to visit her face. Most notably, she carefully controlled, at all times, what was given off to even a familiar and close observer, such as Toby. She remained safe in the thought that years of careful study had brought him no nearer to deciphering her inner thoughts, unless and until she decided to reveal such. Even when talking about reverses to her friends and colleagues amongst the agents, she kept a clear and dispassionate attitude. Known to no one, save for herself, was what happened in private, when she was alone, deep in the night. Here, however, paying their respects to this poor young woman, who had been recently delivered of twins, things were very different. She and Toby could only sit, looking and feeling wretched while the distraught woman poured out all her feelings and felt the need to revisit the sum total of the events of recent weeks. The email that she had found on their computer; the worry it set off, paled into insignificance with what she was now feeling. Although they spent a long time with the unfortunate young mother, none of them was able to understand why he should have been targeted in this way. Toby glanced up at Clancy and for that instant in time, he detected a tear hovering fleetingly in her eyes as the emotions overwhelmed her – the first time he had witnessed it do so in almost fifteen years: since the day they met.

As more members of her family appeared, Clancy and Toby left them to grieve in private. They then took the opportunity to seek more information from the police. Toby concluded, after lengthy discussions with the officer assigned to the case, that it seemed like a professional hit. Also noteworthy was that all Peter's personal effects, including an expensive watch and his wallet were still on him when he'd been discovered. Nobody could grasp why anyone should want to murder, or have murdered, a man who was a successful businessman, but not in any way someone who had made enemies or was in the public eye. Time and time again, the question came round to why anyone would want to kill a CEO of a women's clothing company. His poor devastated widow could think of no one who would have wanted to harm him. This was to set the scene for the conclusions of all others.

Clancy and Toby journeyed north after some hours. Both were physically and emotionally drained. Nevertheless, the same afternoon, they called a meeting at the Salford Quays' offices where things were gone through repeatedly. The more times they went over what seemed incomprehensible, the more elusive were their answers. The meeting room was crammed with agents who'd been able to attend at short notice, but despite their numbers, a disbelieving silence hung over the room. It had been a long time since innocent people had come to harm. Ultimately, all could only hope and pray that it was nothing to do with the involvement of the Horizon team. Indeed, they could all only believe that this was a cruel mistake of some kind; the victim had been selected in a professional hit that had either gone wrong, or had killed the wrong man. They even spent time looking at people who resembled his physical appearance, to see if any of them might have been the true intended target.

Before everyone dispersed, Toby summarised the discussion. Clancy, for once, was completely silent; her expression remained a mirror of impassivity. No doubt, she heard the words but didn't really register them at a cerebral level. Tim looked once or twice in her direction, but her mask-like face hid so many sad thoughts, all of which were in turmoil. Regret stalked her like a ghost in a cemetery. If she'd walked with Peter to a taxi, perhaps things might have been different, was a recurring thought. She was plagued by memories of visiting Mandy at home just after she'd discovered her husband's searches for no-strings-attached relationships. Clancy had promised the distraught new mother that she had nothing to worry about, that she would handle it: everything was going to be all right. She would intervene personally: ensuring that an impulsive enquiry didn't lead to the loss of her husband and marriage. At the same visit, she'd also met the twin girls, not quite six months old, and realised how much they all had to lose. Such thoughts now seemed to be in particularly cruel focus with the poor man lying in the mortuary, awaiting a Coroner's assessment.

"Look, we need to be on this as soon as possible. It has all the hallmarks of a planned professional hit. Close range 9 mm, most likely silenced. One of the shots came from a right-hander and the other from a left. Both pin-point accurate: typical execution style; one shot to the head and one to the heart. No clues, no shell cases; one or two confused witnesses with different accounts; timing was perfect. We will help the police as much as possible. I am in constant contact with the investigating officer, who has no leads, other than those I've just mentioned. Although we feel there are most likely, two shooters, it has all the features of an execution. The only thing that does not fit in this scenario is the victim. I am going to suggest that you, Melody, and you, Brown, liaise with the police force in London." Toby nodded to the two of them in a slight pause in his speech. "You can meet up with Monty, who has opened an investigation of our own. If you could, perhaps, get down there as soon as, and please report back." The two people mentioned got up and immediately left the room to journey to London.

CHAPTER IX

First Horizon

After the meeting, Clancy remained. Quiet, bonded to an all-pervading sadness, descended on the normally bright and airy room. Tim hung back for a moment or two, hoping to catch her on her own. However, when he saw that Toby had also done so, he grabbed his jacket from the back of his chair. Nodding to Toby, he did his best but, inevitably, failed, not to look at Clancy before promptly leaving so that the two could talk. He reasoned that they both had a lot to discuss and although he realised that, if he'd stayed, they would have both been polite, it would only hamper their discussion.

"I know what you are thinking," Toby began. He could detect that tears were a moment away – for the second time in the same day. Indeed, as he'd looked around at the agents while he ran the meeting, it seemed that so many were on the verge of tears.

"You don't!"

"Clancy, how long have we known each other?"

"Don't think you always know; don't think because you've always known me that you really know me. Don't make that mistake. You know only what I want you to know." He could see that his words had sent her the wrong way, exacerbating her wretched feelings; the opposite of what he'd intended. He wasn't quite finished, however.

"Very well then, you can always tell what I'm thinking and, sometimes, I guess what you are thinking."

Deep pools of dark-brown, like discs of Cuban mahogany that had been allowed to mature, darkening in their intensity as they did so, looked back at him. She smiled briefly; at least he didn't commit the sin of overplaying his hand – something that Clancy didn't warm to. Most vitally, however, in that moment her mood had lifted ever so slightly. He smiled at her through his concern.

"Clancy, it's not your fault. Yes, you could have followed him, but, correct me if I am wrong, the plan was to remain behind, having planted a tiny seed in his mind. Once this was done, you were to allow him to leave, in order to reflect on that. Our calculations demonstrated that this was the strategy most likely to succeed. You worked on the maths with me. The subject responded beautifully. I've studied the transcripts. As always, Clancy, you were amazing. You were the only person who could have done that – to remind him of that fine line between his thinking he knew what he wanted and realising what he already had. Wow! Nobody could have done that but you. You know all of this without me saying it."

"It wasn't about me; it was about him, his marriage and those two babies." Her eyes darkened again as she reminded herself of the most painful thoughts associated with his loss.

"So, okay then, you follow him and the guy either thinks he's being stalked, or it blows your cover. Or let's see now, both of you end up getting shot. I take it you didn't have your Glock secreted about you, tucked under that little skirt you had on, perhaps?"

He never admitted to even noticing what she wore, but she knew that this was not the time to make mention of such. "No, just my knife."

He smiled again, not being in any way surprised, because Clancy always had some sort of weapon, either about her person, or in her handbag. He would not have been shocked to hear that she slept with one underneath her pillow.

"I just can't stop thinking about him; an innocent man, dying all alone. If I'd been there, at least I could have given his murderers a run for their money," she ruminated.

"Clancy, it's some sort of terrible *mistake*. I can't tell you why the poor man died; only that he seems to have been in the wrong place at the wrong time, and that if you'd followed him, then, most likely, you'd have joined him."

He realised that there were no more words he could say that would help her; ultimately, the only recourse was to attempt to work through it. He got up, not really sure as to whether he'd helped or hindered her. As he passed her, however, he stroked ever so lightly the top of her hair, feeling its silky smoothness and smelling the delightful aroma that it gave off whenever anyone got close enough to notice. He realised in that moment he had something more to voice and to do. He stared at her, the rich blue of his eyes now descending to their most deliberative depth of colour. She could not meet his gaze. "If you'd have gone, Clancy, been harmed, I mean; that would surely be the end. I wouldn't want to – couldn't – continue without you, Clancy, and neither would they," gesticulating with a sweep of his arm round the otherwise deserted meeting room. He then did something that he'd not done for some time. He gently kissed her cheek, before purposefully moving towards the door. She froze, in that moment, not wanting either to move or to respond.

Toby decided, in the process of walking away, to keep her secret, just as he always did, with no hint that he'd done so. If he'd stayed he might have revealed that he knew far more about her than she would wish. She preferred, needed even, to believe that her face, her expression, was unreadable; only allowing others to see what she wanted, at a time and place of her choosing; her personal thoughts being kept, at all times, impenetrable. Toby knew otherwise. He was aware, without doubt, that she could read him like a book; that his innermost thoughts always had been, and always would be, available to her with one sweep from those beautiful eyes: eyes that could be so clear and yet, at other times, appear so opaque.

What she didn't know, or choose to acknowledge, was that on more occasions than not, he could detect some of those private thoughts in her – certainly more than she would reveal and, at all times, more than he could admit to. He understood, too, that he'd not only take such awareness to his grave, but also do everything he could in order to keep it from her – as now.

They'd known each other so long. So many years had gone by. At the outset Clancy had been surly and uncooperative. Upon arriving, she'd spent what seemed like weeks in her room, not wishing to come out. It was all the housekeeper could do to occasionally get in there to change her bedding and throw some bleach down her en-suite toilet. Those first days were especially torrid. The housekeeper had left trays of food and drinks outside her door which, at first, were not touched. Then, one day, half the pasta and glass of milk she'd left had gone and she was sure that the apple crumble had diminished in size ever so slightly. Toby wondered, from the way she looked at him, on the brief occasions she'd appeared, if Clancy resented his having everything while she had nothing. Their problems ran far deeper.

The grim realisation that he'd made a terrible error in getting to know her dawned upon him. The relationship that existed between them was a more than uncomfortable one – and deteriorating all the time. Her pretty eyes fulminated with loathing and hatred: he desperately sought the reasons why. Then there was her temper, which seemed illimitable and completely uncontrolled. Rage would appear like a plague of locusts at any time, and during even the most banal of conversations. Once triggered, however, it would not subside until everything in its path had been destroyed. To make matters worse it seemed that the only way she could give vent to it was to use it to destroy anything within her reach.

He remembered the day that she'd overturned a cabinet full of expensive and irreplaceable china that had been collected by his mother over many years. The entire contents had been smashed to smithereens. To his shame, he'd toyed with phoning Social Services, to admit the dreadful mistake he'd made and to ask if they could place her somewhere else.

Being aware of the way it was headed, his housekeeper had called him one night to stand with her outside the young teenager's room. The heart-rending and never-ending sobs were patently clear. His housekeeper had been hoping that such things would cease with time but, sensing their unhappy relationship and the fact that it was intensifying, not easing, she'd decided to inform him. He'd stood at a respectful distance while she'd knocked and gone in. To his further shame, himself an eighteen year old, he'd been unable to stomach the horrors of what the housekeeper had discovered, upon entry.

To Toby's credit, however, it was then that he decided he had to confront some of his own feelings as well as to desperately explore hers. In effect, he gambled it all on one last throw of the dice. Putting his cards on the table, he reminded her that he, too, had lost *everything*. The tears had streamed down his face, as she looked daggers at him. He wondered if she would stay for long enough to hear him out, before asking her if she thought that money and opulent surroundings could ever make up for his having lost all members of his family, or whether such things simply clarified exactly what and *who* had been lost, in brutal focus. She remained quiet for some time, itself unusual in light of their many rows that made up those early days. From that day onwards, however, an uneasy quiet began. Toby dared to believe in perhaps a slight thaw and, in his wildest dreams, that the start of a bond had been forged between them. He could only hope that, as the years passed, such a bond would become permanent. Sadly, there was much more torment within her for him yet to discover.

It took him some time to learn the dreadfulness of what she'd been through. At that juncture, being grateful that he'd shown tolerance and patience, he felt ashamed as a human being, and especially as a man, to learn some of the things she had to say. Even more chilling was the detached way, bordering on clinical, and a strategy she had developed, to be able to voice them at all. Moreover, it was almost as though she'd been testing him and his regard for her. This, in a nutshell, explained at least some of the hostility she'd shown to him and also why she'd been most angry when he'd been most friendly. Suddenly, it all made sense. Without doubt, he could not blame her. This fact alone underpinned their mutual understanding. Initially he'd felt sorrow for her; subsequently this was displaced by admiration and, ultimately, feelings bordering on awe. All these emotions he tried his utmost to hide from her. It was only by dint of enormous effort that he'd been able to do so from that day to this.

They never looked back. It was almost as though he'd met a new person. She presented outside of her room: washed and clean. Helping his staff around the house, she even began to converse with them and with him. She started studying; her results at school and in exams got better and better. She seemed more at peace in the environment to which he'd removed her; the resentment in which she'd held him seemed to disappear, albeit slowly. And it had all begun that day; the day he'd had the courage to confront some of her assumptions about him; and his of her. More importantly, her agile mind had been set free from the shackles of anger and, he'd surmised, from despair. Her school and, later, college had never come across a pupil that had improved so much within the space of twelve months. In tandem with her psychological advancement had come the need for physical exercise. Initially, she took up running. Some weeks later, she asked if she could borrow his gym equipment. Following her use, he'd often found the settings on the machines at a much higher level than he could manage. Almost by routine, when she wasn't studying she was training.

As she emerged she was like someone possessed, determined to become fitter, faster and stronger. All this was coupled to an impressive mental agility: for it was as though she now burned with the need, not only for self advancement, but also to escape the horrors of the past. He'd asked her once if she wanted to bring the culprit to justice and she'd told him that she'd handled it in her own way. This was how she'd coped and she would never like to return along that pathway. It made him shudder visibly when she recounted tales of the man who'd been so nice on the outside, but had done such terrible things to her. Someone who'd not only been in a position of trust, but who'd also been expected to assume at least some of the parental role. Toby had respected her views but had itched, on more than one occasion, to intervene with the full force of the law – without her knowledge. However, he recognised that had he done so and she'd later found out, then it would destroy what they'd built and how far they'd come. Moreover, she'd had enough betrayal in her young life.

He kept an old shotgun of his father's. One day, she'd found this and asked him if she could have a go. Months before, this was the last thing he'd have let her use. In a way it was symbolic of how things had changed between them, and he threw himself into a demonstration with enthusiasm. In no time at all, he'd set up the clay-pigeon thrower and she'd started firing over the extensive grounds of his estate. Although she was good at so many things, the shooting was an area in which she excelled. To say that she was a natural was in many ways an understatement. He then bought her a rifle and her marksmanship, within a matter of days, was better than that of many who'd been shooting for years. Not that she allowed anything to elude her: for she continued on her quest to learn everything and to better herself both physically and emotionally.

As the years had passed, they'd grown closer. She'd also developed into a stunning young woman. The affection that flourished between them was clarified one night when they'd both had rather too much to drink and had become a little amorous. As Toby was aware by this time of much of the brutal truth; some of the things she'd been subject to – common sense had prevailed. Mercifully he realised, in those seconds where desire rose, that a mistake on his part would destroy, forever, their relationship. He accepted in that moment that his love for her as a friend, a confidant, a sister or even a daughter, despite their similar ages, would outpace and outlast any attempt on his part to move their relationship on to a more adult footing. She'd smiled at him, as he'd hugged her and kissed her on the cheek before announcing that he'd had far too much to drink, and he was going to his bed in order to sleep it off. He came to the conclusion, much later, that this was the final test she'd set for him: realising at that point how diminished his life would've been if he'd failed – and suddenly were faced with not having her part of it.

From this point on, however, they grew to be inseparable, becoming a close and effective team with common goals. Together, they forged their plans for the future. He was determined that what had befallen each of them, with nowhere to turn and no one to help, would not be visited on others. He recognised, too, that his money and comfortable lifestyle would have dulled him, made him complacent and extinguished his desire to seek out others whom he could assist and empower. He decided that resources were there to be used: to be committed, to bring about what was their joint vision. In many ways the trials that she, and he, had come through set the scene for the work that lay ahead.

It appeared that his answers were also hers. Doing mathematics with statistics and probability at university was almost a distraction, especially while her real learning, what *she* considered more important, was elsewhere. She initially refused. However, when he'd suggested that she needed some formal learning to provide security for her future and a fall-back position, she never complained again and fully engaged with the course. Meanwhile, he'd continued to progress with a strategy of his own. One day, when his ideas were more formed, she listened to them carefully and with interest. How very different her response would have been a few years earlier. Not only did she see merit in his ideas, she also came back to him with those of her own.

At this point, experts in their field were brought in and Clancy showed, once again, that she was a willing and able participant who lapped everything up that they had to teach and was left thirsting for more. With time she greeted the arrival of these experts with some enthusiasm and was keen to compare her expanding skill set against theirs. Viewed with rather less enthusiasm, by her, were the young women and professional shoppers that Toby brought in to teach her about fashion and makeup. Undaunted, however, they whisked her away to hairdressers as well as the department stores of Manchester. In due course, they returned with both her appearance and her wardrobe being transformed. She absolutely refused the elocution lessons, but did agree instead to learn a foreign language, which she accomplished with typical aplomb and rapidity.

Her looks and slim, svelte stance caused those who hadn't met her before to underestimate her. They never made that mistake again. Gone, too, had been the aggression and ill temper of the past; it was as though it had been traded and now used to fuel a more productive growth and portfolio of skills. Clancy found herself able to outperform them, outthink them and outsmart them. Whenever her training called for an adversarial encounter she, more often than not, rose to outwitting them.

It was at this time that Horizon was formed. In conjunction with this, other agents were recruited. She was instrumental in creating the more formal training programmes. These included, but were not limited to, martial arts, self-defence, gun control, endurance, covert operations and IT skills. In many ways he had simply occupied both her mind and body. She'd come to similar conclusions, channelling and using her anger to drive herself to greater heights. Wherever her interest ran, Toby would get hold of an expert who would start by teaching but end up leaving in awe at the prowess of this beautiful young woman. Having mastered most of what the tutors could bring, she then continued to develop new tests and challenges. Without doubt, his was the idea and, yes, the money, but she had given it life, its very own beating heart. Although, in some ways her life had begun anew with no worries about her security, her place, her finances or more recently her abilities – it was the past that continued to haunt her. Sadly he'd seen this lately as their recent mission and Clancy's exposure to people who reminded her of her past and not her future had re-awakened what should have lain long-buried.

Those first missions run by Horizon had bemused Clancy. She was both intrigued and surprised by the 'pickle' that some of Toby's rich, 'toff' friends could get themselves into. They in turn looked down upon her, recognising that she was not from the same background as they. This soon changed, however, when they found themselves owing their deliverance solely to her input and precisely-applied skills. She then found herself receiving considerable attention, from the young males who'd been helped, in particular. With an enigmatic flash of the stunning smile, she'd disappear: moving on to the next mission, without a backward glance. Clancy understood implicitly that she'd had far more unwelcome male attention than her young life could handle and she was careful about whom she acknowledged, let alone responded to.

In the beginning, her activities and her learning seemed to be the only way of distracting herself and staying ahead of horrible memories. Later, she'd learned another way and that was to hide or disguise her emotions, thereby letting very few see behind the beautiful, but impenetrable, wall that she'd built. Toby knew, ultimately, that she needed this, its being part of her coping strategy. In conversation he always acknowledged her inscrutable nature without ever revealing that he could still see beyond it. Paradoxically, this modus operandi had served to strengthen their social and professional relationship, not weaken it. It was plain, however, that despite this there were still eventualities, like today's, that would put so much sadness upon her that the façade would shimmer and crack: more than she would wish to accept.

His strategy was simply to be there for her while she quietly worked through it – just as she had with other traumatic episodes, within her relatively short life, thus far. In any event, he could never voice what he'd guessed she already knew – that he remained spellbound by the skills she'd taken on and of the person who had used adversity, as well as Toby's patience, understanding and resources, to forge them.

She remained in the room in silence. Just as he reached the door, recovering, she said, "Toby, please stop, would you come back? I have something to say to you."

He returned and sat next to her. He'd known for a week or two that there was something she needed to discuss with him. He wondered if it had anything to do with their mission in the embassy that could have extinguished both their lives, along with many others, if their timing had gone even slightly awry.

"Toby, I never thanked you. Thanked you for all the things you did for me. You gave me a home, a roof, shelter. You also gave me respect and self-worth. You showed me so much love and infinite patience. All I seemed to show you was anger, hatred and violence. Just how could you have stuck with all that and not asked social services to place me in care?"

"Penny, that's a very simple one. I could always see the wonderful, amazing young woman that you've become. All your peers are enthralled by you and that is with good reason. It's richly deserved. I'd like to say that I always hoped what was really inside you, what was destined for you, is what I see now. This remarkable and stunning young woman who excels in so many areas."

"But just how could you have put up with so much grief from me when you faced torments of your own."

"Next to your problems mine were inconsequential and in truth, and I hope this does not sound conceited, I just hoped that if anyone could help you and restore you to where you were always meant to be, it was me."

"You did, Toby, and it was, I think, only you that could have done that."

"Why has all this come out now?"

"The other night I really thought we'd get blown to pieces and I'd never get to tell you or to thank you. I can't believe it's taken me so long to say it. I think I was simply too ashamed, all the bad times I gave you, when you were grieving too. You must have thought me so unfeeling and ungrateful. I want to put that right now. I want to tell you how indebted I am, to you."

"That's the other point, Penny, you say you never thanked me but I would disagree. You thanked me every single day, I mean when things had settled a bit." He laughed as they both acknowledged the points he had glossed over. "Your bright, cheery manner, your grace, your enthusiasm, your sheer grasp of life and desire to better yourself. How can anyone not be thankful for all that and so many other things?"

"That's not quite what I should have said. I should have thanked you but, without doubt, I was fearful of showing weakness and human frailty and acknowledging that I owe you – everything. I want to say that to you now and if need be I'll scream it from the rooftops."

"Clancy just saying it is more than enough. Thank you."

"I love you, Toby"

"I know, and you'll know that I love you, too."

He kissed her lightly.

"Clancy, I need to ask. Have I seen your old foe break surface?"

"I'm sorry, Toby, I promise I will keep my *black beast* chained in the cellar." He laughed again. Very few had suffered such problems with anger that they had given it its very own name.

"Oh well, the other thing I need to say is that it's not too late to bring certain felons to justice"

"No, Toby, I said all those years ago I handled it in my own way."

"I won't mention it again but if you need to talk about such things or do change your mind then just let me know?"

"Thanks, Toby, I know you mean well."

He could have said more, but realised that it was time for her to be alone. He pushed open the heavy fire door, walked through and into the corridor beyond.

Tim had hung on outside the door and was carefully looking through the glass panel, hoping that he would get a chance to speak with her. As soon as he saw what had happened and that Toby was walking towards the door, he retreated quickly, to avoid being seen, and went into an adjacent office.

CHAPTER X

Ambush

The following week, Clancy once again, met with Toby in the meeting room. Five other agents had been called in, together with some of the support and surveillance staff.

Toby walked in front of the large screen that held details of another operation. He began, "Clancy, you may remember *Hi-Stak Power*, who design Hydrogen fuel-cells. They called us in a few weeks ago?"

"Yes, they wanted us to flush out their mole, who they believed had been selling secrets to one of their competitors."

"Yes indeed. It's taken weeks of careful surveillance and, not forgetting, Tim and Annya on the inside, to uncover the mole. We believe that we have him. We have a sting operation set up tomorrow night, where we are hoping our suspect will appear in order to sell the leading-edge technology that he's stolen from his employers. What he doesn't know is that the person who'll be meeting him to buy will also be being watched by two of our agents."

Toby looked directly at Smith and Davis as he spoke. "We suggest you hold back until the information is handed over, and then please move in. Bruno, you'll be about, but

I'd like you well away from the action. Can you set up the
Jaunt 360 to cover events, and this should provide us with
accurate and detailed surveillance? We may need some hard
evidence in case it goes to court, but I am hoping it won't
get that far. I think that, when they are confronted, they will
both be very co-operative and *Hi-Stak* can then exclude the
mole quietly without attracting adverse publicity or, in fact,
having any of their secrets hacked. Hopefully, this will
ensure that their share price doesn't plummet. What our
mole is also not aware of is that he's been given false data
for some time. All we need, now, is proof that he is the
guilty party; that he is prepared to gather restricted
information and, subsequently, sell-out the company that
he's been with for five years. This being the case, with luck,
he will be on his way by the end of the night. I think a bit of
gardening will do him good, by the look of things.

"Once the Jaunt 360 is running, then just keep out of
the way please, Bruno, but monitor all communications.
You can act as point man in case there are problems."

Toby looked, once again, in the covert employees'
direction and continued. "Well done, Tim and Annya, you
worked well together and have identified our man quickly
and quietly, which is just how we like it. Even better, you
not only managed to discover where the exchange is to take
place but also have, most likely, exposed the chap who
plans to pay him for the data. He works for a competing
firm, who are obviously desperate to steal a few secrets.
You'd better get off there in order to start work, as usual, in
case you are missed. I must also say that, from what I heard,
you made excellent employees, despite only having a crash-
course in fuel-cell technology. I don't think anyone
suspected that you were not genuine technicians. I'm also

told that you only came close to blowing the place up just the once. And I suspect, for such explosive temperamental technology, that's not bad going." Annya glanced at Tim, who nodded and smiled back. She remembered the first day she'd been allowed in the laboratory and had nearly ruptured one of the main Hydrogen lines. Toby could only think, once again, how well Tim was developing, just as Clancy said he would. His training was moving forward as quickly as the organisation could set it up and his evaluation scores were advancing steadily. The other point, not missed by anyone, was how all the unattached female agents were gravitating more and more to Tim who was beginning to attract a lot of attention.

"Tomorrow night, leave work as usual at close of business; don't go anywhere near the exchange, just in case you are recognised. Although it's not likely, we may need to send the two of you back in. If the mission goes awry and the person who appears is not the one we expect, we may need to keep you in there until we have clarified things. If your cover is compromised, then it will not be possible. If you would, however, let Clancy know when our mole leaves, just to make sure that we are up to speed with our rehearsals. If everything goes well, I will let you know and we can arrange for you both to be transferred out in the next few days. We'll prepare suitable and credible exit scenarios for you both. So, Tim and Annya, if you want to get off to some real work, then we will expect to hear from you later. Try not to blow the place up you two, as we are hoping to help *Hi-Stak*, not wipe out their factory."

"Understood, boss," came from Tim, as Annya continued to look a bit sheepish when recalling the close call with the main Hydrogen feed. Clancy smiled at them both as they left the room like excited students being told they could leave school early. They both departed without further comment.

Toby continued, going through details of the rendezvous, which was the following evening. "I am not expecting any trouble, it's only going to be a couple of employees, up to no good. One of them will be selling secrets and the other buying. They won't be armed, so two active agents and one in surveillance should be more than enough. By all means take your revolvers, but you are unlikely to need them. Bruno, I'd like you to set up the monitoring, just in case there are any legal wrangles later. I should imagine when we apprehend the two of them they will both start singing like canaries. A bit of detailed surveillance footage can't hinder in case one of these characters tries to wriggle out of things." Toby detailed the layout of the all-night bus station and exactly where the exchange was to take place. He marked the position of the two front-line agents and also of Bruno, the one who would be conducting remote monitoring.

The following night, the team were in place. Clancy took up her position in the surveillance van, parked some distance away, as Bruno set up and sent through the detailed and sophisticated video-feeds that would make up their surveillance; for discussion later, as well as for future training.

Just after midnight, the bus station, though technically an all-night depot, was deserted. The last bus had pulled out and the next was not due for almost an hour. A dark-blue car approached the quiet, but brightly lit, station and parked just by the main approach road. A few moments later, a nervous chap got out and waited. He lit cigarette after cigarette as he stood there, leaning against his car, but didn't really smoke any of them. He looked with surprise at the small pile of discarded ones lying at his feet, when another saloon car, in white, drove up and passed him. The second car then parked about fifty metres away, just near the ticket office and waiting room.

As instructed, Bruno had set up the Jaunt 360 video camera. This was a special camera that the Horizon team were using increasingly to provide surveillance for their operations. It stood like a black ball on a tripod. Once activated, however, it could render a high definition image of the entire scene in three dimensions. By using a virtual-technology headset, the team could then view the scene as if they were really there. It was especially useful for quality surveillance, monitoring and, as always, and much beloved by the whole team – for training. The 4G feed would also ensure that they received images in real-time. This could then be viewed remotely, or saved for the purposes of future training.

Their mole stubbed out his latest, barely-smoked cigarette and withdrew something from his car. He then walked quickly over to the buyer, who had vacated the white car. His nervousness persisted, since he continually looked around and over his shoulder while he walked. It was almost as though he'd had a premonition that something dreadful was about to happen to all who bore witness that night. After a few minutes, he'd traversed the distance; all the while, the cold December wind swirled around the bus depot. The pair shook hands and the corporate spy handed over a small package that presumably contained data sticks with the confidential and sensitive technical information. Few words were exchanged by the two men, but the directional microphone that Bruno had set up detected and recorded their conversation and moreover, fed the sound to Clancy, in the surveillance van. The automatic camera faithfully recorded all the available images relating to the whole scene. The buyer then opened the rear door of his car and produced a laptop from the back seat. Inserting the flash data stick in one of its ports, he wanted to check the information and make sure that it was the material that he'd been sent to purchase. Studying the screen intently for a few minutes, he nodded excitedly with a smile forming on his face. He closed the laptop, satisfied that he had the information that his company had been hoping to acquire. Pressing the remote control, he opened his boot. From the boot he withdrew a large, black holdall, which he unzipped and angled towards the corporate spy in order to reveal the bundles of notes contained within. On seeing the money, the company mole smiled enthusiastically in anticipation. He'd thirsted all of his life to be able to get his hands on what was contained in the canvas holdall and it was now within touching distance. More words, simple pleasantries, were exchanged by the two men and the buyer made ready to zip up the bag and pass it to his source, who'd come through for them just as they'd hoped he would.

The two Horizon agents held back, just for the moment. They were waiting by the side of the waiting room, out of sight. They knew that the images from the camera would be available to Bruno who was a little way off, crouching behind a low wall which ran along the nearby main road. Clutching a pair of binoculars, allowing him direct line of sight, he in turn was relaying messages to the two agents so that, although they were hidden, they would be fully informed of the events. Images and messages were being relayed to Horizon control in their offices at Salford Quays and also to Clancy, parked some distance away. The van could be a little conspicuous; therefore, they usually kept it well away from the action in case any of their subjects grew suspicious. A few more minutes and it would be time for the two Horizon agents to intervene and rush forwards in order to apprehend the two men. Bruno relayed the go-ahead and upon receiving the signal in their earpieces they moved from behind the waiting room in order to confront the two men effecting the exchange.

Just as the buyer held his arm out with the weighty holdall, a high velocity round was fired, instantly killing the mole with a precise head shot. In a grisly scene, both he and his car were spattered with blood and material that the buyer dare not even contemplate. The horror of what he'd seen and felt was nothing compared to the sense that he was now in grave danger and he knew that he had to get out of there as quickly as humanly possible. The buyer now panicked and dropped everything, including the holdall and the laptop. He turned to get back into his car. It was the last move he made. He touched the door handle, a feeling of abject dread overtaking him. He knew that he simply could not move any faster – terror enveloped him. A similar head shot despatched him before he could even release the catch. The still-unzipped bag disgorged its contents on the tarmac as both men died instantly – falling within a foot of each other.

A tall man approached, wearing a black leather jacket. He carried a revolver in his left hand and a sniper rifle in his right. He looked briefly, but disinterestedly, at the two dead bodies. He paused as if he were waiting for someone, or something, else.

The two agents came forward quickly, making ready their revolvers as they did so. They crouched behind the white car. Once they had secured cover and brought the tall shooter within their field of fire, they called to him. Meanwhile, the images continued to be fed back to Horizon control. Bruno spoke with Clancy in the surveillance van.

"Oh, oh, lots of trouble here. Did you see that Clancy? Both our corporate spies have been killed. Both suffered precise head shots; it has all the hallmarks of a professional hit. Smith and Davis have the shooter covered."

Clancy's words rang in their ears.

"Use extreme caution. I have a bad feeling about all this; proceed with great care and take no chances. I am packing up here and will be with you as soon as I can get there."

"We have you covered, drop your hand gun and the rifle, lay them on the ground, kick both away from you and then raise your hands," came from Davis.

The tall chap smiled a little, but otherwise did exactly as they had demanded. After kicking the weapons away, he then brought himself up to his full height of somewhat over six foot and held both arms aloft.

Davis and Smith now approached, coming out from behind the white car. Both had their weapons primed and ready and trained on the assassin. He remained perfectly still as they came forwards. The agents moved forwards slowly, neither taking their eyes off him.

They had only moved a couple of feet, however, when a similar high velocity round hit Smith with an instantaneous kill shot to the head. Realising that the shell had come from behind them, Davis crouched down and turned. He knew he was in an exposed position and quickly moved back towards the car in order to gain at least some cover. Bruno detected immediately the danger that Davis was now in. Deciding to leave his post, he could only think that Clancy would be here soon, but he knew that he had to take action now. He drew his revolver, unlocked it and went forward to provide cover for his remaining colleague.

Clancy studied the images with horror. She feared that all had been drawn in to a trap. Sensing the extreme danger that the two remaining agents were now in, Clancy offered firm instructions down the earpiece.

"Bruno hold back, it's a trap, do not engage. Do *not* engage, backup is on its way, simply stay where you are. Stand down! Acknowledge? I am on my way, stay where you are."

Unfortunately, Bruno's need to support his colleague had taken over completely. Although the logical thing would have been to remain out of sight, he knew he could not live with himself if he held back in order to save his own neck at their expense. Sniper shots approached now in rapid succession and all Davis could do was to attempt to shelter behind the white car, as round after round peppered the car body. As soon as Davis sought shelter, the tall chap ran towards his revolver. He seemed to know exactly where Bruno would be coming from and shot him with two shots as he approached: one to the head and one to the heart. Bruno fell just as he drew his sidearm. At the same time, Davis managed to fire a couple of shots. Tragically, not only was his adversary too far away for his pistol to be effective, but also, the sniper was concealed in a dark area, so that not even the flashes from his rifle would reveal his precise location. Davis continued to return fire, but then became aware that the first shooter was approaching him from

behind. He stood and turned. Just at this point a sniper's
round found him. He fell to the ground, surviving the chest
shot. He lay gasping on the smooth concrete surface. The
tall chap in the leather jacket approached. Displaying an
unfeeling smirk to his face, he kicked Davis' revolver away
from him and then shot him twice through the head.

Five men lay dead. A small fortune in bank notes
fluttered round like confetti, marking only a scene of horror:
completely unwanted and absolutely no use to those who'd
paid with their lives, for reasons which now seemed
unimportant and incomprehensible. The tall man waited. He
was to be soon joined by his partner, who walked
nonchalantly from the opposite side of the depot. He looked
as if he had simply been on a training exercise. They both
turned their attention to the surveillance camera and began
firing. It faithfully continued to relay images but, after
several direct hits, it was fatally compromised and the scene
went dark not only in Bruno's now-deserted position, but
also in Horizon control. The bank notes continued to fly
round the depot, being caught by swirls of wind as it was
channelled through the bus shelters and hard standings,
where the buses would park.

A black cab appeared a minute or so later. The two
assassins got in and the taxi made slow and unruffled
progress away from the scene of devastation. Horizon
agents were despatched at once, but they were simply too
far away. The last images received by Horizon control were
those of two men, one converging from the left and the
other from the right. They wore identical black leather
jackets; one carried his revolver in his left hand and the
other carried a sniper rifle in his right. The cameras went
blank a second later.

Clancy and her driver drove in as fast as the vehicle would carry them. Although she appeared within a few minutes, she was unable to arrive in time to either support her colleagues, or even see who their adversaries were. What was very clear was that this was a professional operation; the people who'd launched it were well aware of when and where Horizon would appear; also what their strength and disposition would be.

Another sleepless night awaited both Clancy and Toby. This alone would have been of little consequence, but the thought of losing three agents, in what had seemed a routine operation, was deeply disturbing and intruded so forcefully on both of them, thereby preventing all but a few minutes of snatched, fitful sleep. Things seemed even worse when they took into account the casualty rate among largely-innocent civilians who had been cruelly targeted, so it appeared, purely on a whim.

The following morning brought no respite for the Horizon team as a state of numb incredulity descended on the agents and their backup staff alike. Clancy studied the footage that had been captured. She began by looking carefully, frame by frame, then repeated the process; starting once again from the beginning. The most vital piece of information was recorded in the last few seconds before the cameras were destroyed.

"The assassins would not have known that our cameras are 4G. They look like simple video cameras, recording to a hard disc or memory card. They wouldn't know that they would generate high-quality information, including video, in a continuous stream that we could monitor and record remotely. I think, maybe, we have a little break.

"Look here, the big chap moves in from the left of view carrying his weapon in his left hand and the other guy comes in from the right with his weapon in his right.

"More importantly, the rifle he is carrying is a Dragunov, if I am not mistaken. This is a weapon still used by Russian Special Forces, the FSB. It's not as accurate as the AI sniper rifle and is not as powerful as the American M1. It uses a modified 7.62 mm cartridge and it's most likely that this is the murder weapon used for the long-range shots. I wonder, too, if the rounds fired by the revolver seen here," she said, as she pointed animatedly at the screen and continued, "will match the one used to kill Mandy's husband. Surely, these events are linked and I'm guessing that it's us they are after. Those who are subjects in our missions are killed as if by cruel reminder, in some sort of spiteful collateral damage. Even more disturbing is that they know who we are, where we will be and what strength we will be fielding. Something is not right here and we need to find out what pretty quickly or we will lose our entire force. Something is very wrong and I think it's right under our noses."

Clancy stopped; she looked at the walls with the array of screens and the interactive whiteboard. Words failed her at this point as puzzlement and worry overtook her; she sat down. She then looked at the large screen where final plans were gone through for each and every operation. The same screens would be used to display calculations of probability, of chance, as well as lessons from their rehearsals and surveillance footage – in fact, just about everything to do with a mission. She knew, too, that the room was swept daily for bugs and also how painstaking the whole organisation was with all things related to security.

"Time for a coffee?" she motioned to Toby, Tim and Brady. Suddenly, she rose from her chair rather precipitously so that the three men and one of the secretaries gave a little jump with the rapidity of her movement. She then left the room in a hurry and waited for them in the corridor. Furthermore, rather than go to the in-house coffee bar, she took them out of the building and to the Costa along the Quays, between the BBC studios. Very little was said by any of them as they struggled to keep up with the pace that Clancy had set.

Getting there just after the others, Tim came in just as two had gone to sit down and Toby had gone to buy the coffees.

He was immediately spotted by Janet who came over. "Oh, Tim, so nice to see you once more, and so soon!" She lowered her voice, looking at Toby and Brady. "Are they your work colleagues, and I see *she's* here with you again. Is that your mother?" She looked daggers at Clancy.

"So nice to see you Janet, yes, I'm afraid it's a bit of an important meeting, hush-hush, you know." He put his finger to his lips and Janet took the hint and went to serve some more customers as Tim sat down. Before she did so, however, she managed to squeeze in another malign look at Clancy.

Toby approached with the coffees.

"What are we doing out here?" asked Tim, breathlessly.

Toby nodded to Clancy, having guessed at least some of her thoughts.

"Clancy, here, thinks we've been bugged."

Her voice dipped to its most conspiratorial, lowest key as she looked carefully at the three men who'd followed her. "We have either been bugged, or we ourselves have a mole.

The latter is something I cannot believe. Consider if you will. They just know too much about us. Mandy's husband leaves the bar. He takes a little walk and within a minute or two gets gunned down. Our men last night were ambushed from both ends as if their assailants knew precisely where they would be hiding. They'd also anticipated Bruno's intervention as if they had foreknowledge of where his station was. I believe they were aware of where the surveillance van would be and how long it would take to get there. Then, did you see the way they came looking for the Jaunt camera? It was right where they expected it to be. I am sure we can discount a mole among us, so that means our friends have, somehow, found a way to breach our security.

"What's more, I know those two. I have seen them before somewhere. I am going to ask Sheila, in surveillance to try to scrutinise the images we have and let's see if we have any matches in our photo files. I bet we will have them somewhere, if I am not very much mistaken." Clancy nodded to them as she spoke, knowing that she possessed vital information somewhere deep in her memories. Despite the unremitting sadness, all four felt as if a corner had been turned and they were now on their way back. They should have known that the recovery pathway was rarely a smooth one.

"One thing's true, they are using SVD Dragunov rifles." She continued, "We don't see many of those used as sniper rifles these days. It's all M1's for the serious sniper or the Accuracy International for the Brits and NATO. I'm guessing that these blokes have been trained on the SVD and they don't want to give them up.

"One thing, too, is for sure; despite our elegant countermeasures, they have found a way to spy on us. I can't help but think that the answer is in that meeting room. It's the only thing that makes sense. I'm guessing that they know where we'll be and what we are going to do, because *we* tell them. If they managed, for instance, to get a look at the summary screen or are privy to what we say, that would be enough for them to be ahead of us at each turn. They can then, given this information, sit back and wait for us to show up.

"We've lost three agents, three innocent people have been gunned down and these blokes are after us. We need to be very careful and the first thing, as a matter of urgency, is to find out how they have breached our security. We start with that room. I suggest nobody mentions anything in there that we don't want them to know. The other thing is that none of us are safe. For the time being, we should restrict what we say both in the offices and also by mobile. Perhaps if we communicate by digital telephones with scrambled signals for the foreseeable future; it should slow them down a bit." Although Clancy was pleased to have made some progress in solving the mystery that held them dead-centre, she couldn't escape the sadness that washed over her for all those who'd been gunned down out of what amounted to wanton spite and revenge.

They finished their coffees and, although she was serving, Janet managed to notice and wave at Tim as soon as he stood to go. Toby's curiosity was aroused and he leant his head forwards just as the other three were preparing to leave. "Who is that?"

Clancy diverted her eyes upwards in frustration as Toby and Brady both looked at her.

Meanwhile Tim's normally pale features were drenched in a shade of pink embarrassment.

"It has nothing to do with me," and now looking a little irritatedly, "That is Tim's friend," Clancy said.

Toby then remarked, as he detected another hateful look directed at Clancy, "Doesn't like you, Clancy?"

"Yes, I don't know why, but she sees me as competition. I think she thinks we are together," Clancy said quietly while pointing at Tim.

"Can't see that, what a funny thing," offered Toby

Still retaining the humourless expression, Clancy said "Yes, I'll have to deal with her later. Suppressed rifle fire from just over there should give me a clean kill shot, nobody will know it's me. Soon as she finishes work."

Both Tim and Brady now looked horrified, while Toby's face began to form a laugh.

Tim and Brady stared at Clancy with incredulity, not seeing the joke; suddenly she laughed. "Only joking, boys, you are gullible. I like her; and Tim; she'd be great for you! You should ask her out."

Suddenly all three men laughed, Tim with a mixture of nervousness and relief, as Clancy walked to the door leaving him to wave to his admirer, disguising his discomfiture, and Toby and Brady to work through a mix of incredulity and delight.

It was only that night that a vital clue came to Clancy. For some days since Peter had been shot, she'd had only snatched moments of disturbed sleep. However, that particular night she was blessed, courtesy of sheer exhaustion, with an hour or two. Of most significance was that, by the morning, she'd recalled the abseiling window cleaners. She remembered thinking that the cleaning company had returned a bit early. All the windows had only been cleaned a week or two before, instead of the usual two or three months. She'd also noted that their action was awkward. This could only be because they were either new to the job – or, as she now realised, they weren't window cleaners.

As an added bonus, no doubt feeling a little refreshed from at least having a couple hours of sleep, another idea came to her as she drank her cup of coffee.

CHAPTER XI

Vital Clue

As soon as she was dressed, she phoned Toby to meet her at the 'NV apartments'. These were a series of three luxury blocks of apartments, standing side by side and although they were some distance from − they were, otherwise, directly opposite − Horizon offices. He wasn't unduly surprised to receive a call from her at 5am although he suggested that, as he had an urgent meeting at Horizon headquarters, she might like to wait an hour or two and then phone Tim to see if he was available. Clancy looked at her watch a little dispiritedly, but then agreed to at least wait for daylight and then take up his suggestion.

She'd brought a very powerful telescope that was mounted on a rest. Tim met her there. He seemed a little surprised and puzzled to get an early morning call from Clancy who had explained very little. They went up to the tenth floor of the apartments and, seemingly at random, she banged on someone's door. In point of fact, Tim realised later that this particular apartment would give them the greatest vantage point for what she had in mind.

The owner came to the door and saw the couple standing there. She was carrying a large telescope on a long pole, which she tapped on the floor, as if to announce their arrival, as soon as he opened his door. He had never seen these two before in his life, and vice versa, but this did not hinder Clancy, whose imaginative mind swung into action just as the stranger stood staring at them.

"Excuse me, Sir, might we come in?" Clancy asked, forming an accent that any elocution teacher would have been proud of – given the chance.

The owner was somewhat fazed by the two of them appearing in this way. What was more, he was expecting an Internet delivery of all his shopping and not this pair of strangers, who looked like rampant naturalists with this large telescope finished in a green-camouflage pattern. All that they seemed to be missing were woolly cardigans with big pockets and similarly camouflaged hats. For all he knew, they were about to camp out on his sofa and proceed to take all their clothes off. Thinking that it would be best to not let them in, he quickly considered which excuse would be the most fitting. He looked the woman up and down and also Tim. They were both smartly dressed, he in a quality jacket with an expensive watch perched unobtrusively on his wrist and she in a wonderful skirt suit. She strode forwards, even before he could reply to her question.

"I'm Rubinia and this is Kevin Snodgrass." She offered him a half-hearted, token, handshake and even withdrew this when his bedazzlement left him a little slow off the mark. "We are from the RSPB, Salford Branch. We have reason to believe that the Golden-Crested Warbler is nesting in that building over there," said Clancy.

She nodded enthusiastically and pointed a long accusatory finger in the direction of the offices, as if she expected the puzzled flat-owner to have knowledge of this.

She saw the array of glass windows and the balcony that made up the side of the room she'd indicated: it was perfect for their needs.

"Now, sad to say, if I am correct, then you'll have thousands down here just trying to catch a glimpse of the nesting pair. They could be on their way *right* now, this very minute. The Cleethorpes branch are especially vocal – the people I mean, not the birds! What! It was rather busy on the roads this morning; they do like to travel by hired coach and their favourite: camper vans. Of course, I am hoping that I am wrong, but would you mind if we do a quick recce through your front windows? I must inform you that it's a rare event that I *am* wrong. It won't take half a mo. and we'll be out of your, uh, hair," she offered, her speech slowing a little, as she caught sight of his thinning hair-line. "What a spiffing apartment you have here, my man: quite splendid, if I might say so. It won't take long, at least no longer than two shakes of a donkey's tail, what, Snodgrass, old bean?"

The owner nodded, passively. Somehow, he'd become locked in an image coursing round his brain of all these people on the loose in his apartment and with no clothes on, as they made cooing noises, whilst looking for a terrified pair of nesting birds as they did so. The only crumb of comfort that appeared to the startled apartment-owner was the fleeting image of this pretty, young woman perhaps joining in. Before he could cherish such an image, she was on the move. Again, without waiting for him to reply, she strode towards the windows and set up her telescope. Its rest was plonked firmly on the Wenge, solid wood flooring; giving off a firm, thudding noise as she did so. She peered through the telescope, her face alight with expectation.

"Look, Snodgrass, I say, what do you think? Come here, Snodgrass and give me the benefit of your views." She invited him to look through the coated, highly-polished lens and steadied it with her free hand, as he did so.

Clancy had covertly identified the area of interest. A tiny box about the size of a pack of cards had been placed outside their meeting room window. She knew that this must be a sophisticated bug that would record images and probably also speech. This was, undoubtedly, the source of the leak.

Tim played his part, and ummed and ahhed, quite loudly, before finally saying. "No, Rubinia, you are quite wrong, that is just a family of Lesser-Spotted Tits that you have identified. There isn't a Golden-Crested in sight, truth be told, old gal. I can see how one might have made a mistake, although it's not like you to get carried away like this. They are frightfully similar. As you are aware, however, the Lesser-Spotted is, in fact, frequently spotted, if you'll excuse the jest, my Dear."

"Surely *not*, Snodgrass, I'm rarely wrong about such things. I could be certain I'd seen a couple of Golden-Crested over there."

"Well, Rubinia, old gal, you are on this occasion – quite wrong! Take another look and we'd better cancel the sighting report pretty smartish, or these poor people will be overrun by this afternoon. They won't be able to move for bird fanciers. And once the twitchers get here, it could turn nasty. I'm terribly sorry about this old chap, seems like a false alarm. Don't worry, however, we'll make sure we put a false sighting report in pretty pronto. Should only find twenty or so will turn up. There are, sadly, always the ones that try to think we're deliberately putting them off and turn up anyway. They are unlikely to stay more than an hour or two. They will set up a few cameras, a long-range microphone and a camouflaged gazebo; eat a couple of sandwiches and down a quick flask of cocoa. They'll have cameras and binoculars on large tripods and they may play the recorded mating call of the Golden-Crested, to try and draw them out. We'll make sure that they don't leave the dock side, they'll have more than enough room down there to set up. After a while, though, they will realise it is, after all, a false report and they'll be on their way, until the next sighting, of course. Thanks for this old bean, we'll get out of your way," came from Tim. "Come, Rubinia, we'd better beat a hasty retreat and get those reports corrected."

"Frightfully, sorry about this, my dear man. It's all for the best, and hopefully you won't have too many out there. Of course, it's a sad day when one finds one is wrong and it seems the Golden-Crested has eluded one, on this occasion at least."

With this, they walked out through the flat, taking their telescope with them. The owner continued in a paroxysm of curiosity and incredulity, but still hadn't managed one word.

They walked away with a stiff formality, the only things missing were a clipboard and a pen on a chain; the resident watched them as they went down the corridor to the lift. As soon as the lift door closed they both laughed like kids upon entering a fun-fair. She looked at Tim with nothing but admiration.

"Tim! You were superb! Well done, you carried it off beautifully. We'll make a bird-fancier out of you yet, or maybe even an actor."

"I'll have you know, Miss Clancy, I was asked to play Joseph, two years running in our school play, when I was seven and eight."

"Well, Tim, if it doesn't work out here at Horizon you can always try your hand at treading the boards." Her pretty eyes seemed to be enlivened as they ascended the spectrum of visible light to their most enticing shade of creamy caramel. He looked at her just as she looked at him. Silence intervened. Their eyes met and, for a brief moment, neither seemed to want to look away. He then realised that he could only risk a brief gaze as her eyes continued to glimmer at him. Words failed for both of them at that point and neither knew why that should be so.

Suddenly she became more serious and the moment was over. "Something has been attached to the outside of the window, just in the corner I indicated. I don't think we could see it from inside. It seems our friends have been using this to spy on us. All we need now is to know who they are working for and how many of them there are." Tim nodded in agreement, doing his best to think of serious matters.

"Let's go and find Sheila to see if she has had any luck with the grainy images we have of our two snipers armed with Russian hardware." Clancy suggested. They walked over to the Horizon offices and met up with Toby, who had just finished his meeting but was keen to hear of their discovery that morning.

At that moment Toby's phone went off. His face creased into a smile as the caller's name came up.

"Alexis, so nice to hear from you. What! Has anyone been hurt? Are you okay? Where are you now? I will be there as soon as I possibly can. I will fly down immediately.

"Yes, the cellar seems like a good idea. Get everyone in there and lock yourselves in. Please wait for me and don't trust anyone. There are some professional hit men targeting anyone who has any connection at all with Horizon; innocent people have been killed. Don't open that door to just anyone. I'll get Monty to head over as soon as he can. At least he is someone you will know. I am on my way; I'll be there as soon as I'm able. Now, lock that door. I'll make sure Monty lets you know that it's him. When you first met him he gave you two things, one of which was a tablet. Do you remember what colour it was? That will be the secret word; don't open the door until he has spoken it. I will telephone him now."

Clancy remained calm even as Toby's anxiety rose, "Tim, would you be able to see Sheila to see if she's made any progress, I'll go with Toby."

Tim went immediately, after deciding that now was not a good time for questions. As soon as Toby terminated the call, Clancy quizzed him.

"A bomb's gone off outside Alexis' offices in London. Nobody has been hurt. I need to get down there, Clancy, and make sure she is all right."

"Of course, I understand. I'll come with you, Toby. I'll drive," she nodded, already reaching for her car keys.

She drove him to Manchester City airport, where a helicopter took them to Manchester International. There, a private jet awaited them, which took off almost immediately. It landed at London City airport in the Royal Docks and within the hour they were approaching Alexis' offices. En route he had phoned Monty to investigate as soon as he was able, in order to ensure that Alexis and her employees were safe.

"Be careful Toby, I think it's a trap. They know you will respond and this is just what they'll be hoping for. You turn up, do the frantic boyfriend thing, and they promptly pick you off with the Dragunov," cautioned Clancy.

"I can't not go. The poor girl is terrified and this is because of Horizon. Besides, I never do the 'frantic boyfriend thing'."

"And go you shall, frantic boyfriend," she smiled, reassuringly.

"I have to find her."

"And find her, you shall. But, I'll go in with you and I have a little trick up my sleeve. Please let me speak to Monty so that he can get the stuff we'll need?"

Toby nodded a minute or two later, as he heard her suggestions. "Just love you, Clancy, where would I be without you?"

"I know, to the former and I dread to think, to the latter. Now, let's just have a pause, here, before we go rushing in." Clancy continued. "I am worried that they are waiting for you and they will pick you off as soon as you show yourself. Consider, for a moment, if you will. A bomb goes off in the centre of London. The Police, Fire and Counter-Terrorism will be all over it. They will be crawling over the area as we speak. First, they will need to make sure that the locality is safe. They will shut the road and seal the whole zone off. I suspect that even you would have trouble getting in to the place. This will be to your advantage and will give us more time. I'm sure that one or two more will not be noticed. Time for a bit of dressing up, Toby?"

Clancy was correct, the Police and emergency services had responded very quickly. Another team, however, went in carrying large, metal cases, wearing riot gear, bullet-proof vests, helmets and tinted goggles. People drifted in and out of the offices all morning. At Clancy's insistence, Toby had arranged for extra surveillance to scrutinise the roof tops and surrounding vantage points for any snipers. In particular, they'd been asked to concentrate the perimeter of search at a distance within the effective range of fire of the Dragunov sniper rifle, which was about 800m. If the assassins were hoping to pick off more targets, they'd need to be within this. Clancy was certain that they would be aware of the limitations of their hardware, just as she was.

In a particularly effective move, so typical of Clancy, the perceptive would have noted that more than one Counter-Terrorism van had pulled up outside. The most observant, however, would have seen that more acute-response unit officers came out of the building than had gone in; some with ill-fitting uniforms and some gazing intently at the surrounding skyline, as they did so.

Toby, Clancy and a couple of the London-based agents got in the back of the extra Counter-Terrorism van. They were joined by four others, some of whom walked clumsily in the baggy outfits. Once they were in the van, the door was closed; they all took off their goggles and loosened the jackets, which were very warm. Alexis, Peter and her staff removed their helmets too. The van immediately sped away.

"Great disguise, Toby, can I keep this for our Christmas fancy dress party?" asked Alexis, her panic and fear now being swept away by the team's presence and especially Toby's.

"Mm, yes I am sure that can be arranged. It could do with a bit of taking in, though."

He kissed her.

Clancy smiled, "Are you okay, Alexis?"

"Perhaps a bit shaken, but we are all right. Glad to be out of there. We were very lucky to be down in the loading bay, looking at some samples that had just been delivered. Good job I need my Financial Director, Production Manager and trusty secretary to be with me when I do this."

"She doesn't do a thing without us," offered Hilary, her secretary. "Except meet you, of course," she continued, with a wistful look in her eyes, as she looked at Toby.

"I'm so sorry about all this, Alexis. Someone is targeting Horizon and we are not quite sure who or why, at the moment. Our agents, our subjects, even the innocent are coming under fire. Nobody is safe at present. We need to get you, all of you, to safety." Hilary's eyes brightened as Toby continued, "*Ma Puissance* is in the Western Med; we have asked it to divert to Gibraltar. We can have you, and as many as wish to go with you, on a flight within the hour. You remember Monty?" The agent to his right, took off his helmet.

"Ah yes, Miss Alexis, it's so nice to see you again, my Dear. I do hope you can forgive me?"

"I think all that is in the past now, Monty, and, of course, you were positively charming at all times. I certainly remembered the red tablet you gave me and how can I forget the 'unsafe in taxis'. That was really clever; everyone needs a bit of intrigue and a bit of spice."

"Yes, I must say that was Clancy's idea. Our figures showed that…"

Clancy shot him a glance; in that instant, he altered his intended sentence. "Oh, well that's all in the past, too."

"You were a perfect gentleman, Monty, and I thought you played your role perfectly," she offered, sensing that he was more embarrassed by the episode than, perhaps, he deserved to be.

"Well, Monty, and Miss McCready, both of whom you know, will be accompanying you to the airport, will travel with you and will embark with you, as soon as *Ma Puissance* makes harbour. Moreover, they will remain with you, keeping you all safe, until we have this sorry mess sorted. Think of it as a bit like a Mediterranean cruise," came from Toby.

"Can you come with us, Toby?"

"No, sorry, Alexis, my place is here in the UK. I have to stay and find out, with more than a little help from Clancy here, who is trying to kill us all. As soon as we have all this figured out, then I will be on the next aeroplane out. Until such time, I want you all out of harm's way."

"In that case, can I not stay here with you?" Alexis asked.

Clancy looked at her very carefully as she said this. It was clear that Alexis would rather stay with him, albeit in danger, than leave without him. She wasn't in any way surprised that she'd said this. In point of fact, Clancy's strategy, in bringing the two of them together, had been predicated on such a belief.

"No, Alexis, we are not sure just how deep this goes and, just a couple of nights' ago, we lost three agents."

The young businesswoman saw the sorrow and tiredness etched to his face. Knowing, ultimately, that displays of loyalty were not what he needed, she nodded and did her best to smile.

"As soon as it's over, and we have concluded our business, I'll come and find you. If we ask her nicely,

Clancy here will show you how she catches fish with her bare hands and a sharp knife secreted about her person."

Clancy shook her head. "Actually, the only catching of fish I do is at my local supermarket, but it's best to just let him carry on when he's in this giddy mood. I suspect it's down to seeing you, Alexis. We've been working him so hard recently that he hasn't been getting out much."

Alexis nodded even more vigorously, managing to wink at Clancy, with a little nod aimed specifically in her direction.

The Incident van made steady progress away from the scene of devastation and, so they hoped, out of danger. Alexis and all her staff were dropped off at London City airport. Toby relayed some final instructions to Monty and Miss McCready. Most importantly, he warned them not to trust anyone and always be on their guard. They were not to hesitate to use lethal force if they felt the situation warranted it.

Sensing that their impromptu meeting was over, Alexis approached and kissed Toby.

"You can probably get a change of clothing later?" he suggested.

"Well, at least we won't have any problems getting through security dressed like this. I am definitely going to keep it." She waved, after kissing him for a little longer than his blushes would have sanctioned.

"Please keep yourself safe and come and find me as soon as you can get away?" Alexis asked him, beseechingly. The party of six walked away from the transport towards the runway, with Hilary in particular barely able to contain her excitement. They then boarded the private jet that had brought Toby and Clancy down from Manchester. As they took off, Clancy and Toby took the train from Euston, heading north to Piccadilly. Meanwhile, *Ma Puissance* was making all possible speed to meet up with Alexis in Gibraltar.

Clancy sensed his thoughts as they journeyed north.

"I'm sure that Monty and Karen McCready, will look after them. This way, they'll all be safe and we can get on with sorting this mess out."

Clancy's phone rang. She mouthed to Toby that it was Sheila.

"Oh yes, Sheila, I knew I'd seen these two somewhere before. Yes, print the file for me, if you will, and leave it on my desk. Nobody is to go into the meeting room unless given express instructions from either Toby or me. I will explain more at our next session."

Upon silencing the phone with a quick dab from a long finger, she turned towards Toby, who was sitting next to her as the train ran north.

"Toby, at last we have some identification. The Ruganov brothers, twins in fact, are ex-KGB. I knew I recognised them from somewhere. Antonov and Leonid are identical twins. One is right-handed, however, and the other is left. You can see how they take advantage of this when they start shooting. After the KGB, they were trained as part of the Russian sniper force in Afghanistan. More recently, they transferred into the FSB. Unfortunately, with the decline in the Russian economy, the FSB started recruiting a load of poor-quality agents, who embarrassed the whole agency. These two left a few years ago, being disgusted, so we are told, by the lack of capability on the part of their contemporaries. They both went freelance a short time later. Obviously they decided that rather than stand on their principles they would simply go for the money. They will have been trained up on those Dragunov, which can probably be regarded as special equipment for the Russian forces. These two, these days, are effectively guns for hire. They will do anything, if their price is met. Killing innocent dads who are just walking the streets is second nature to them." As she spoke the words, disgust appeared on her expression. Toby could see her inventive mind already plotting a way of bringing them to battle.

"Yes, I think they were sending us a signal. Having gone this far, then I am sure they will not stop now. I wonder who can be paying their expensive bills. I'm told it's ten million, USD, a hit. So, someone with deep pockets has obviously engaged them. It can only be someone who, clearly, bears a grudge against all at Horizon. Trouble is we run so many missions that it could be any number of people."

"Well, at least we know who, and what, we are up against."

"Yet, this is a little excessive; it's way over the top and this is why I am glad Alexis is out of the way. It's almost as if they are killing for the sake of it, just for fun. I don't think they would stop short of shooting her, if they got the chance, or just about any of us. You saw what they did to the agents, up close, at the bus station. They gave them absolutely no quarter. I am not sure who has hired them and why, but at least we know who they are if not who has sent them. We need to find them, and quickly, in order to start changing the odds in our favour. Tim is picking us up at the station, so we can perhaps talk in the car?"

Chapter XII

Breadcrumbs

The following day, Clancy gathered some of the agents in the meeting room. The screens showed details of their next operation and the key targets and objectives of that mission. She made sure that the brightness was turned up more than usual. She also spoke more loudly than anyone could remember, almost as if she were talking to someone who was hard of hearing. The screens, as always, directly faced the windows that looked out on the Quays. Clancy, as was her wont, stood in front of the screens and paced up and down as she summarised the salient points.

"This is a simple job. One of our clients has reported that his son is buying drugs from a dealer on the London embankment. So, if you look at the aerial view, you can see it's a small car park and, late at night, cars pull in. As soon as the deal is made, money changes hands, drugs are handed over; nobody is any the wiser. It's a small-time operation, so it should be quick and easy to sort out.

"I will drive down in my white F-type with Brady. I will then just wait until the dealer appears and simply ask him, very politely – as you all know, if it might be time for him to suspend operations of selling drugs to kids. If he is not enthusiastic about such things, I will go on to inform him that his next conversation will be not with me, but with the Police. Hopefully, this will be more than enough to make him see the error in his ways – at least for now and for our client's son.

"Very well then, we are live tomorrow night. Just two of us should be more than enough. It's only a kid selling, so we do not need to go heavy-handed and, of course, we won't need any firearms. Any last questions? Good, okay then, let's get down there and do our concerned citizen bit, shall we?"

Clancy came out of the meeting room and whispered to Toby, "You owe me a new car."

"Clancy, if we can wrap this up, then that will be my pleasure. What would you like?"

"Oh, same again, I think. That boot takes my sniper rifle perfectly."

"Most people say something about golf clubs at this point, not sniper rifles." She looked at him askance, thinking why on earth would she need golf clubs, when she had a perfectly good sniper rifle to fit in that boot. He continued, realising that he wasn't getting very far. "All right then, Clancy, same again it is. I will phone my contact and we should be taking delivery in the next few days. Do you want the same colour and the same extras? I take it you want the more powerful engine option?"

Clancy looked at him, wondering if he really needed an answer to a question that did not need the waste of breath to pose. She drew a breath to speak, but otherwise said nothing.

"Oh, just checking, I should know, the way *you* drive, you'd want the quickest one possible."

"Look, I only got fifteen speeding tickets last year."

"You know my influence only extends so far, Clancy?"

"You just love bailing me out of trouble; it reminds you of days gone by."

He smiled, "I'll just order the car, Clancy. You wrap this up, finally, and perhaps we can all get out for a cruise on the Med and, if we do okay tonight, we might be there by Christmas."

"I'll do my best, Toby."

Just then Tim came up to her in the corridor. He'd clearly been waiting for her to leave the meeting room and seemed more nervous than usual, despite the excellent suggestions he'd made *before* the meeting. The other inescapable point noted, not just by Clancy, but by all the other agents, was his growing confidence. Clancy was keen to acknowledge the contribution he'd made; the fact that he'd challenged her strategy and suggested one of his own, which seemed to be more effective, made this even more important. "Tim, that was a brilliant idea of yours about the meeting room. I think this gives us an excellent opportunity to finish this once and for all."

"I, I hope you didn't think me interfering, Miss Clancy?"

"Tim, no, not at all, my thoughts on the matter were incorrect and would not have given us half what I am hoping your ideas will deliver. Thank you, Tim." At this point she was just about to turn away in order to pop in and see her secretary, but she noticed that Tim was a little reluctant to leave. "Sorry, Tim, was there something else I can help you with?"

"No, not really, not exactly..."he began, falteringly. "Tim, what can it be? Just tell me!"

He'd clearly been observing the female agent, his idol, and her strategy of calming herself before a crucial shot. Following suit, he now took a deep breath and then said, "Miss Clancy, I was wondering if you'd care for some lunch?" Clancy was aware of one or two eyes being on them as people dispersed from the meeting room. She was just about to decline when something – perhaps it was a slight pang of unaccustomed hunger – diverted her thoughts.

"Tim, that would be lovely." She could only wish that his face hadn't illuminated with such unabridged pleasure. Mercifully, most people had gone by this time and only Toby glanced quickly in their direction as he walked past.

"Ooh, that's great, Miss C. Downstairs in ten?"

She smiled to herself; he had such boundless enthusiasm that he was a hard person to disappoint. Perhaps she felt a little more carefree with the first positive plans they'd put in place for weeks, or it might have been simply that she was hoping to reward him for his unstinting efforts. What she could not acknowledge, or even consider, is that there might have been something far more complex in play, just at that moment.

She waited on the corner just as Tim pulled out of the secure park in a beautiful red E-type she'd never seen before.

"Tim, what a beautiful car." He blipped the accelerator as she got in. The day was clear and bright, but cold. The fans had begun to infuse warmth into the foot wells from the heater as he passed her a scarf and a pair of oversized sunglasses which, initially, seemed passé, but then she tried them on and he whooped with delight.

"You look marvellous, Miss C," he couldn't help but say as his unmasked delight at having the woman he admired, more than any other, in his car, overflowed. He did his utmost, but ultimately failed to limit his thoughts to that. As they drove along, he also did his best to look directly at her and managed to avoid his former habit of staring at her legs. She thought to herself, as they whisked along, just how far he had come in such a short space of time.

"This is Series I, if I am not mistaken?"

He nodded, having guessed that she'd know exactly what she was being transported in.

"Well, I never thought I'd sit in a Series I OTS (open two-seater). Is it a 3.8 or a 4.2?"

"Four point two" he clarified with boundless delight, full of admiration for, but in no way surprised by, her knowledge.

"About 1965?" she cooed, with her lips, as the sheer delight mirrored his. Staring along the length of the car she couldn't help but remember how one motoring correspondent had said that the reflection of Heaven itself could be seen in that bonnet. She understood in that moment why he'd said that. The scarf restrained by just the right amount as the slipstream toyed with her glorious head of hair. His blond and slightly wavy locks were tousled more thoroughly and she couldn't help but notice the more rugged look that this gave him. She found herself staring more in his direction each time she approached him with another question about the car.

"So, better brakes, synchromesh, reclining seats?" she queried. He deliberately raised his eyebrows a little suggestively at the mention of the latter and this seemed to resonate with the light mood that their journey, and especially their mode of conveyance, had created.

Heads turned as the office workers around the Quays went to lunch; many heard it before they saw it. The magnificent engine purred away with a stimulating, slightly-earthy note as it carried them along. He looked over his sunglasses as he chanced another glance at her. Just as he did so, a bright shaft of late morning winter sun caught him full on the face. For the first time, or so it seemed, she noticed the pale-blue eyes, much paler than either Toby's or Alexis'; in point of fact they looked as if they'd moved further along the spectrum, from the blue – approaching even indigo.

He found the southbound motorway and thirty minutes later they approached the village of Alderley Edge. He took a sharp right, gassing the gears in precisely as he changed down, thereby maintaining a higher level of speed and a smoother gear change, and eased the work of the synchromesh as the revs rose briefly.

"I didn't know you could drive? Where are we going?"

His only reply at this stage was the enigmatic smile he offered in her direction that left her heart fluttering, for reasons which she struggled to contemplate. She had to admit, for once, that whatever was happening was due to something even more exciting and compelling than fear.

The road to Prestbury wound a little round the headland. Even from this distance, she could see the magnificent house on the lofty curve that lay ahead. It in turn had unparalleled views down towards the Cheshire Plain and past the wooded sandstone ridge of the Edge itself. Even without calling upon the skills of the wizards who were said to have once inhabited this area, she knew, without being told, this was their destination. This is why he'd not answered her.

She laughed as they approached and she was rewarded once again by the smile that had not been absent since she got in the car.

"Go on, say it, I am waiting?"

"Nothing, I was just thinking why are there no poor people like me in this organisation."

"You know, Miss Clancy, you're better than all of them, and they'd all swap places with you in a heartbeat."

Clancy was not so sure about this, but events encouraged her to continue in her carefree mind-set that had been absent for some time. It was only later that such simple and inoffensive words would catch up with her.

A few more bends and he pulled off the main road. The rear end broke away, just for a second as they traversed a patch of damp and icy leaves. Tim corrected it immediately with a slight flick of his wrist. She nodded, "You really can drive, Tim, and you've not been on your advanced driver's skills training yet."

A private drive led, after a further half mile, to an enormous pair of wrought-iron gates suspended between stone pillars that she decided would not have looked out of place as a feature in an ancient Egyptian tribute to the gods.

Coming to a stop, the engine now burbled reassuringly as it idled with a slightly uneven note. He pressed a little button on his key fob and the gates slowly and noiselessly began to swing open.

The car then swept along a semi-circular drive that led to the most beautiful house she'd ever seen. She noticed the magnificent, double front door with glazing panels above it in a semi-circular arc. Standing in front of the partly-open doors was a delightful couple who'd clearly turned out to welcome their son and his guest. A flight of curved solid-stone steps came up from the level of the drive to the glazed canopy that extended from the house, forming a porch. Through the partially open double doors she gained a hint of the square hallway with its hardwood floors, panelled doors and lofty ceilings. Providing illumination was a large circular cupola above the entire hallway made up of leaded lights in bright colours. On either side of the foyer ran symmetrical staircases that led to the gallery rail that in turn led to the upstairs bedrooms running off in both directions from the hall, making up two wings of the building. Either side of the doors were long, rectangular windows that were set in a pleasing symmetrical pattern. The only thing that broke up the expanse was a circular bay that had been brought out from the frontal elevation featuring matching, but curved, windows that extended round its periphery, inviting light into the room at all times of day.

Above the entrance was a large, circular window with original leaded lights that matched the cupola. As one's eyes were drawn up the facing wall, the vast slate roof was interrupted only by dormers set four either side and, at the back, one could make out the six chimneys that sat in regular intervals above the whole, beautiful edifice.

Clancy laughed, "Tim, what am I doing here?"

"Lunch, wasn't it?"

"I thought you had in mind a quick snack in the chippy?"

"Come on, they are dying to meet you and I promise they won't bite. We'll have a code; as soon as you say 'pomegranate' I'll know you've had enough and want to leave?"

Far from biting her, the couple, who looked in their late forties, could barely restrain their excitement.

Indeed, as Clancy approached she could have sworn that the woman was hopping up and down. She noted immediately where he'd got his pale-blue eyes from, as his Mother's were identical to his. The older lady could barely wait for Clancy to ascend the steps; she'd begun her own journey down them to meet up with their guest a bit sooner. "At last Tim! We've been so looking forward to meeting you, my Dear. I'm Margaret and you, of course, are Miss Clancy?"

"Penny, Mrs Wainwright, please call me Penny."

Tim whispered to her, "Told you it was only a matter of time before you let it slip." Clancy conveyed a magnanimous but rewarding smile as she conceded the point happily.

"And in that case, please call me Margaret and this proud Dad is Arthur."

Clancy shook his hand after noticing a quick look down at her legs.

'Can only be Dad' she thought. "Pleased to meet you, Sir."

"Arthur, please. We are so pleased that you were able to come. Tim has been speaking of nobody else since he joined you at Horizon," Arthur managed, whilst dipping his voice despite the fact that there were only the four of them present. "We've given the staff the day off as we wanted you to feel at home and not have to be careful what you said. Tim has sworn us to secrecy and never reveals any details of missions."

Margaret then began again and spoke to her son almost as if Clancy wasn't there. "Tim, you said she was a pretty one, but you didn't say just how gorgeous she is."

"Maybe, because Miss Clancy here is my *boss*, Mum, that might have something to do with it."

She smiled good-naturedly; there was something intrinsically uncomplicated and genuine about these two parents. The younger woman could not help but wonder how her own parents might look after all these years and if a tiny tear formed just for an instant it was subsumed by Tim's Dad linking her arm unceremoniously and guiding her into the impactful hall.

"What a beautiful home you have Mr Wainwright, uhh Arthur."

"Thank you, Penny, we are very happy here."

Within a second Margaret had appeared on her other side and Tim had been relegated to bringing up the rear. Their collective enthusiasm for meeting Tim's boss seemed to spill over in an endless string of questions. More than once Clancy thought to herself, 'Well, I know finally what's made him so inquisitive'.

"We've been begging Tim to bring you for weeks and he's made excuse after excuse. We wanted to thank you for what you did for him. He's not been the same person since you offered him a place with Horizon." Margaret now whispered as if she was about to turn round to make sure they were not being overheard. "We came across Toby via a mutual friend, Bernard Pollofino?"

"Ah yes, I know him well."

"Yes, Penny, he was so impressed by your efforts at 'rescuing' his son. We were spellbound, though he said there was only so much he could tell us," Arthur said, conspiratorially.

"We aim for discretion so that all parties are protected. Please remember, too, that it's a team effort and we are all part of the whole."

"Now, Arthur, don't remind the poor girl about her work. She's here to have a bit of lunch with us, not stand by being bored while you quiz her about confidential things."

Margaret now started on Tim. "I've been asking Tim to bring a friend over to see us for weeks. He used to bring lots of friends back with him, but not one since he began at Horizon. Penny, you are the first friend of Tim's we've seen for months and months. But you, you Penny, are well worth the wait!"

Arthur looked a little irritated, "You go on about me and there you go embarrassing the poor girl, just when she's got here. She'll never come again," Arthur concluded and now started shaking his head.

Tim decided that a change of topic and or scenery was needed, and quickly. "Come on, Mum, is lunch ready, I'm famished? I hope we can eat in the kitchen?" He started rubbing his abdomen enthusiastically in an attempt to move along the topic of conversation.

Margaret looked deliberatively at Clancy. "Yes, not formal, Tim, is that not what you asked? I've cooked your favourites, well, the things Tim tells me are your favourite."

"Mum, are you going to only partially embarrass me, or will you go the whole hog? It's a good job you don't work for Horizon, we wouldn't get to keep many things secret."

"Nonsense, Tim you know Penny here would see through every little secret, anyway. Didn't you say she's the best agent you've ever seen?" Tim decided that her comments were unanswerable. For her part Clancy had latched on to a trait shared especially by the couple – talking about someone as if they were not there.

"Yes, thanks again for that, Mum, and judging by the puce colour my face has just gone, that must be true, too."

Clancy was used to meeting up with devious people who had things to hide, or even secrets to uncover. This straightforward couple seemed to demonstrate nothing but friendship and unambiguous mannerisms that she found both delightful and refreshing.

They were about to sit at the table, two to either side. Unfortunately both Arthur and Margaret were keen for Clancy to sit next to them. An active discussion between the parents then ensued. Eventually, sensing that a stalemate was in progress, Tim declared that he was hungry and perhaps Miss Clancy could be allowed to sit next to him but, initially at least, facing his mother. The table itself was filled to capacity with the things that clearly Tim had remembered she'd eaten since he'd met her. Arthur poured the drinks.

If they'd seemed a little direct, things went up another notch or two as soon as their guest excused herself to visit the bathroom. She'd barely left the table when Margaret turned to Tim at once. Clancy did her best to hurry from the table so as not to eavesdrop. The volume and insistence in his mother's voice made this very difficult.

"She is stunning, Tim, and what a beautiful girl. She'd be perfect for you. I do hope you've asked her out."

"Something with her being my *boss*, mum if I might remind you"

"Well that doesn't mean a thing, Tim, she can only say *no*."

"Or fire me, perhaps, Mum."

"I do hope you'll bring her again and for longer next time, how about a weekend?"

"Mm, I'll have to see what my *boss* says about that, Mum."

Margaret reached for his hand over the table and squeezed it. She looked steadily at him. "Tim, my love, life is short; just ask her out." A well of tears appeared in each eye as she spoke.

He looked away, being aware of her discomfort, and a reminder of a person not present meant he was not quite able to meet his Mum's constant gaze.

Clancy returned some moment's later and created a little cough to allow them to change the subject. Margaret was still exploring the same theme.

"I was just saying to Tim, he'll have to bring you for longer next time. How about a weekend?"

"That's so kind, Margaret, it's just that we are always so busy."

"Well, as soon as you have a day or so to spare, then, you'll be welcome. In fact, you'll be welcome at any time. Come on your own, we don't need Tim here, do we?"

Clancy had also hit the point where words were difficult to return and a little laugh escaped from her lips.

"Tell me, Penny, is there someone special in your life, or are you married to your work?"

"Mum, will you stop interrogating Miss Clancy?"

Clancy laughed, "Tim, I don't feel as if I am being interrogated, not at all. In truth, as you've guessed, I am married to my work and tend to live for it."

"Well, that's no good for a young, pretty girl like you. What do you think, Arthur?"

"I'm sure this intelligent young woman has it all worked out, Margaret." Clancy smiled, detecting the first attempt at discretion since she'd arrived.

"Our Tim is going the same way, he says he's always working."

Arthur offered quickly. "Well, Margaret, that makes a wonderful change, and we are *so* pleased. It's down to you, Penny."

Tim blushed again. "Miss Clancy, what can I do with parents like these?"

After just over an hour and much to both parents' disappointment it was time to leave. Although Clancy had not had to use the code word, he sensed that their guest had more than enough exposure to his parents than was wise.

Margaret, in particular, hugged and kissed her, doing her best to extract promises of a return as soon as possible. Arthur was no less enthusiastic and managed another long glance at her legs as they were retracted carefully into the low-slung sports car.

"Miss Clancy, I am so sorry. You can tell they don't get out much."

"Not at all, Tim, I liked their uncomplicated, straightforward approach."

"Bordering on brutal!"

"Well, perhaps not for the very shy!"

The car weaved its way back along the roads and eventually found the motorway.

Clancy remained quiet for much of the journey. Tim wondered if she'd been simply polite and, in point of fact, she'd been offended. However, if he'd had occasion to look in more detail he would have seen that the young woman was deep in contemplation.

So many thoughts now intruded. For the first time, she'd been given insight into a normal family life, with parents who embarrassed their children even at twenty-eight, and also their guests. Ones who talked about girlfriends and weekend sleep-overs. Clancy couldn't help but draw a parallel with her own life, one that ran firmly on professional lines and featured someone who was always at work. In some ways Toby's recent liaison with Alexis had exposed this and Clancy had known at the outset that it threatened to destroy the life she knew. She just hadn't realised it would be delayed until today. All the things that her life lacked, including two loving parents and a normal boy-girl relationship, had been revealed to her in a couple of hours over lunch – the things absent from her own life stood in stark and unforgiving relief.

More merciless thoughts then followed. Every relationship she'd ever embarked on had been prematurely terminated, as Clancy was simply not sure if she could ever trust a man to want her for who she was and the person she'd become, rather than as someone who could deliver sexual release. The abuse she'd suffered at the hands of someone who was supposed to be in a caring parental role, at a critical phase of her life, had forever damaged her chances of seeking balance in a relationship of her own. How could she ever let her guard down and find someone who would love her unconditionally and not simply expect sex? Surely, in today's environment such a man only existed in fairy tales and one's febrile dreams. Even Toby had assumed that she could have any man she wanted with a snap of her fingers. She didn't thirst after this, in many ways she was holding out for a man who loved her enough to provide almost an old-fashioned courtship; not the current norm of trying on sexual partners and seeing which ones might fit.

At least her lunch had shown her that relationships like that among decent people and well-structured families were out there and perhaps she now just had to find a man who could help her create one similar – but of her own.

Although she accepted that had it not been for her work – and Toby – she would have been at all times desperately lonely, she now knew enough to at least plot the direction that would lead from her romantic isolation. Once again she was grateful to Tim and, without doubt, his parents.

The car pulsated smoothly as they retraced their route. After many minutes she spoke. She took off the glasses and allowed her hair to be claimed by the wind as they progressed. Looking directly at him she said, "Thanks for taking me, Tim. I had a super time."

Tim assumed she was being facetious. "Oh, I am sorry, Miss Clancy, I know they can be a bit over the top. I like it when they start on each other and of course they wonder why I don't bring anyone."

She laughed, "No, seriously, I had a great time."

By this time they were approaching the secure car park.

"Would you like me to drop you off on the corner?"

"No, Tim, let's see where you have been hiding this little beauty." The garage was much darker than the sun-washed streets. Lights came on as he drove into his spot but they were inefficient and ageing fluorescent tubes that would take a while to assume their maximum brightness. He turned the engine off.

She paused, her words appearing as a prelude to something much more significant.

"Tim, thank you, really, for taking me; they are wonderful people."

"Why, thank you…"

Suddenly she'd leaned towards him. He at first thought she was about to reward him with a peck on his cheek; he even stuck his chin out expectantly.

He then became aware of her stunning eyes closing with his, these were the first things he'd noted the night they'd met in the casino; these and her winning smile, had captivated him totally. This is why he'd used the card at the outset and why he simply had to look away when they were in the lift. They burned with a conflagration of emotion like a comet passing through the corona of the sun − only now they were millimetres from his. He closed his eyes as she approached and did his best to support her and hold her while she did so, sensing something momentous was in progress.

It was only then that he realised those beautiful lips that he'd encountered in his dreams for months were around his. He could hardly move, let alone breathe; her intoxicating presence flowed through him − not that it mattered, such things as breathing had suddenly become a secondary consideration. Long fingers from her left hand had gently fixed on his right shoulder while those of the other hand had run their frantic course up the back of his neck and through the thick, blond hair that still smelt of fresh air and sunshine.

As she pressed herself to him, through her firm breast she could feel his heart pulsating explosively within his chest. He, in turn, felt her tremble as the emotion coursing through her frame discharged through them both like a burst of electricity that mortal flesh could barely contain. He continued to hold her and would happily have done so until the Earth had dissolved into elemental dust in the infinity of space.

She eased away from him after what seemed like an age. Gently biting her own lip she looked down, first at his mouth engorged with the tumult of passion and then at his eyes that now glowed like hers. He desperately wanted to speak her name but something told him that by doing so he would shatter the moment forever. He was therefore content never to speak again if need be. Her eyes dipped further and, raising a flat palm, she gently pressed against his heart that still raced uncontrollably like water flowing off a cliff edge. Her light caress sent goose bumps coursing through his muscular torso. The fleeting glance, they'd shared, in the lift had achieved something of far greater significance. Their eyes now met unequivocally with a passion that felt as if it were conveyed more by physical force than just light.

It seemed for Clancy, in that moment, years of pent up frustration – of disastrous and inappropriate relationships, of men who sought very different things from what she needed or wanted, together with horrible tortured memories of how sex could be used to fuel liaisons that had nothing to do with love or indeed what was right – were expunged by a burst of sheer emotion that left both of them exhausted and left him completely stunned. He'd seen first hand, on numerous occasions, the precisely-directed, almost surgical, blows her svelte form was capable of marshalling; but now he'd experienced the deft touch of her soft caress, which without doubt was even more impactful.

As they parted he released her from the grip he'd assumed on her lithe, toned form; the delightful smell from her perfume and shampoo lingered even as his lips still tingled with excitement.

"I'd better go. Forgive me, Tim."

In a fleeting moment she'd opened the door, had vacated the car and had started walking to the exit still bathed in the sunshine.

He locked the car, but was then in a desperate quandary as to what to do next. Tantalising thoughts formed in his brain; some that he wanted to declare, and some to ask; but he knew in that moment that he couldn't voice any of them.

Clancy, too, was not quite sure what had driven her. Maybe a glass of wine, the enchanting, relaxing company amongst a real family, the wondrous drive and company of a man she'd realised was both desirable and a delight to be with – or perhaps it was something even more important, signifying a break from her lonely past and a way to access a more normal future. In the days ahead she would recall that there had definitely been a moment, ill-defined perhaps, but certainly not *nothing*, passing between them – in that lift. What had just happened in the car was something that even her acute mind could not even begin to compass – for now. What was clear was that very soon she would clarify it – and at such time she would grant him the courtesy of an explanation.

"Please forgive me, Tim," Tim heard her say, he believed, for the second time. He wasn't at all sure what had just happened; he was sure of only two things. Firstly, that no apology was needed and secondly, that he would wait until the seas had consumed the land if necessary to have the chance of a repeat.

Clancy, if questioned, would probably at that juncture know very little more than he. She had remarked more and more of late about his increasing maturity. He called upon its fullest width and depth now as he spoke.

"Miss Clancy, did I just dream that and, if so, then please don't wake me?"

He sensed her turmoil – something that she didn't need or want; he could never do such a thing to her as forcing its clarification when she was clearly neither ready nor even perhaps able to do so. Tim knew only that silence could not carry what now lay between them. He understood with some nervousness that the wrong words would destroy the moment like a detergent bubble coming off a child's loop on a summer's day. Once shattered, his fear was that it would never return. His plan was simply to preserve it by passing it into the future; to save it, if at all possible, for a day to come – when they could both, if they wished, and were able, acknowledge what had happened and, as his heart gave summersaults at the thought, reclaim it.

He walked next to her for a few vital seconds as his head cleared and his heart calmed. In any event her thoughts were not unlike his and as they walked he spoke first.

"I know this is not the time to talk; I know you have to finish this. I know you have a difficult mission tomorrow night. Perhaps when we are through this there may be time to do so if you would like to?" They walked a few more steps, which gave him a little more time to think and to somehow allow him to preserve intact what he realised was the most important thing in his life, to date.

"I promise to never ask you, nor to voice what might have just happened but, if ever, at all, you feel you can tell me, then that would be great. Until that time I'm going to assume that I am still asleep and can't be sure what's real and what's a dream; that my alarm clock is about to wake me and, until such time as you are ready, I am going to assume it was just that." He paused again, desperately wanting to look at her for a reaction – any reaction, and yet frightened to do so as he feared what that might be. His only recourse now was to acknowledge that he could do no more – then simply hope. "Thank you for coming to lunch, Miss Clancy."

He held out his hand and she took it in a more formal handshake that signified his acceptance that more serious things faced them, and particularly Clancy, than his trying to prolong something she might have done purely by spontaneity and that she might now regret, even though he knew he'd treasure what had happened in his memory forever.

She smiled a weaker and more depleted smile than he was used to. "I'll phone when we complete the mission tomorrow. Thank you for inviting me, I really had a super time. We'll talk soon, Tim, I promise." And with that, she turned. The beautiful smile now laced with a hint of sadness over the years and feelings that had been lost to her.

He walked away leaving her to find her own car.

The following night, it was just after 1am and the white F-Type pulled into the car park, just off the London embankment. The engine revved for a moment, but then was silenced and the headlights turned off. All the windows, including the front screen had been darkly inked, so that the occupants could not be seen. The car remained stationary, as the engine cooled with a gentle ticking noise, against the light breeze blowing over the Thames.

A few minutes later, two men appeared in front of the car. The surveillance camera inside the car that had been mounted on the dash recorded the, by now familiar, image of the two tall Russians dressed in black leather jackets. As they walked forwards, each held an AK-74u, shortened submachine gun, capable of delivering a ferocious volley of rounds per minute at close range. Without any further delay, they started to fire and walked round the car initially with vehemence. They now laughed enthusiastically, delighted to be making more inroads into bringing the Horizon organisation down and accumulating significant wealth, as they did so. They looked forward to the payday and bonuses that they'd been promised. Judging by the number of mistakes that their enemy was making, they obviously had no clue as to where the leak of information was coming from. They were being taught an expensive lesson. Tonight, it seemed, they had just lost their best agent. They'd heard that Clancy was very difficult to defeat and yet here she was; dying from multiple gun-shot wounds without even getting out of her car. Perhaps, one so sloppy did not deserve to live. In any event, she was no threat to them now. The assault rifles went on discharging 700 rounds a minute into the Jaguar and the magazines were soon empty. The pair then pulled out the empty ones, discarding them, then clipped in fresh ones, before continuing the withering fire. The car was hit with a deluge of bullets. Several magazines were used; a small pile of discarded ones appearing around the car as they continued. Within a few minutes the car exploded.

Clancy had kept her eyes closed as the car went up. She knew that the intense light given off would damage significantly the low-light accommodation that her eyes would be making and she would need, she assumed, any minute now. As soon as the noise died down, she opened them once again and, though the car continued to burn, the intensity of the light was much-reduced and was also of a deep yellow and red colour, rather than the intense white of the explosion. Snipers who used the so-called 'starlight' scopes that employed night-vision equipment could have their eyes damaged by suddenly looking at a very bright object through such scopes.

Clancy knew that, tonight, her AI with the Schmidt and Bender PII, offering lowlight capability, but no light amplification, would be more than sufficient.

The car continued to burn. The Russian twins approached; merriment clearly evident. Clancy wondered if they would still be laughing soon. They fired the last of their ammunition and prepared to leave. In that moment, however, two of the Horizon agents rushed in, their revolvers primed to shoot and pointing at the twins. Both wore bullet-proof vests, which would be capable of stopping small-arms fire.

"Hands up, you are both under arrest!" came from one of the agents.

Clancy chambered the first round from the magazine of five bullets.

Antonov, to the left as the agents looked at them, immediately raised his arms. His twin, on the right, Leonid, turned outwards in a counter-clockwise motion, passing behind his brother, who kept his arms raised.

"Stay where you are, you are both under arrest," repeated the first agent.

"Freeze, or we'll fire," came from the second, who hesitated as one man surrendered and the other continued to move. Such hesitation was about to cost them their lives.

Leonid continued to pass behind his brother, completing the full circle, but now appeared to his brother's right. He had used the distraction to wield his revolver in his right hand and transferred the revolver in his brother's waistband, at the back, so that it was now available for him on his left. He came round, now emerging from behind his twin, having completed his circular motion. Both guns were unlocked and primed. Leonid shot immediately, choosing a head shot, so as to deny the agent protection from the Kevlar in the bullet-proof vest. He died instantly. The other agent prepared to shoot him. In that moment, Antonov grabbed the gun that had been presented on his left side and fired.

Both agents fell to the ground dead from, what appeared as mirror-image head shots – one from the right and the other from the left.

Clancy fired immediately. The round was despatched in less time than it took one to blink and would reach its target, from that distance, in under a second. Antonov died at once, the bullet passing to the left of his sternum, shattering the fourth rib as it did so, and travelled onwards, directly into his heart. She would have chosen a disabling shot, had she felt that it was safe for her to do so. Having seen, however, how quick and merciless these two were, she knew that only a kill shot would suffice. The other distasteful point is that they were deliberately abusing the accepted rules, as regards surrender. They had exploited the agents' willingness for them to give themselves up and then suddenly flouted the rules, giving them an unfair and detestable advantage in murdering their opponents in cold blood. Clancy was determined that it should end, and do so tonight. She chambered another round and prepared to despatch the second twin with a lethal shot to his skull.

Again from his rear waistband, Leonid pulled a flare and held it in front of his torso as it went off before he dropped it on the ground in front of him. The bright orange naval flare gave off a lot of heat and smoke. Most crucially, it also gave off a copious amount of intense light, which temporarily blinded Clancy, as she prepared to squeeze the precision trigger. For a vital second she could see nothing through her sniper scope.

Leonid moved under the cover of its intense light and used the distraction to run down towards the river. He didn't glance back at his brother, who lay in a pool of his own blood and could not have survived such bodily insult. Clancy was a little way back, picked up her rifle and also moved to the banks of the Thames, so that she could cover it with fire. She saw that a speedboat waited for him. Both engines on the speedboat started as soon as the Russian approached. Clancy did not have much time. She saw that a person waited in the boat; he must have been the one who'd started the engines. As soon as Leonid clambered aboard, the boat took off and set a course directly across the river, which appeared inky black, with only a little swell, against the night sky.

Clancy remained calm. She had a direct view over the river, but the speedboat was fast disappearing into the darkness. It bounced up and down as it crossed the waters of the Thames. Even worse was the fact that a swirling wind had got up and this, when combined with eddies over the water, would make her job of estimating windage much harder. Such unpredictable gusts could only make the bullet's flight more difficult to gauge and be more erratic. Many shooters would be unable to get results under such conditions.

It was, however, times like this that separated the adequate shooter from the superlative one. Clancy was firmly in the latter group. Tim had asked her why it was that she was such a good marksman. Firstly, she remained cool. It was only by adopting such a strategy that her body, in conjunction with her skills, would behave in a predictable way. Secondly, though she would not hesitate to use instruments; those that would estimate range and windage, ultimately her instinct was worth much more when assessing a shot. She knew when to trust the instruments and, above all, when to trust herself. This had caused almost a charmed life where shots had been sent on their way in difficult and seemingly impossible conditions, only for her to hit a target when others had not come even close. Lastly, she was blessed with superb vision.

Her optometrist had told her that she had what could only be described as perfect vision. The maximum scrutiny he could put her eyes under was for her to read the 4-metre line at 6 metres. This was the so-called 'six over four' vision. It was the highest range that he could test with his equipment. Although he could not prove it unequivocally, Clancy managed this without hesitation, and he suspected that she was capable of reading the 4-metre line at much greater distances. When combined with a sniper scope, her visual acuity was unassailable. Most crucially, her reliance on herself, and not so much on her instruments, meant that she could, when called upon to do so, table a shot much faster than all others. This would make up a telling advantage when targeting a fleeing opponent – as now. If one then took into account her other skills, it meant that none of her contemporaries could match her.

She'd seen men, in particular, brag about their expertise and be confident that 'this woman couldn't shoot her way out of a paper bag'. Shooting was, after all, a male preserve and no doubt Clancy could always make the cups of tea. Within no time at all, they'd received comprehensive and painful instruction from the person who, they concluded, was the best shooter they'd ever seen.

She unfolded the bipod at the front of her rifle, which she then supported on the wall of the embankment. She chambered a Lapua Magnum cartridge. Although this was a standard 7.6 mm cartridge its 'magnum' designation meant that the shell casing was longer, so that it would contain more propellant. This ejected the projectile at higher speeds and also meant that it would not only have greater range and accuracy but also would be less affected by windage. In addition, the higher velocity of 2,800 feet per second meant that it had massive potential for damaging a target. The price that would be paid would be a higher recoil force, but nowhere near as much as that of some modern rifles that had been known to dislocate shoulders.

The speedboat was making a rapid crossing and was bobbing about on the water. Staring intently, her eyes dilated in the low light. She felt the breeze play over her face. She estimated the wind, its force and its direction; rather like a captain who might look up at the topsails in order to estimate the best course for his ship and how much canvas the spars would carry before coming away. She caressed her rifle with her cheek, rather like a snooker player making millimetric adjustments with his cue, or a tennis player managing his racquet as an extension of his arm in order to place a stroke with unnerving precision.

Her first shot hit the port engine, which immediately exploded. Flames erupted well into the air and were dragged a little behind by the speed of the boat. She closed her eyes briefly as it went up. The starboard engine was still running, but fuel was sprayed over the two passengers. Both men were deafened by the sound created by the forceful explosion; their eardrums being damaged by its proximity. Only the slipstream of air flowing over the boat, as they crossed the Thames at speed, prevented the flames from venting forwards and igniting such fuel; as well as the starboard engine.

The second shot pierced completely the port rear tube of the inflatable dinghy. As it passed straight through, a leak began and the inflatable section started to go down. It remained afloat only because of the other intact partitions in the side tubes. It would, however, now be a race to see if they could make the far bank and remain sufficiently buoyant.

Her third shot hit the speedboat driver. The shell entered via his left loin, passed through the left kidney and then continued on at a slightly oblique angle, which was enough to rupture the aorta. Death was instantaneous. He slumped forwards over the controls. The boat now veered wildly off course and, in so doing, threw his body out of the dinghy.

Leonid had to act fast. He had been doused in fuel from the port engine. This was an irritating and inflammable mix of nine parts petrol and one of pure ethanol. He could barely see as the noxious combination insisted on seeking out his mouth, nose and eyes. He used his sleeve frantically in an attempt to clear his vision. Grabbing the steering, he compensated for the loss of the engine and also for the fact that part of the port tube was rapidly deflating. He crouched down in the boat as low as he possibly could, for he knew that it was only a matter of minutes before a bullet met up with him. Clancy's fourth shot hit the wooden board just behind him, the splinters flying everywhere, but somehow deflecting the bullet, destined for his spine, at the last moment. Even so, the projectile still caught his left hip, and grazed it with a non-lethal, but intensely painful, open wound. Both she and he knew the next would hit him. Clancy chambered it in the time it took the long lashes to caress her pretty eyes within their next sweep. She knew she would end it in a second or two. Just as her right finger prepared to squeeze the precision trigger, a large barge swept quickly down river, with perfectly infuriating timing, thereby blocking her line of sight and frustrating the kill shot that she'd prepared. Clancy was not one for liberal use of expletives; Toby had always, by example, steered her away from such things. However, she permitted herself one such now.

Desperately trying to compose herself once again, she waited patiently for the barge to clear her field of fire and pictured the bullet that would meet with him, shortly. Fortuitously for him, none of these things happened before the dinghy hit the opposite bank. He scrambled ashore without looking back, either at the boat, or at the opposite bank where his brother had met his demise. He was also very lucky that the fuel mix he'd been covered with had not erupted in flames coming from the explosion as the engine went up. He knew that on this, the opposite bank, there were lots of places to hide and eventually to melt away.

Clancy ran back to her car and stowed the weapon in her boot. The nearest crossing was some distance away. She knew that he'd be long gone by the time she had made it to the other side. Other agents converged on the scene and conducted a search, but by the time they had all appeared on the opposite bank, Leonid was nowhere to be found. A helicopter with night-vision apparatus was also brought in. The Russian was used to hiding in unfriendly territory and had also done a tour of duty in Afghanistan where being captured by Muslim insurgents would be very bad news indeed for any of the Russian forces. Even as the other agents organised a comprehensive search: he had disappeared.

The following day Clancy met up with Tim, Brady and Toby in the meeting room. She held the little box that had been removed from the outside of the window. She nodded towards it as she spoke. "It's certainly a handy piece of kit. It contains a wide-angle camera that could obtain images from inside the room. Not only this, however, but because the pane of glass acted like a sounding board, the microphone in the unit was able to pick up conversations within the room even though our bug sweep was not triggered. We are going to need to look at our security not only inside but also outside the building. Perhaps, we have been a bit too complacent here, and assumed that because of our hidden floors, we have been immune to eavesdroppers." She continued. "I'd also like to thank you, Tim, for your excellent suggestions regarding leaving the box to draw them in and also the remote-controlled F-Type, complete with two dummies!"

"I was hoping that our ambush would have led to the capture of at least one of them," Toby offered.

"Losing two more agents. That's five we have lost in almost as many days," confirmed Clancy, looking grave.

"Yes, it's a long time since we lost an agent, and now we seem to be doing so on a regular basis!" agreed Toby, "and when this is all over we need to take a look at our operations as a whole and not just the counter-surveillance measures. It is some time since we have been up against ruthless killers and, of course, it was never an arena in which we sought to place either ourselves or our agents. However, Tim, what is not in doubt is your wonderful suggestion to leave it in place so that we could entrap them and turn the tables. Also really good were your ideas about the sting operation. We nearly had both of them. Well done."

"Sorry it meant loss of your car, Miss Clancy."

She laughed. "Oh, don't worry, Tim, I usually get through one every six months and I'd had that one a bit longer than usual. I'm sure it was due for replacement, eh Toby?" Toby looked a little pale at this juncture but smiled anyway as she continued. "It led directly to at least removing one of them and I know I wounded the other. That will slow him down a bit."

Toby nodded in agreement, picking up the positives from the mission. He was keen to keep up the impetus. "I will begin a review as soon as we have Leonid captured or neutralised," he said, while remaining deep in thought.

"To be fair, though, Toby, we always look at the importance of the mission, not how much danger it offers. We all sign up with this thought uppermost. As one of the newest recruits, Tim, what do you think of this? Do you think we should avoid dangerous operations?" queried Clancy.

Tim looked grave, his message as serious as it was important. "No, I can't agree with that. That tricky bastard who threw his own man in front of the car needs sorting and because of our 'flexibility' we are the team to take it on; not shy away from it." Brady looked at him and smiled while he thought how far he'd come in such a short space of time. "The other point is, look how one minute these Russian blokes surrender, or don't surrender, then they start shooting. It all seems a bit ruthless, a bit below the belt, to me."

"Tim, you are quite right, it is self evident that we are not used to dealing with such ruthless people and perhaps we have to re-plot our strategy accordingly. On a happier note, *Ma Puissance* has made Gibraltar, collected its passengers and I am told Hilary, Alexis' secretary is having the time of her life," offered Toby.

"I bet she's spending most of her time in the engine room," Clancy suggested, with a wicked smile.

Toby had more information. "The other piece of good news is the pilot of the boat. We recovered the body from the water and also managed to identify him. We have discovered that he works for a man called Dimitry Romanonov, who works out of Rostov."

"Who is that?" they all asked in unison.

Now smiling, Toby clarified. "You remember our old friend Alexandre Ciesciu?" They all nodded, "Well, Mr Romanonov is well-known among those who operate above the law in Southern Russia, he is the chap who bankrolled Mr Ciesciu and it seems his tentacles extend into running girls out of Africa, hence the part played by our other old friend, Mr Mdombku," They continued to nod as Toby continued.

"So, our suspicions that it might have been him were well-founded. At least, we now have some evidence to tie him to the Russian pair. So, just to summarise, one Russian sniper is in the mortuary and his twin is on the run. We have no clue as to where he might be, although there is a massive manhunt for him, involving Horizon, the police and the security forces. I am told he is a top priority. Then, we have Mr Mdombku, who is untouchable in his mini-fortress in deepest Niger. Any operation against him would be easily detected before we got within sight of him. A lone sniper being sent in might just be successful, but he or she would almost certainly be on a suicide mission. I am not sure we could extract such an agent before his vast security team had found them. This would be bad news, because if he or she were discovered, I'm certain they would be torn to shreds, or worse." Somehow, as Toby said these words he managed to avoid looking at Clancy, for he knew she'd be the first to volunteer if it meant she was in with a chance of bringing him down. Moreover, he had to come up with a better plan, and quickly, as he knew she would be soon putting him under intense pressure to allow her to go.

"Now, at least we know what we have to do to tidy all this up. We need a solution in place and quickly," offered Brady.

"Yes agreed, we need to rebuild the team. Morale is very low and we have lost so many good people and the ones that remain have lost friends and peers. We can't do this while we have loose ends," concluded Toby.

"So, we need to shore up what we have. We will begin looking at areas of weakness and also look at training in the arrest situation. Perhaps we might routinely use Taser guns to neutralize those who have surrendered and then, at least, our agents won't be ambushed or caught off guard by them later. And, though I do not relish such a task, at least the surveillance footage we have will allow us to look at where things went wrong and why," Clancy suggested.

"I suspect it will be a long time before we are up against such ruthless assassins, but looking at their methods can only help," agreed Toby.

The meeting broke up. Toby looked grave. "Clancy, could you stay behind for a moment, I have something to discuss with you?"

Tim and Brady left, allowing the two of them to talk. They were both curious as to what might be the topic of conversation, but they realised that it had something to do with tidying up loose ends that Toby had alluded to – and quickly. With such low morale, the sooner they had taken definitive action the better. That same night, Brady received a call. He was asked to travel immediately to the airport where private transport awaited him.

The following day, Clancy met with half a dozen agents and some admin staff in the meeting room. Mood remained low, but Clancy wanted to gauge their views about further training and lessons learned. In addition Toby had suggested a Christmas shutdown, provided that Leonid had been captured by then. He'd promised to fly them all to Barbados, something that he'd been promising for years, but had never quite found the time to put in place. He was determined to draw a line under recent events and work on restoring morale.

The meeting broke up an hour or so later. It was still early and the darkness was only now starting to lift over the waterways of the old docks. Clancy walked along the dockside for a while. Without his guileless eyes betraying a flicker of what, if anything, had passed between them, Tim asked her if he could tag along. She looked at him carefully as she thought how much more accomplished he had become in masking his feelings that only a short time ago would have been on display to all. For some time, she walked in silence and Tim was content simply to walk with her, doing his best to quell his inquisitive steak, his thirst for information and desire to discover all that he could. He had learned, above all, that when Clancy needed time to think, then there was nothing else for it but to allow her to do precisely that. He kept glancing in her direction but was content to just allow her to think and remain within herself; as on many occasions was her wont.

After walking for some time, she said, "Come on, I'll buy you a coffee."

They walked on to the nearby Costa.

Clancy was a regular sight around the Quays. Although people recognised a familiar face, nobody seemed to know exactly who she was, or what she did. Some had assumed she was an actress, most likely used to being photographed; some were of the view that her role was as a producer behind the camera. Still others were convinced that she was a high-powered executive in one of the businesses that were springing up in the Quays. The only thing they realised after further deliberation was, what they did know was not very much at all. It was beyond doubt that no one would wish to ask her. The more times she was seen, the deeper the mystery that surrounded her, yet, the more distant the answers.

Tim insisted on peeping round the plate-glass window to make sure that Janet was not in work that day. Clancy waited like an offended Traffic Warden insisting that it was time for the two women to have an adult conversation, but Tim had prevailed and in any event it was a moot point when he discovered that she was on her days' off.

Tim brought the coffees. She looked up and a depleted smile rewarded him for his efforts. He'd been thinking for some time about what he wanted to say and he knew that now was as good a time as any.

The topic he really wanted to talk about was the one that he knew he could not approach. She would signal when it was time, if ever, to talk of the things that had oscillated within him from the lofty uplands of hope to the dim depths of despair. Mercifully for Tim's agile and inquisitive mind, there were lots of other things he wanted to ask.

"Clancy, I'm sorry. I didn't pick up on what you told me. He really did pull you out of a train wreck, didn't he?"

Hazel eyes surveyed him carefully. Little clue came either from her steady gaze, or from her expression, as she deliberated whether to reveal any of the truth and, if so, how much.

"Yes, in a manner of speaking; it was a long time ago. They'd been working on the points. I was going on holiday with my Mum and Dad; we were heading north on the West Coast line. The points failed as the express train went over them. All the cars from the fifth onwards were derailed. At that time they were still putting bogies at each end of the carriages. These days, as I'm sure you know, the bogies run between the carriages on all the high-speed trains." He'd never heard of this, but he did his best to nod knowingly, as if it were obvious to all. She smiled for a second, in so doing acknowledging his attempt at subterfuge in the interests of allowing her to continue. "Anyway, also, as you'll know, the old configuration caused more instability in the event of one of the bogies being derailed. The carriages of that time would have been thrown further out of alignment. The further towards the rear you were, the greater the disruption as it spread along the train. We were in the last car: me, my Mum and my Dad and, sadly, many others. They were killed instantly. Every single one was killed." She snapped her fingers. "I'd gone to the bathroom. I was the only survivor out of the whole carriage.

"I was orphaned in two minutes at the age of just shy of fourteen. That was fourteen years ago.

"There was nobody to take me in. Social Services intervened, and so I was fostered. My stay with foster parents was a difficult time. The guy was a sexual predator, shall I say, and his wife was of the view that the sun shone from him. She could not possibly comprehend that her view of him was flawed. She didn't ask, neither did she want to hear, what happened when darkness fell, nor some of the things that he put me through.

"Toby had just lost his Mum, Sister and, not long after, his Dad. He was a few years older than me. He learned of my predicament quite by chance. He was attending court the same day as my case came up. His case very different from mine: he had been bequeathed a fortune and I didn't have a penny, or even a safe place to sleep. I wanted to be allowed to live on my own. I didn't want to go and live with some rich toff. Social Services wanted me to stay where I was. It took Toby ages to get permission to take me in. I became like his ward. He was just eighteen. Mercifully, he had a lot of friends with influence and retained some pretty high-powered legal counsel: moving heaven and earth to help me. I was allowed to go and live with him under social service supervision, until I reached the age of eighteen. By way of thanks, I gave him hell; I don't think he knew just what had hit him."

"That, I find hard to believe, you are so close now!"

"Ah yes, but it took a while, I can tell you. If he ever regretted it, he never said.

"I wasn't quite finished with my former foster dad, however. Before I left, I made sure he was alone. I held a kitchen knife to his throat. I assured him that I would return and that I would use the knife on him, but not start with his throat, if I ever heard that he'd misbehaved with any of the people he was paid to protect. I then wrote an anonymous letter to Social Services, saying that they were an unfit couple to be allowed to foster. They interviewed me as part of their investigation. I asked them what he'd said. According to them, he'd denied everything. I suggested that they ought to interview him again.

"I remember walking out of that house with a couple of plastic bags containing the only things I owned in the world. Waiting there for me, standing on the pavement in front of this house, was Toby. And waiting for him in the road, the engine running, was his driver, sitting in a beautiful new Bentley. Toby was never going to be some spoilt, rich kid, if you'll forgive me?" She looked at him carefully at this point hoping that her words had not offended him. He smiled unconcernedly, but acknowledged her point and her sensitivity towards him, as she made it. "Soon after, when I'd calmed down a bit, we started working together. He wanted to help people in tricky situations who could not rely on, or did not have, established avenues of assistance. His vehicle for doing this was, as you're aware, Horizon: I was his first recruit. Not that I didn't continue to rebel a bit. I didn't see the need for continuing my education when I could be learning to do other things, like hand-to-hand combat! He insisted, however, and also advised me that it was part of the deal struck with social services. I didn't give him, well, not *much* more, trouble after that point. I was the first Horizon if you like; his first mission."

"And your former, pervy foster dad?" asked Tim.

"Mercifully, I never did have the need to revisit him and no doubt his wife still thinks he lightens the eastern sky."

Typically, with Clancy, it was not what was said, but what had been missed out. Though at times she could be an accomplished liar, what was barely recognised by her was how she could lie to herself and avoid unpalatable truths that she simply could neither face at thirteen, nor face now. For Clancy could never return to face her tormentor; the man who, instead of protecting her, had abused her in ways that, even now, she could not contemplate. Her inactivity against this person continued to plague her, and her anger expressed towards both Toby and, more significantly, herself was simply displaced from feelings that she really wanted to vent upon her foster parent. Even when Toby had suggested that they pursue him and bring him to book she still could not face the prospect of doing so. Her self-perceived weakness had tortured her so much that she had chosen to bury it in the deepest recesses of her memory. Her anger became personified as the 'beast chained in the cellar' with the tacit view that, though an unpleasant part of her and what she always regarded as a weakness, it had nevertheless fuelled her advancement in so many difficult areas and allowed her to master so many challenges. Her dealings with the abusive paedophile on the African subcontinent had brought such buried angst to the fore once again. Although Toby had guessed some of this, he could never be aware of the degree to which it unequivocally had returned to haunt her.

Tim continued with his animated queries, "You do love him, Miss Clancy, don't you? Just tell me, it'll be our secret."

"Who, Toby?" She now had an incredulous look on her face.

She presented an indulgent smile that an adult might offer an inexperienced person wrestling with something new, yet complex, and then he was rewarded by the melodic laugh. One or two men in the coffee shop used the gentle sound as an excuse to turn and look. They couldn't help but stare at her and also Tim, the man lucky enough to be in the company of such a gorgeous woman.

"Ooh, Tim, I can see how curious you are. I can't help but think that you are reading quite a lot into our relationship. We are close; yes of course we are, affectionate even. Added to this is that I owe him *everything*. I dread to think what would have happened to me if I'd stayed with wandering-hands, abusing foster dad. It is also true to say that I do *love* him." She could detect a crestfallen look on his face as she said the words, while he struggled to hide his inner thoughts. She then continued, "You may know that the ancient Greeks talked of six different kinds of love. Perhaps, simply, I love him in a way a sister might love a brother, rather than in the sense you mean?" He nodded and she saw a brightening of his expression as, once again, he struggled not to reveal something of his thoughts. "This being said, we work closely alongside each other and personal feelings – not that I am saying there are any – would only get in the way. Surely, Tim, you can see that? What have I been trying to *tell* you all this time? Do you think I am somehow exempt from these things or that Toby is, for that matter? Furthermore, you cannot have missed the way he looks at

Alexis and how he goes all gooey-eyed when someone mentions her name. You saw for yourself the panic on his face the other day when that bomb went off in front of her offices. He couldn't wait to get there, but wasn't entirely pleased when I suggested he was doing the 'frantic boyfriend thing'. Of course, he feels the loss of the agents just as we all do, maybe more deeply. I dread to think what would have happened if Alexis had been harmed. I think, though he hasn't said so, this will be one more reason why he will look at a complete revamp of our organisation." She drank some more of her coffee. Tim had fallen silent, desperately trying to form an orderly pattern to his thoughts.

"Oh, on a separate note, and while I am talking of doing the right thing for the organisation as a whole, everyone, all your colleagues, have remarked how professional you are, and that you are behaving like a seasoned agent." She broke eye contact at that moment, not wishing to embarrass him any more.

"Is that one who's covered in salt and vinegar?"

"No, I had something else in mind, but we can do this for you, if you'd like, perhaps leave that to Janet?

"You know, Tim, all of us have personal feelings. We all have to decide sooner or later whether we act on how we feel or behave for the greater good of the organisation."

He had a sneaking fear she was about to deliver bad news. He wanted to say that people felt what they felt. It wasn't always possible to simply switch off one's feelings: disguise and mask them perhaps; this he knew, he had been doing so constantly for weeks. He was of the view that, sometimes, such feelings would just not die.

Mercifully, just as Tim held his breath she moved the conversation back to his progress.

"Also, if I may say so, everyone is most impressed by your performance and how quickly you have learned the ropes. Furthermore, you have a good instinct and a good feel for the crucial mission parameters. You certainly earned your recent 'Golden Gun' award. More importantly, your peers voted for you. Some people never learn in a lifetime what you seem to do by instinct. Well done!"

"Thank you, Miss Clancy, it means a lot coming from you. So, where do we go from here?"

"Well, we've had one hell of a beating. I need to sit down with Toby and we need to look at some painful truths. I am wondering if we have become complacent. Perhaps we've taken too many routine jobs. This has led to some of the more complex and dangerous ones being backed by insufficient depth and cover. I worry, especially, that when we knew we were under threat we should have put more resources in. In effect, we spread ourselves too thinly. Of course, we were not to know that two paid assassins were after us. Hopefully, and at last, we are getting up to speed, but it has cost us dear. Anyone can be wise after the event. We need to rebuild and regroup and, in so doing, airing some of our failings, and maybe looking at some of *my* failings, is going to be painful."

Tim sensed her lightening mood. She had learnt to recognise, after weeks of careful observation, when he would begin his questions.

"So, may I ask, then," he began, right on cue. Most likely, the pause would come next; whereupon he would formulate the most efficient way of getting to the information he sought. One more question, among the millions, that she knew, he would never tire of posing. She waited patiently.

"Whose idea was it to recruit me?"

"Well, you know, you'd been under surveillance for some time. Your Dad was very worried about you and, as you know, it was he who first brought us in and asked us to help. We spent a lot of time just following you round, I suppose is the best way of putting it. We needed to understand how bad things were for you and if there were any prospect of us helping you to turn it around." Clancy paused again, looking for non-verbal clues from his expression as to whether her words were causing discomfort. "We were so sorry to learn of your sister." Clancy nodded in his direction and looked both grave and concerned, imparting to him that they knew all about his younger sister, who'd drunk herself to death after a failed relationship and unremitting depression, but did not feel the need to clarify further.

"Forgive me," she continued, "but it seemed that you were wasting your whole life. And yet, the more we looked, looked into your life, the more surprised we became and the more good things we found. We certainly didn't find a hopeless case: someone who would not change no matter how many times he were bailed out. Your father was very wealthy, but this caused you to rebel a little?"

He laughed, "Well, more than a little it has to be said."

"It didn't start out like that. You gained a first, no less, in Mathematics at Cambridge; you were regarded as the brightest in the whole year, if not the whole department. So many firms courted you. Microsoft flew you to Seattle and made you an offer of a starting salary of $100,000. Google got wind of this and entered a bidding war for you. You could do no wrong. Then, it all went pear-shaped, your sister's illness, you dropped out. I think your Dad was first alerted to problems by the bills you were racking up. This is when he called Toby, but as I said the more we looked, the more impressed we became. The restructuring you carried out at your friend's charity; I believe that it was about to close with massive losses. You went in, trawled through the numbers, weeded out those who were skimming off the business and slashed fixed costs. You didn't charge him a penny for those months of work you put in." She nodded and offered him an almost triumphant smile; she was about to tell him something that few knew. "Then there was the time you were crossing the Atlantic, with your Dad in his personal jet. They had miscalculated the fuel at loading. You weren't sure if you'd have to divert to the Azores or perhaps make Newfoundland. You performed the calculations, gave the pilot cruising altitude and speed to ensure greatest endurance. You made it to St John's, Newfoundland with a teacup to spare."

"Anyone with an I-Pad could have done that."

The melodic laugh appeared again. "This was years before an I-Pad, you were *fifteen* and you made the calculations in your head!"

"May I ask, then, who saw that? Who decided that I wasn't a hopeless case?"

"Well, to be truthful, it was Toby," she lied. "You know, this is one of Toby's favourite scenarios. He likes to find the 'diamond in the rough'. You, it won't surprise you to learn, were perfect because Toby felt that, with a little polish, you'd come through nicely. And, it seems, he was right." She lied so convincingly, at this point, that Tim would never have known who had seen such potential in him. He, in turn, became very thoughtful. Although he liked Toby very much, he'd never guessed that he would be involved at such a level. Clancy knew instinctively that this was the only way to answer his questions and satisfy his need to know – just about everything. Seeing something of the 'truth', he'd now become very quiet.

She looked steadily and unwaveringly at him, her face like a waxen mask, betraying nothing of far more complex thought and emotion within. This, without doubt, was one of the things that he had not learned: not learned about the most gorgeous woman he had ever set eyes on. For, surely, no one who was that pretty could possibly part with even a tiny untruth and it not affect them, in some way. She'd hinted, for sure, on many occasions that skills were being applied, but he'd underestimated just how consummate a liar she was. On the contrary, no one could lie like Clancy. Every word she spoke on such occasions; when her lies were the deepest, the most confusing, or the most diverting – looked the most genuine.

Detecting a slight flicker of disappointment on his face, she also saw something much more significant. She knew, in that moment, he had almost mastered his personal feelings: their relationship would change as a result – and Horizon as a whole could only benefit. His growing maturity and self-awareness, possibly; or, perhaps, the blows and sadness that had been inflicted on the whole organisation, had brought rapid and necessary change. Things between the two of them were on a much more professional footing; both she and the rest of the team had learned to be able to trust and respect him more, as a result. More than that, his performance, for one so inexperienced, was exceptional. Moreover, it had been a long time; Toby would say, not since Clancy herself, had they seen someone who had grown into the role as quickly. This is what

Horizon needed: also what he needed. Her own feelings were, for the moment, deeply submerged and held in total abeyance.

"And here's me thinking it must have been you,"

Not even the smile betrayed her, as she offered its full intensity in his direction.

"We are *all* delighted to have you on the team."

"You know, Miss Clancy, the day you came for me, the day Toby sent you; in that dreadful back room of that casino – you were amazing. As soon as you gave me your card, I knew, I just knew, that my life had changed. From that moment on, I wanted to be someone and something better. I cannot thank you, I mean, Toby, nearly enough."

Had it been anyone apart from Clancy, it would have been apposite for him or her to be deep in thought. She recognised, however, that the situation demanded a very different approach. Her strategy called for distraction next, moving the conversation on seamlessly. "You have handled yourself so well. And to think you have barely begun your training. Let's see, there's self-defence, bombs and explosives, setting and disarming – that should really tax you. Then, there's my favourite, endurance and fitness training."

"Mm, I am not looking forward to that. They say you achieved the fastest time ever when you completed it?"

"Tim, I was just lucky, the weather was milder than the forecast, visibility was better and it didn't rain. It just seemed to fall into place."

This was the only time that he could detect her lies: when she was talking about herself and had been forced into obscuring just how amazing she really was. He nearly challenged her that he'd been shown the performance tables;

she appeared at the top of just about all of them. He decided,
however, that this was neither the time nor the place to call
into question her self-effacement and simply nodded, whilst
her deep brown eyes looked steadily at him. Nor did he
guess that when she took the exercise, the weather was
atrocious, with gale-force winds followed by one of the
coldest nights on record. He thought later that Clancy was
not someone that one could confront about anything. Not for
the first time, a further question covered his awkwardness.
"So, is it true, then, about the exercise? Do they just drop
you off by helicopter on a remote Welsh mountain, in the
dead of night?"

"Well, I wouldn't like to spoil the fun, but let's just say
I am sure you will get through it whatever they throw at
you. I can't see you coming all this way and then failing."

"And do you think I have come a long way?"

"Toby assures me that you have," she lied once more.
Not for the first time had she anticipated his likely next line
of questions and where the thread of those questions would
lead. She knew that he hadn't quite satisfied his own need to
know just why he had been chosen.

"I must thank Toby for showing such faith in me."

She paused, managing a blink from the constant gaze,
suddenly lost for words. Tim would have gained vital clues
had they not been interrupted.

An independent observer might conclude that she was
being needlessly dishonest in deliberately misleading him.
Furthermore there may have been a time when she was able
to tell herself that this was purely for his benefit and would
protect him. In a moment of clarity she realised that it
wasn't so much about him but her. She needed a construct
of lies as a defence against her own feelings. She knew that

this was the only way she could concentrate on the job in hand and finish it once and for all. This could only be a good thing; the organisation was so badly shaken that its on-going repair and functioning must take precedence over personal feelings.

Not for the first time, she had deliberately avoided recognition of the feelings deep within that would haunt her in the days to come. For she could not contemplate, let alone solve, the questions as to what had really happened in the lift and just before she vacated his car.

Her phone buzzed gently in her handbag, "Excuse me Tim, I am sorry about this. I think it might be a message that I just have to read. Forgive me for a moment?"

She rose from the chair. An uncomplicated walk she made to the door, combined grace and a flow of perfectly co-ordinated movement that any large cat would be proud of. She read the text on her phone and also checked the time with her phone and watch. Only then did she return to her seat.

He guessed that something momentous was in progress.

"Are you able to tell me?"

"Oh, it's only that a mission is 'go'."

"Is it *just* a mission?"

"Of course, Tim; it's not all cloak and dagger, you know." She sensed his disappointment and decided to reveal just a little more. "I could tell you but, trust me, the less you know about this particular phase the better." She looked at her watch once again and then at him darkly, 'probably too late to back out now' she thought to herself. Tim detected the change within her in that instant; something truly earth-shattering must be in play.

Doubt was not something that afflicted her very often, but this would be one of the occasions when it would wrack her mercilessly.

"I'd better get going, Tim, before Janet comes on shift." She looked round quickly crafting fear on her face as he smiled. "I'll see you at the meeting tomorrow?"

Tim looked at her for a few seconds, having learned not to stare. He knew that it made her uncomfortable, although she denied that it was so. He had also successfully learned to hide the thraldom in which he held her. Moreover, he understood that this was a good thing. She had advised as such; and she had been correct. She must certainly never learn the truth, nor the supreme effort he made in treating her, the most wonderful woman he'd ever set eyes on, like just another member of the team. Perhaps, in not telling him, she had served a kindness upon him after all.

Chapter XIII

God of Thunder

What Clancy had learned was something momentous; for it marked a new chapter in the way they conducted their operations. That morning, in the, so-called, graveyard hours, an A400M, Atlas, military transport plane had taken off from an RAF base. Both its destination and its cargo were known to very few, and then only those at the highest level. The list of those in the *know* included Toby, who'd requested that the mission take place and Clancy, simply because it had been the only way to prevent her from taking the task on personally.

It was only in exceedingly rare times, like this, that Toby called in favours. Although they were more often than not granted, it was on condition, solely, of a need to know basis; that in future all knowledge would be denied and that it was never spoken of again. Notwithstanding this, Dame Helen had at first categorically refused. Toby had gone on to remind her of all the covert missions that Horizon had carried out and the times when the British Government's blushes had been spared – as a result of their efforts. He'd advised her that Horizon itself was now under threat and their very survival in the balance. This was a way to correct this and settle scores. Dame Helen, in turn, had had to take her request to her own political masters and it was only a mixture of insistence and pleading that'd won them over.

Eight-bladed, large, swirling propellers soon got the massive aeroplane, and its payload, airborne. It banked a little as it then clawed skyward somewhere over Andover, in the small hours of the morning. It flew steadily south-south-west for four hours over the disinterested waters of the North Atlantic.

At a pre-defined location, the Atlas flew straight and steady; its payload was released. This was made up of an unusual craft which, within a second or two, dropped a few feet from the transport. At the same time, a radar station in West Africa detected a new heat signature occurring at exactly the same spot as the location of the RAF transport plane. High-efficiency Rolls-Royce engines had gone through their pre-heat cycle and ignited a second later. As the two craft separated, the military transport banked sharply to starboard; after observing, briefly, that all engines were alight on their precious cargo, they set a course bound for the Azores.

The Taranis drone then fell a further hundred feet as it completed its pre-flight diagnostic checks. It alerted the remote pilot surveillance and telemetry station, somewhere on the Isle of Wight, that all systems were operational. As the signals were being exchanged, the engines came up to full power, their after-burners glowing red then white with the heat given off. The drone sped off into the night, an awesome force, now quite alone, apart from the instructions that had been programmed into it and the sophisticated command and control systems that pulsated through it.

During this time, Brady had crossed the border in northern Niger from Nigeria and headed north-west. It was dark when he'd set off but, with careful use of his headlights, he made good progress. The one or two occasions when he felt that he was in danger of being spotted, he killed the headlights and activated his night-vision equipment. The light given off from the magnificent stars in the otherwise absolute-black of the African night was more than enough to steer by. Dawn produced a majestic sunrise and the promise of a beautiful day, which accompanied him. After checking his position, and the time, on several occasions, he continued his journey. Some minutes later, upon encountering a deserted part of the landscape, he opened the rear door of the Land Rover and pulled down a ramp. On this he slid down a large quad-copter surveillance drone.

Firstly, he made sure that the power cells were fully charged and that the remote control systems were operational. Ensuring that the numerous cameras were working and were sending him clear signals, he finally stood back and activated the four rotors, which were positioned at the corners of the unmanned aerial vehicle (UAV). Contra-rotating, but vertically mounted, propellers gave more lift, a faster response, greater range and a rapid climb rate. Moreover, such blades could be tilted to allow fine control of direction, height and hover for the drone. These attributes were very much in evidence now as, without further ado, the quad-copter's engines gave off a determined buzzing. Within a second or two it was airborne, precipitously soaring above him. Lastly, it was sent on its way, bound for deeper territory in the north-west of Niger.

Cameras mounted on the UAV reported ground images back faithfully to agent Brady in control, assisted by eight GPS satellites, which ensured that its course and movements were obeyed perfectly. It continued to fly north and west. After checking that the correct course was being followed, he poured himself a cup of coffee from the hot flask and sat in his transport to wait.

Meanwhile, the Taranis drone was given final course co-ordinates from its base and these were accepted and confirmed by its on-board navigation computer. It flew inland over the west coast of Africa. It immediately went into its most efficient fuel-saving mode and continued on its route using similar technology to that of the quad-copter. Both were bound for the same location. The radar installation of the Liberian military hinted at an inbound target, but sensors on the drone immediately detected such scrutiny. Going into stealth mode, the geometry of the trailing surfaces and the shape of the wings altered to make it far less visible to radar waves; the trace immediately disappeared, as might a flock of birds temporarily dispersing, as it did so. The radar operator gave no more thought to the fleeting signal. The drone flew east.

The stealth software had been assessing the terrain over the assigned flight-plan and fed back that a lower height was indicated, therefore the drone dropped to hug the terrain at less than one hundred feet, making it even harder for radar to detect. It was spotted, visually, over Ghana and a surface-to-air missile was launched. On-board sensors detected without delay that it was under attack. A series of Chemring countermeasures, in the form of a pattern of white-hot flares and chaff, were discharged regularly in its wake while it flew on. The heat-seeking missile was confused with the profusion of targets, each more noteworthy than the drone, which had now masked and shielded its engine emissions, so that they gave off less light and heat. Eventually, not being sure of any target, the missile self-destructed as the drone continued on its assigned course to head east.

The quad-copter was finally in position over the presidential palace of Mr Mdombku. A steady stream of high-definition images came back to agent Brady, who now pored carefully over the pictures being fed to him. He waited. Just after 8 am, local time, a woman with her two children was escorted by a coterie of security guards towards a waiting armoured Range Rover. Two security guards got into the front seats and drove towards the substantial front gates, which were manned by more guards. On seeing the passengers, they opened the gates immediately and the Range Rover swept out of the extensive palace grounds. Upon receiving such images, Brady reported back to mission control that a woman and two children had been driven clear of the compound. The information was relayed to the Taranis control on the Isle of Wight. In light of this information, final attack and launch codes were uploaded to the Taranis. At this point, messages were sent to both Toby and Clancy with the option to override the operation, should they so choose. Neither of them did so.

Sweeping in from Nigeria, the Taranis drone armed twin racks, one either side, each containing three Brimstone II missiles. The missiles appeared from recesses, which opened, where the wings met the fuselage. Launch codes were confirmed and the rails containing the missiles were unlocked in the final stage before launch. Detailed images of the target were fed to the missile-launch computer and an attack algorithm calculated. This meant that all six missiles could be activated in a 'fire and forget' pattern. This would ensure not only that the entire armament could be launched at the same time, with no risk of them colliding, but also that maximum damage would be carried out on the target. Only a slight whooshing noise betrayed the missiles' launch: all glowed with deadly intent as the propellant was consumed, while they followed their assigned path to the target. As soon as all the missiles were away, the Taranis drone ascended quickly with the sudden loss of its payload; turning towards a secret location in Kenya. The quad-copter remained and continued to transmit accurate images of the scene and events now unfolding.

Mr Mdombku was waiting eagerly for his men to deliver his mistress. He was looking out through one of the upstairs windows, impatiently anticipating her arrival. In any event, his wife had been given instructions not to return until late afternoon.

He was about to turn away from the window when he saw a black shadow, which must have been some distance from the palace. He thought it was a flock of birds or possibly a vulture, but then he recognised it to be an aircraft of some description, for it was moving so fast. Now, intensely curious as to what it might be, he saw it bank sharply to the east and fly away. As it did so it gave off a muffled soaring noise, as the engines cut in to effect a course correction. He gave it no further consideration and, once more, was about to move away. Only then did he become aware of six black dots that must have originated from the aircraft. His subsequent thought was that the small dots appeared to be fanning out in a complex pattern, becoming much larger as they approached. The attack sequence ensured that all rockets would continue on their pre-assigned pathways, despite the Taranis drone already moving away at increasing speed. In that last second, as the roar of the missiles could be heard, he knew exactly what was coming for him and that it was now unstoppable and unavoidable.

The palace and its compound were comprehensively destroyed as the warheads struck home. The despotic warlord would not die immediately from his massive internal bleeding, but some time later. Several members of his medical team were shot dead by his few remaining guards, in an attempt to motivate them. However, with limited resources and a multitude of injuries received by his significantly overweight body, the task was a futile one. Death came to him within two hours of the strike – allowing him time to reflect on what sort of human being he had been during his life, and what sort of memories of him would be retained by others.

The Taranis continued eastward, bound for its next destination, just inland from Mombasa: port of Nairobi. Surveillance footage was captured by the quad-copter drone and relayed back to mission control and also to Horizon headquarters. Individual messages were sent to Toby and Clancy. As soon as he received images of the extensive destruction of the compound, Brady recalled the drone and awaited its arrival a short time later. Quickly recovering the UAV, he loaded it into his boot, before driving south and back over the border with Nigeria, where transport awaited him. A large wooden crate containing the drone was, in turn, loaded on as cargo.

At the same time, but nominally two hours ahead, in Rostov-on-Don, Mr Romanonov was occupying his preferred table just as he did every day at this time in his much-loved German restaurant, Schieder – Weisse. He was sitting having lunch with his girlfriend who was, in reality, one of the escort girls that he used regularly. His two minders were sitting at a nearby table. As he was about to take a sip of wine a tall woman with long flowing glossy-black hair bumped into him causing him to be knocked forwards and, in so doing, nearly spilt his drink. The slim woman leant forwards. She sported a low-cut neckline and seemed to linger as she leant apologetically towards him. Her intoxicating perfume filled his nostrils and his head. Initially, at least, her stunning décolletage did much of the communicating for her. She produced a string of fluent German and, though accepting her emollient tones, he had no clue as to the words she spoke. Sensing that he was unable to understand her, she then switched to less capable English and once again did her best to apologise. The minders stood but he waived to them to remain seated. His escort, sensing both competition and trouble, stared daggers at the voluptuous young woman who tottered a little unsteadily on the really high heels she wore.

Out of nowhere a young man came forwards and started shouting in English at the attractive woman. Far from being cowed, however, she stood up to him and shouted back in her less confident English. The table separated them at this point but as he moved to come round the table his words became more insistent and his anger more apparent.

"What are you doing talking to this man when you are supposed to be meeting me for lunch?"

"Yuri, I zimply stumbled, I do not know zis man."

"You always say that: you are up to your old tricks again."

"No Yuri, I beg you, I do not know 'im."

Yuri prepared his left arm and started reflecting it across his large torso keeping his palm flat as if he was about to slap the woman with it.

She now wailed plaintively as if this scenario had been played out before.

Mr Romanonov stood at this point and moved to pass between the young couple. His minders both darted forwards.

The poor young woman gripped the tablecloth for support as Yuri advanced. She sheltered behind the Russian oligarch as Yuri pushed him.

Yuri then shouted at the top of his voice. "Move out of the way, this whore is always chatting up other men behind my back, she should be taught a lesson."

The minders moved quickly and restrained the deeply-agitated man, each taking backwards one of his large and muscular arms as they stood behind him. He continued to spout at his date whose short, black-sequined dress now shook, as she did, in the overhead lighting. However, at the point of maximal confusion, she quickly moved her right palm that still gripped the pristine table covers, broke a small vial in her hand and slipped the clear liquid so liberated in his glass of wine.

Dimitry snapped his fingers and pointed to the door. His minders understood immediately and Yuri was dragged, as he continued to scream, to the exit at which point he was ejected forcibly. He continued to rant for some time but the minders remained at the entrance and although no words were spoken they managed to convey with sufficient menace that it would be unwise for him to attempt to gain re-entry.

Meanwhile, the girl in the black-sequined dress continued to thank her saviour while his escort continued to look daggers at her.

"Would you care to join us, my Dear," came from the Russian in oleaginous tones.

"No, You haff been mozt kind. I vill get a taxi hom, but I zank you mozt sincerely."

Dimitry's escort was delighted when she moved away. By the time she left there was no sign of her angry partner. Dimitry resumed his lunch and drank more of the excellent glass of wine as he did so.

Tracy, the young woman in the tight, black dress walked down towards the river. The majestic river Don was reaching its widest point here, just before it joined the Sea of Azov. She took off the high shoes that were killing her feet and her pace picked up a little. She did her best to pull down the hem of the short dress but knew she would never succeed to her satisfaction. She accepted, however, that it had more than done its job. She made for a large motor cruiser that was moored at the river's edge and, after a quick look behind, went aboard.

Griff met her below decks. "Well, that went well Tracy; you were superb, nobody noticed the little extra you added to his drink."

"And so were you, Griff; you really had me scared when you started ranting. Good job I had my valiant Russian to protect me." She reached up and took off the glorious, black wig which revealed hair of a similar colour but much shorter. "That feels a bit cooler. I'll just go below and slip into something far more comfortable!" She pulled determinedly upwards on the plunging neckline, but stopped this quickly when she realised that as she did so the hem rode up even more.

Griff smiled and raised both eyebrows at the tantalising sight of his fellow agent in the sparkly mini-dress. "Okay, time to get under way; he should be another half hour, I guess, so if we go up river, move to the opposite bank and then start to move down, his car should be here to collect him soon."

Right on cue the armoured limousine appeared, ready to collect the oligarch.

The clear mix contained liquid versions of no fewer than five readily-available drugs. One was a diuretic used to expel excess fluid from the body; this would have the effect of lowering his blood Potassium and Magnesium and therefore the heart's resilience. The second was a common anti-sickness drug that is available to buy over the counter. In addition there was a clear, colourless solution of a commonly-used anti-depressant taken by millions around the world each morning. Then there was a simple antibiotic, which had also been added to the mix and finally, a drug used in calming psychosis. All these drugs were widely available and all suffered from a potentially-lethal side-effect when used alone. When used in combination this made the lethal side-effects much more likely, and almost a certainty when five such agents were used. This so-called prolonged QT-interval was increasingly recognised by doctors as causing a fatal arrhythmia in a person's heart. Because low doses of common drugs were used, detection would be nigh on impossible.

Mr Romanonov came out of the restaurant. He was feeling a little sleepy, but no doubt this was the wine he had drunk. His girlfriend walked with him. She didn't so much mind the depravity he subjected her to, as he paid well, but she had taken the step of making sure that he drank more than he'd intended so that, hopefully, he would fall asleep before his proclivities were visited upon her.

His car appeared right on time. The two minders opened the car doors to allow the couple to enter. Just as they did so sniper fire was aimed repeatedly at the armoured limousine. The incoming shellfire was difficult to locate; some appeared to be coming from the opposite bank of the river but the report seemed to be coming from behind them, from the city centre. The minders realised that even accurate sniper fire like this could not penetrate the armoured protection of the limousine. As a precaution, however, they advised Mr Romanonov to leave the city and head for his safe-house deep in the country. In that instant they sealed his fate.

Griff turned to Tracy who lay prone on the deck next to him. "Nice bit of shooting, Tracy, Clancy would be proud of us both."

"You know, Griff, I don't think even she could have done better. That was a brilliant suggestion using the suppressors on the rifles. Just as you said, it threw all the sound forwards and made them think it was coming from behind them."

"Yes, Clancy taught me that a good silencer can disguise the rifle's report as well as hide the flash. And I agree; I don't think even she could have done better; let's have it?" he held up a large, flat palm and the high five was delivered in return with enthusiasm.

The limousine sped away only minimally damaged by the precision shots. The agents' intention was a simple one;

to make sure that their target was far enough away from mainstream medical services when the arrhythmia in his heart started. Specialist and urgent medical care would be needed and this in turn would depend on proximity and also knowledge of whether he was taking any routine medication. Both these things were now denied to him. As Griff steered the large motor-cruiser downstream and made ready to enter the Sea of Azov, bound for northern Turkey, their target would suddenly collapse. It had all the appearances of a heart attack. The minders did their best to perform CPR but he was now at least half an hour out of the city together with the equipment that might just have saved his life. Though they continued for some time, it became clear that they were fighting a losing battle and both men gave up as exhaustion claimed them both. They reflected that heart disease had taken another of their heavily smoking and drinking middle-aged countrymen.

That night Toby phoned Clancy. Although he did not acknowledge it when she told him that she was about to phone him, he'd guessed as much.

"Are you ok, Clancy?"

"Yes, just peachy," she offered with more sarcasm creeping into her voice than she'd intended.

"I thought I'd phone you to make sure you are all right." His repetition had the desired effect and she brightened, something he recognised immediately, despite his not being able to see her.

"I'm fine Toby, thank you for asking and also for phoning me. Are *you* all right?

Have we done the right thing, Toby? I am just worried that we crossed a line today."

Toby knew that given half a chance Clancy would have happily had herself dropped into Mr Mdombku's presidential estate, so that she could confront him directly and either bring him to justice or else, die in the attempt. This would have been the outcome: she would have died in the attempt. It might have been on a purely selfish level that he'd proposed an alternative strategy, but he knew, in any event, that he could neither continue without her, nor would ever wish to do so. This, put simply, was why he'd called in favours: and lots of them. He'd been aware for some time that the forces had been testing a new type of British Aerospace drone that embodied stealth technology, and had significant on-board detection, surveillance and self-defence programmes so that it could insert itself deep in hostile territory in order to carry out precision attacks and then withdraw. Once it had been discussed with him, then he'd begged and pleaded for an immediate strike to take place and had provided sufficient fact and figure to interest those who could authorise and undertake such an operation.

"You know, Clancy, that these two were really bad men. We removed one of them today in a place where no one will care and the other, more surgically, in a place where no one will guess. You have seen, first hand, how they operate. People are expendable to men like these, whether men or women, loyal or otherwise. Do you think the world will be a tiny bit better for not having them in it? In fact, near misses don't act as a warning to them; they are an excuse for them to escalate the response. Look at the poor Nukumobos; he was a good man with a young wife and daughter. Those two Russian assassins they let loose. You were quite right, Clancy, you told me the African bloke would do something stupid and he did. It seems as though the Russian chap helped him. We could argue, maybe, that our agents stood in the line of fire; perhaps, one could say it was their job, at a pinch. What's more, to be gunned down in the most appalling of circumstances is bad enough, but then, suppose we factor in all those innocent people who were killed, just to make it more ugly. I can't forgive that."

Clancy had felt a little guilty about telling Toby that she should have shot Mr Mdombku when she had the chance. She now accepted, as always, something of his words and his logic. Moreover, he knew that Clancy had been determined to face him. Given this, Toby's efforts in setting in motion a remote, cleaner, but final, result to remove this low-life despot and his sponsor, who'd both believed they were untouchable on their home soil, made perfect sense. When one factored in that Clancy had been protected too then doubts, if any, disappeared within seconds of his confirming the strike. He, for one, would never regret that. His purpose in phoning Clancy was purely to make sure she didn't either.

"You know, Clancy, none of us would have been safe while these men lived. Not you, nor me and none of the missions. You know what we said all those years ago, that we did this; set up Horizon, to try to help people, to improve their lot or extract them from sticky situations – not get them killed. If I crossed a line today, then yes, maybe I did." The fact that he took all the responsibility on to his own shoulders at this point was not lost on her and this is what made him a wonderful partner to work with, someone she would follow into Hell and back and why she loved him so much.

"No, Toby, I am okay with it and I do thank you for phoning me. I do feel that *we* made the right decision for everyone and in truth I can't say I am sorry. I would have liked to have confronted Mr Mdombku eye-to-eye, me up against him, but I suspect the last thing he would have offered is a fair fight."

"Too right, Clancy." Toby went quiet for a moment. He knew what this man represented; he understood, too, that he symbolised all the things that Clancy hated. This was why she'd wanted to go and get him; sacrificing herself, if needs must. It was his fault; he'd re-awakened those monstrous thoughts within her and this is why he'd taken definitive action, and so quickly.

"No, I am at peace with it and good riddance. We just have to apprehend the last Russian now and hopefully we can rebuild and get on with new missions."

"I think we'll all have earned a few days on the *Puissance*; eh, Clancy, before we make a start on that; the others are off to Barbados, but I wonder if you'd like to join us on the yacht. Anyone you'd like to bring along?"

She ignored his question. "I agree, let's get hold of this Russian and I can hang up my sniper rifle, for a little while."

"I'll drink to that Clancy. As I said, I just wanted to make sure you were okay. Night, night."

"Thank you, once again, Toby, and goodnight to you, too."

Chapter XIV

Dagger No Cloak

The following day, Clancy met with Tim in the shooting shed. Toby had insisted upon his instruction going forwards and that training for all agents was not put on hold as a result of their setbacks. The temptation to delay, or even stop such things, remained given that the ex KGB assassin was still at large and thus far had eluded all attempts to find him, a strong one. Ultimately, however, it was decided by unanimous agreement that the organisation would continue to train, repair and rebuild and now, of course, recruit, despite the Russian still being on the loose. It was to be Tim's final session in the shooting shed and it would be followed by an assessment. If he passed this, then he would be allowed to progress to open-range shooting.

After a couple of hours practising on the static targets and also in the timed trial, they walked back to the Horizon offices.

Clancy was ecstatic and walked with a gentle spring in her gait.

"Tim, a brilliant performance! You sailed through. Not only were you very quick at identifying targets, but you were also very accurate. I see that the old lady came through unscathed. What wonderful scores you ran up."

He looked away quickly, feeling a mixture of satisfaction and embarrassment. "Thank you, Miss Clancy, I have been practising."

She did her best to look surprised, but Clancy had already heard that he'd been in there on every available free occasion.

"Well, it shows, Tim, and I can say you have passed with flying colours. Just a bit more training on the setting up of snipers' rifles and we will then move you on to field trials, where you shoot targets out in the elements. I can see you will pass this with the skills you have already acquired. This means that you'll have earned your first badge, and I believe that makes you the quickest recruit to do so." Although Tim did not challenge her, he knew that Clancy would hold such a title, and no doubt, if he had access to it, her file would confirm it. He knew that it was typical of her not to brag about her own performance; though he guessed, should she have the need to do so, there would be a lot to brag about.

"I think Toby just wanted a word; he's going to meet us back in the offices."

They entered Horizon HQ and she accessed the lift that would only ascend to the top floors when a fingerprint was recognised as it was applied to the display screen in the lift. Most people never knew that there were two floors, on top of the building, that were restricted in this way. The lift was also programmed to operate in a whisper-quiet mode and a false illuminating progress bar always indicated that the lift had arrived from below, whenever someone attempted to summon the lift from what they believed to be the top floor.

The offices below were always complaining about the lift as on more than one occasion they could have sworn that the lift had appeared on the top floor but simply not opened. No one had guessed that it was working perfectly and was simply transporting down those that had already got into the lift from the hidden top storeys.

Upon reading Clancy's fingerprint, the panel offered the further floors. She chose the uppermost level, where the meeting room was to be found. Toby met them at the lift. He showed the two of them into his office, just facing the meeting room.

"Well done, Tim. Excellent scores. He pointed to the file that Clancy had given him. We are delighted with your progress and, if I may say, with the insight and quick thinking you have shown whenever you are in the field. It seems you have come a long way since meeting Mr Ciesciu in Kyrenia."

Tim gave a playful shiver as the name was mentioned.

"Mm, don't remind me. Those minders of his looked as if they were going to tear me to pieces with their bare hands."

"Sadly his sponsor suffered a fatal heart attack yesterday. It was so severe that he did not survive." She looked steadily at him as she spoke the words allowing him to draw his own interpretation. After the slight pause, she continued. "In any event, we suspect that things will be very different after your combat training and hand-to-hand fighting course, which we have scheduled to begin next week. You'll be able to take on anyone after that, either armed or unarmed. And so, you may have realised that your trial period is now over. We are ready to make you an offer, though I realise, for you it won't be about the money, but hopefully about something much more valuable? It's time to come to a decision if you wish to continue with us or cancel your membership of Horizon. Nobody will think the less of you if recent events have put you off."

"You must be joking. No, they've made me more determined to see it through and become a fully-trained member of Horizon. That's if you want me?" He did his best at this point not to look at Clancy in case some of his deeper thoughts might betray him.

"Oh, no doubt about that," came from Toby, enthusiastically.

"I'd also like to thank you, Toby, for having faith in me and sending Miss Clancy to come and get me from that Casino. She tells me that it was *you* who saw something in me that you thought was salvageable."

Toby went very quiet at this point and only glanced fleetingly at Clancy, whose face was a mirror of neutrality, betraying no emotion whatsoever. He was not as consummate a liar as Clancy, but he shared a similarly acute mind, which saved him in that instant. Only when he'd seen Clancy's expression at these words did Toby glance back at Tim and offer, "Don't give it a second thought, Tim, I always pride myself on being able to spot the potential that some people have. I like to think that it's one of my better qualities, actually," he confirmed, whilst at the same time studiously avoiding looking at Clancy. Had he done so, he would have seen her eyes look up at the ceiling as she thought that, perhaps, he was both overplaying his hand and enjoying himself at her expense. He then went on, so as to tease her a little more. "Clancy tells me that this is one of my sharper skills; that I am able to see potential in people right from an early stage. I sent her into that casino to bring you out and also to offer you this job that I thought you'd be perfect for." Her expression had rapidly changed to that of one who was about to commit murder, very slowly and painfully. His smile became even deeper as he enjoyed Clancy's discomfort.

"We think you are an ideal new recruit and, truth be told, we will be looking for more in the days ahead, owing to sad events here."

Toby did not linger with such thoughts. "Anyway, look, off you go, you two. I believe you have more training tomorrow, Tim, and Clancy here will be following some leads about our Russian friend, who is now minus his twin, but probably twice as deadly, so please observe caution. I will be flying out to Naples to meet up with Alexis who is cruising in the Med with most of her employees from London. We are hoping to travel east to meet up with Tracy and Griff. Hopefully, when we have all this wrapped up, we can start to get back on an even keel."

They went down in the lift. The person who was waiting at what he thought was the top floor was convinced that the lift had just moved past him and pressed the button irritatedly. Meanwhile, in the mirror-walled lift, Clancy managed to find something about her shoes to stare at and simultaneously Tim found a light bulb in the ceiling of the lift to capture his interest. Neither agent could either manage words or risk even the shortest of glances in each other's direction as the lift conveyed them almost noiselessly downwards.

Tim walked out with Clancy.

"Very well then, Tim, well done again, good luck with your self-defence and unarmed combat courses. I am sure you will do brilliantly. I can see I am going to have competition on the shooting front so, well done for that, too. I am so pleased you have decided to stay. I'll most likely catch up with you in a few days. I just hope we can get this chap who is on the loose, as I have a feeling nobody will be safe until we do."

He wanted desperately to ask her if she really meant it; that she was glad he was staying, but he knew that he could never frame such a question.

They turned the corner and started going up the short flight of steps. The shell that met him must have been aimed straight for his heart and it was only the movement upwards that caused it to penetrate just below. His torso was rising up the steps just as the bullet hit. Notwithstanding the fact that it missed his heart, it ripped through his spleen, causing massive bleeding, which began immediately.

She heard the report from the high velocity rifle as it echoed round the tall buildings and the waterside frontage just after he started to fall.

In the event, it was the taxi that had been coming along the main road that they had been about to cross that saved her. The sniper's second shot, aimed straight for Clancy, was interrupted by the unfortunate black cab driver that had been coming along the road and was slowing for the roundabout at the end. Although this protected her, the cabbie was hit on the side of the head and died instantly. He slumped across his wheel, the vehicle then banging into the kerb, where it stalled.

Clancy crouched beside Tim. Both agents were shielded, for the time being, by the taxi. The body of the vehicle was made of mild steel. Bullets at this range were capable of passing straight through. By such means, the gunman was hoping to hit her with a lucky shot, or at the very least leave the two of them trapped as they cowered behind the bodywork.

Most vitally, it allowed Clancy to collect her thoughts. She could see that Tim was badly hit. The profuse bleeding began to spread and soaked into his shirt like a river bursting its banks. The rate at which it did so was, to Clancy, ominous.

The one benefit it afforded her, apart from time, was that she could identify the shooter's position. Her sharp eyes homed in on the landscaped area just in front of the NV apartments, which lay on the far side of the nearby stretch of water, the Huron Basin, that used to make up one of the docks but was now used for open-water swimming and water sports. Using the black cab for cover, she peeped through one of the back windows just as he fired. She immediately identified the flash from the gun as another projectile was sent on its way. She reasoned that he had abandoned use of a suppressor, as this would adversely affect the performance of the rifle even at this fairly close range.

"Tim, are you all right? Seems we have found our second Russian," she voiced, doing her best to keep the concern from her voice. She immediately removed her cashmere cardigan and rolled it into a tube and then stuffed it under his shirt and applied compression to the wound. It rapidly became blood-soaked. She then moved and tightened his belt to continue the pressure while she lifted his legs and placed them against the side of the taxi. The wound continued to gush alarmingly. Clancy knew she had to keep cool and under no circumstances would he be allowed to see how concerned she was for him.

He looked at the cashmere shrug, "Ah, pink, my favourite colour, Miss Clancy"

"Now I know what to get you for your birthday," she returned. "Actually, it does suit you, Tim."

He started gasping, breaking up his speech, as the pain conspired with the bleeding to make him feel dreadful.

She saw that the knitwear had been immediately soaked with his blood. Furthermore, she reasoned that very soon his situation would be critical, if not terminal. As if to mark the event, he turned a deathly pale colour. At the same time, his breathing sped up; he began panting with short, shallow breaths.

She knew they would be pinned down for a while. She understood he no longer had sufficient time for her simply to await backup. More significantly, she accepted she had to do something – and quickly. Clancy pressed an app on her phone. The screen then glowed with an unusual pattern. Reaching into his shirt, she grabbed the barcoded tag that was on a smooth chain around Tim's neck.

"I've been waiting for you to get your hands on me," he panted, as he winced with the spasm of pain.

"And isn't it your lucky day," she whispered, as her voice found its deepest register.

"Clancy, each day working with you has been *my* lucky day."

Had the situation not been so urgent she would have paused at this point. She offered him a smile and tried to make it as unconcerned as possible, for she now knew that he'd grasped that he was badly hurt. The app on the phone immediately scanned the barcode she held up to it.

The screen changed again.

"AGENT 147a. Confirm?" appeared on screen. She was supposed to ask the fallen agent this question, but she knew that shortage of time no longer permitted such niceties.

She pressed the 'confirm' button. Setting the phone down, she knelt next to him and pressed with renewed vigour on the bleeding point.

Sister Munro had been in theatre since the small hours at nearby Hope Hospital. It was the end of her shift. She was tired and thought that she'd simply put her coat on over her scrubs and head for home. Her phone beeped and buzzed in her pocket; she recognised the tone immediately.

Leaving the department, forgetting her coat, she went straight down the nearby stairs and into the blood bank. She approached the technician at the window. No words were exchanged; she simply showed him the mobile phone.

He read the 4-digit code that had appeared and immediately opened the secure refrigerator behind him. He withdrew the correct package and brought it back to the window. She applied the phone to the barcoded tag attached to the bag, which contained ten units of cross-matched blood. The phone beeped again and a message came up 'Match Confirmed. Proceed.'

Nodding to the technician by way of thank you, and still with no words being exchanged, she moved swiftly from the department. She grabbed the package firmly, making sure that she did not drop it as she descended the stairs just outside the blood bank entrance and made for Casualty. Someone tried to stop her to engage in conversation, but she rushed past him with the simple words. "Sorry, that's my crash bleep." He could have sworn he hadn't heard anything, but stood aside quickly to let her pass.

Paramedic Evans was parked in his Skoda estate, rapid-response vehicle just down the dock road about a mile away. This ran alongside the waterway that then journeyed through the locks and into Salford Quays. It had been a quiet day and he sat in his green and yellow check-patterned car with the window down as he studied his rota for the next few days.

His phone activated with a similar tone to that appearing on Sister Munro's phone. The message came up. 'Paramedic/Driver – respond?' Dabbing decisively at the 'respond' button, he started the engine immediately. He activated the lights and the emergency klaxon and then drove straight to the assigned meeting point just outside the Casualty entrance at Hope Hospital.

Mr Charles, A&E consultant, sat in the office in Casualty. He had been called there because his junior staff were worried about a young lad who'd crashed his motorbike and looked as if he'd sustained a nasty fracture of his left leg. They'd asked him to assess him to see if the fracture was going to need repairing with metal plates and screw.

His phone went off with an urgent tone. Everyone in the office became aware of it. The unmissable tone only stopped when he pressed the 'respond' button. He spoke to Jenny, the senior ward sister and asked her to contact the Orthopaedic Registrar on duty as he had been called away urgently. She wondered what this could possibly mean as no crash alert had been given off, and the ring she'd heard coming from his phone she'd never experienced before. The other thing that she'd never seen, from the laid-back consultant, was such a speedy response as he left the room hurriedly and ran through the entrance to Accident and

Emergency. Even his speech seemed to be faster. As he approached, the bright yellow and green Skoda had just drawn up and the engine was still running. A couple of minutes later, Sister Munro ran through the entrance door, opened the rear hatch and placed the blood-transport bag inside. She saw that Mr Charles was sitting in the front seat and got in the back.

The Paramedic touched the screen on his satnav, which gave him the destination and the shortest and quietest traffic route. The device began to count down.

"Everyone all strapped in. Are we all set to go?" came from the Paramedic.

Both Mr Charles and Sister Munro confirmed that they were ready. He activated the sirens and the car got underway at speed as it emerged from the covered section outside A&E.

Clancy looked at her phone, which buzzed and glowed with a message 'Emergency response unit in progress'. She looked at the cardigan, which was heavily soaked with blood.

So many would advise CPR at this point, but she knew this would be futile. She lifted his legs a little higher in an attempt to keep his blood pressure up.

A young man on a bike stopped. She advised him to stay down as shots continued to strafe into the taxi and some had hit the wall above their heads.

"Please keep down, we have help on the way. Could you support his legs for me?" The young chap grabbed his bike and used it as a rest to keep Tim's legs up.

She knew that the bleeding had barely slowed and they were dealing with hypovolaemic shock. This was caused simply by blood loss in the circulating blood volume, which was usually of some eight litres. She was aware that this was rapidly seeping out of Tim's circulatory system and soon the heart would be unable to work without it.

She could already see that his breathing had sped up in an attempt to drive what remained of the blood a little harder and get it to transport the vital oxygen the brain needed in steady quantity. For certain, too, the heart would play its part to compensate for the loss of volume, by speeding up. Without the blood available to pump round, however, there was only so long that this strategy could be maintained for. Even the strongest heart could not work at this pace forever and as the blood became scarcer, its job became more difficult. The heart, too, needed blood to fuel its progress and it was being denied this just at the point where it needed more oxygen, not less. Adrenaline and Cortisone would be coursing through his body in an attempt to control the bleeding and shut down non-essential areas. The aim, at all times, and at all cost, was to preserve the vital circulation to his heart and brain.

Sadly, the splenic artery had been ruptured and such a wide vessel under such pressure would continue to haemorrhage. She knew that his life could now be measured in minutes if nothing was done. After this, it would be a downward spiral, from which neither he nor anyone else, for that matter, could recover. She thought she could hear a siren, but could not be sure.

A frantic burst of gunfire continued to go off. More rounds poured into the taxi and some continued to pass through completely. Bullets rained down and the young man looked terrified. She spoke calmly but quickly to him. "Thank you for helping us. Please keep down and you will be safe. If you can get down at the side of the engine block, the bullets won't pass through there, and you will be protected. Help will be here soon."

She knelt beside Tim, she could definitely hear a siren but it was still some way and vital minutes off.

In a single moment of clarity, Tim read her thoughts.

"Finish it, Miss Clancy, I'm okay," he lied, with far less convincing expertise than she could apply. "This is your chance to end it, get over there and sort him, Miss Clancy. Don't let him get away."

She nodded, "I'll be back as soon as I can."

She gave last-minute instructions to the cyclist about maintaining pressure on the wound and also continuing to elevate his legs.

Seemingly oblivious to the danger, a passing news team from one of the nearby TV studios had stopped their van and, despite the bullets that continued to fly, were about to set up a camera and start filming.

Looking carefully towards the NV apartments, she knew that their assailant was established behind the low brick wall before them. She understood that if she could just get over there, then she could end it or silence him.

She reached inside her handbag and retrieved the sharp blade that she always carried. She also found a spare pair of hold-up stockings. She then lifted the hem of her dress to expose one of the gorgeous thighs, around which she tied one of the stockings. She looked up to find both men staring. She pulled the stocking tight and then slipped the blade underneath it so that it was held securely against her thigh and would not interfere with her plan. Looking up, she found both men still staring; even Tim, in his state, had temporarily held his breath.

She then stood up as if paying no regard whatsoever to the hail of bullets that appeared as she did so. She held a flat palm up to both men who continued to stare. Neither embarrassment nor fear crossed her face as she pulled herself up to her full height. "Gentlemen, could you close your eyes, please?"

Both men complied, sensing her next move. For a moment she reached above and behind her; she grabbed the fine-wool wrap dress that she now slipped over her head.

She stood before the two men, doing their best to keep their eyes firmly shut, for a second, standing in her bra and pants. Tim couldn't help but look. She understood why.

"God, Miss Clancy you are absolutely gorgeous! Forgive me for staring," and he did his best to shut his eyes again.

"Tim, it's all right, I understand."

Her figure was tall and willowy. The toned musculature had been honed by years of physical exercise and of resistance training. Her skin was slightly sun-kissed, but otherwise both soft and yet firm. Her ample bosom supported by, but not needing any enhancement from, the perfectly fitting bra. The young cyclist still struggled to clamp his eyes shut as his pale features blushed uncontrollably.

"I need to tell you....to tell you, Miss Clancy. I need to tell you now...." Tim began.

"I know. I know. I'll be right back," she said softly, like a mother comforting a sick child as she kicked off the high shoes.

Realising that they were in the middle of a scoop, the news team had started filming and the sight of this beautiful woman standing in her bra and pants occupied the screens.

As she moved away, once again she held up her palm to the camera to deny the intrusive shot. The editor pointed at the monitors; he would have his work cut out later to make it suitable for a family audience. Little did he know what horrors awaited.

The young cyclist, at this point, was overcome by his hormones, so much so, that he just had to risk a glance and gulped very hard at the sight of this pretty girl, who ran quickly behind the taxi and over the road.

The angle of fire quickly changed, but the Russian had not anticipated this. He immediately concentrated his fire on Clancy, as she darted towards the water.

She approached the edge of the dock and, without a moment's hesitation, dived in. Utilising a strong thrust that her legs had made off the edge as she did so, she used her momentum to change direction once the water had covered her, going as deep as the time constraints would allow. She hoped that this would confuse him and make it much harder for him to estimate her position. The water was very cold. It had been a frosty but dry December and the water temperature was deemed so chilly that open-water swimming, usually carried out there, had been suspended until March. Even then, no one ever went in without a wet suit. Clancy knew that she was fit enough and fast enough to make the transit before hypothermia overtook her – despite being in just her underwear.

From the tenth floor of the NV apartments, the owner whom Clancy and Tim had visited had sensed a kerfuffle on the other side of the road. He could have sworn that he had seen the lady called Rubinia, who he knew to be with the Salford RSPB run across the road with next to no clothes on and dive in the water. Wondering if there had been another sighting of rare birds, he could only conclude that some people's attention to their job, and their cause, was second to none.

Leonid saw her enter the water. He understood that he had to move and quickly. Coming out from behind the low wall, he carefully scrutinised the surface of the canal for any clues as to her position. He believed that she would not be able to stay under for the whole width without surfacing for air and directed the fire from his rifle towards her likely position. Deciding to aim along her anticipated direction of travel, he knew exactly where she was headed – straight for him.

Continuing to fire into the basin, a little desperation now creeping in with thoughts of a target he could not see. Most significantly, the water represented a very different medium from the air that his bullets were designed to fly through: the liquid being much more dense. If one then considered the angle at which the bullets would enter; this could only cause their trajectory to be unpredictable. At best, their lethal potential was dimmed substantially and, at worst, would be a waste of time – and cartridges.

Clancy knew all this. Surfacing just for a moment, she used the time to take frequent and deep breaths, one after the other, in rapid succession. Realising that he would have to anticipate where she would appear, she was determined to deny him as much information as possible, by remaining under water for as long as she was able. He saw her, but was far too late to respond. By the time he'd re-trained his weapon, she had submerged.

She appeared again and saw him abandon the Dragunov and reach for his hand gun. She plunged below the surface as soon as she'd seized the opportunity to draw more breaths. Once more, he saw her, but could not react quickly enough. If he were to have a chance of stopping her, he had to approach the edge of the water, to speed up his response time. The dilemma before him: either to break cover, or run away and plan another ambush. He accepted that either he or she would die that day; his skills and training would ensure that it would be her. The assassin approached the far bank and maintained position with his revolver drawn. He believed that the next time she appeared, he would shoot her dead; she would never leave the water; he would discard her lifeless body there as he made his escape. In so doing, he would have revenge for his brother and would live to fight another day, with many more assignments coming his way. Once word had spread about his performance in killing the Horizon agents, there would be many customers.

He fired into the place where she'd submerged, but Clancy had already moved ahead and also just to the side. Approaching initially from his left, she moved diagonally across him whilst under cover of the water. Holding her breath throughout this time, she reasoned that by remaining deep in the water he would no longer be able to tell where she was.

As she swam the fastest time she had ever done in her life, she realised that she'd gained the advantage. She knew she could make the far side without breaking surface. He would have to rely on guesswork; a handgun could only hold so many rounds and a man could carry only so many magazines. She thought it likely that the Glock sidearm was his backup weapon and he had been hoping to rely solely on his rifle. In so doing he would be moved out of his comfort zone. It would also mean that he'd have fewer shells for his revolver, as his rifle was going to be of little use to him now

– being neither quick enough, nor versatile enough to intercept her.

The level of water was slightly down, meaning that the dockside stood proud above its surface. This would make his observations more difficult and would also mean the nearer she got, the closer to the edge he'd be compelled to approach, which was just as she'd intended.

Clancy was not only very fit, she was also very fast; her speed of shooting only matched by her prowess at running, climbing and, without doubt, swimming. All her frustrations over recent events came to a head and the cruel ways of her opponent were channelled into her arms and legs as she powered forwards. More importantly, he had underestimated the woman and had assumed that her progress through the water would be not only much slower, but also that she'd be forced to surface more often in order to breathe. Crucially, he had believed that she would have to get out of the water in order to close with him. All he had to do was wait and she would come to him. He was about to learn that nearly all of his assumptions were incorrect – most vitally his underestimation of her, which was a particularly dangerous folly when assessing Clancy – at just about anything.

She came to the Basin's edge; she could see his figure exactly where she'd hoped he would be. His body was silhouetted against the sky. However, the murky depths of the canal continued to obscure her true position.

She broke surface and gently brought an arm up so that she could gain a purchase on the coping stones of the dock edge. She could see he was looking the wrong way, still clinging to the thought that she would surely swim directly across the waterway and also that even a fast swimmer would not be approaching yet.

With her other hand she grabbed the sharp blade and made ready. She gently felt its weight between her thumb and index finger as if renewing the acquaintance of an old friend. She knew that her right arm gave her a slightly longer throwing range, one that was matched for accuracy only by her left. This was another reason for her swimming at a diagonal across the water.

It was not to be. The gods, so long her greatest advocates, who had denied her neither success nor victory, all deserted her at this crucial juncture. It seemed for sure that her tragic but charmed life had now drained from her and had been bestowed upon another. Moreover, her nemesis, the 'black beast' chained in the cellar was on the loose, had been given free rein and came to claim her without further ado. She felt it fulminate like boiling mercury within and knew it was about to defeat her with disastrous consequences.

So many agents and innocent people had been massacred as if they simply did not matter: her breathing sped up. She thought about Tim who must surely be slowly dying over the road: her right arm started shaking. So much blood coursed through her head: her vision started pulsating in time with her furiously beating heart. She remembered Peter, the man who'd recently become a father and whose twins had summarily been orphaned: she felt her legs wobble in the water. The anger and rage began to consume her totally: her whole body started to tremble uncontrollably.

Worse than all these things − she no longer saw the Russian but the face of her foster parent, which came to taunt her now. His weak, simpering smile; the way he cozied up to his wife the following morning after doing dreadful things to her in the night. His feeble jaw and rancid beard, behind which there was nothing. The lies he told and the threats he made that she would be taken away and have nowhere to live but an orphanage where worse things would befall her if she denied him or spoke of the simple warmth he asked for from her. He'd threatened that she could not tell a soul. Who would believe her anyway when it was his word against hers?

So much hatred overwhelmed her in that moment: her arms started going into spasm. Detecting that anger was unequivocally overtaking her, she understood that it was, at this point, the last thing she needed if she were to perform with the predictability and accuracy that would be required. Moreover, she would only have one throw and, if she missed, it was unlikely that she would live long enough to feel even the agony of regret. She clasped her free hand to her forehead. She panted rapidly, her head became dizzy and her vision began to blacken. She could neither see, nor think. She knew in that moment that she was incapable of throwing anything let alone a knife with even an approximation of the precision she would need: for this was the thing about unrestrained anger, it could neither be contained nor subject to the grace of reason.

She'd failed. How could she take down a trained Russian assassin? Perhaps it would be best to simply accept the lethal shell that he'd planned to visit on her presently. Even easier, would be to just let go of the dock side and sink below the cold waters: like a floundering boat on rocks before the high tide – a craft with no survivors.

She thought of Toby, the person who'd saved her, who'd stood by her despite the sheer hell she'd put him through and who had never lost faith in her. He'd protected her and had sought nothing in return – not even thanks. She then considered all those who looked up to her and who depended on her to be their inspiration and their champion. In losing today she would let not only herself down but every one of them, too. Moreover, her abuser's laughing, taunting face would ultimately have beaten her, along with the anger that triumphed both over her psychologically and the ability of her trained physical form to function.

She came then to her final refuge: something of the wonder and admiration she'd seen not only in Tim's eyes, but also his parents as they'd fidgeted excitedly on the threshold of their house. Their belief in her was both unmistakable and unshakable. She needed to see that too. Ultimately, it was her recollection of the words she'd spoken to him about being part of the weapon, of bonding with it and sending a little piece of oneself with it on its journey, that helped her now. She accepted that she had to remain calm - a cool, dispassionate air would assist her. How hard it was, however, with all the pent up frustrations of recent weeks. She knew, too, that her aim was at its very best when she remained focussed, yet relaxed. She struggled with this but she knew what was demanded of her. She calmed; her respiration slowed, her mind focussed, the shaking stopped and so did the panting. Most vitally, her anger was defeated and in that moment she was on the training range again with a difficult but viable target to be aimed for.

She closed her pretty eyes, but briefly, knowing that she needed this moment of absolute calm despite the danger she was in. If he'd seen her during this time she would be perfectly vulnerable to a well-aimed shot – without doubt, which he had the skills to mount. She knew however that she had to use this time to prepare. Her eyes opened now, her vision restored, with an edge that mirrored her honed blade – she was ready. The knife with its perfect weight and very sharp point was poised.

She pulled herself up using her left arm, which rested on top of the edging stones. This caused her torso to rise up and out of the water. He was standing approximately thirty metres further up the dock, having gone the wrong way. He was also looking away from her.

She knew that if one strike were to end it, he would have to look towards her. She grasped the tip of the blade and brought her arm backwards behind and above her shoulder. She readied to extend her wrist as the final step before reversing this and allowing its release.

Leonind had expected her appearance to be ahead of him and about now. Every slight ripple of the water in front of him was fired at - all to no avail. He realised that he was running low on bullets for his 9mm sidearm, he could only wait for her to attempt to get out of the Basin, whereupon he would fire immediately and despatch her on the spot. The more he looked the less he could see; the water had a dulling effect on his vision and he feverishly thought he could see shapes forming in the surface that could only be her head breaking surface but – at each occasion – wasn't. The more this went on, the more uncertain he became: panic rose within. He took to running desperately up and down the edge of the dock, scanning the water feverishly, but less and less productively.

She understood that her chance was about to present and that it was the only one she would have: she waited for him to move towards her. She prepared the direction of travel for the knife in her mind and also the precise point where it would come into contact with him.

It seemed that he still had not seen her, but he was at an ideal range of about 25 metres. If someone attempted to slash their own throat they often looked away from the blade before applying it to their necks. It was a grisly thought, but she knew that this movement caused the sternomastoid muscle, which ran from the breastbone to behind the ear, to tighten and also to cover the carotid artery, which was one of the main arteries in the neck and the body as a whole. This made their intentions harder to achieve.

She called to him; his head turned towards her; the muscle relaxed just as the one on the opposite side extended. As it relaxed it exposed the carotid artery, which presented as a target. This was perfect. Her strategy was predicated on there being only one survivor: she applied it now. She breathed quickly once, a sharp intake of breath. She held it just for a moment and then exhaled.

As she did so, she extended her wrist just before her arm came forward precisely with a well-rehearsed and dependable progression as the wrist went into full flexion. The blade flashed for a second, but was on its noiseless way along the track she'd assigned to it. He saw her. He was in the process of bringing his gun to bear, rotating his torso to engage her, but his neck remained relatively fixed.

It was too late, far too late; the blade was ready to meet him and it followed its prescribed path with precise and lethal efficiency. Long before he'd even pointed his gun, the knife was in flight and as he finished turning, it was all over. The Russian's ideally-positioned neck was kissed, unequivocally, by the cold blade: such an embrace was more than sufficient. The honed edge met, did its work, and continued right on through, also transecting the windpipe, having already severed the artery completely - a millisecond after it had pierced his skin.

People would always underestimate how much blood a severed carotid artery can produce. Having come directly from the heart and being responsible for supplying the brain, it was under intense pressure. This was demonstrated graphically as blood sprayed several metres into the air. Sadly, one or two bystanders had appeared after noticing the shots. At first they had run away but then sensing that he was firing into the water they had paused to watch. It was only then that they saw the young woman appear on the edge of the dock and call to him. They saw the slim blade glint in the available light and they only realised exactly what had happened to it when they saw the big man fall in what amounted to less than a second. The blood going everywhere caused an impactful but horrific scene. One or two fainted with the violence and explicit nature of the man's demise. The blood continued to spurt for some time but had covered much of the dockside and for a considerable distance. They knew that no one could survive that degree of injury.

Clancy understood it too, and as soon as she'd released the knife she knew that he was already dead. Many would hold the view that a revolver was quicker, more definite, but Clancy knew otherwise and now, had he lived, Leonid would know it too. She did not wait to see any more, missing the perfectly dreadful display of torrents of blood that issued from his neck. All stared as the stunning woman pulled herself out of the water wearing what must be a bra and skimpy knickers that were completely wet and quite transparent. From seeing the grisly scene, bystanders witnessed something else entirely and girls and wives covered their men-folk's eyes as she tore round the edge of the dock over the bridge and back to Tim's position.

The gods' countenance was restored. She had fought her greatest enemy – anger – and triumphed. It was clear the worthy contender had earned her chance to seek a place among those in the pantheon of the greats. In the days ahead they would see if she were capable of this, too. Sadly, not even a god could stop or divert the torment and unremitting sadness that was about to come her way and would hit her with the force of an earthquake.

The Paramedic had blocked the road with his estate car. He and his two colleagues had rushed forward to make an assessment of their patient. Another siren from an emergency ambulance could be heard approaching.

Tim's condition had deteriorated. He looked deathly pale and his breathing had sped up to form short, sharp and rapid panting. So much so, that he could barely speak.

She knelt by his side as the medical team worked on their casualty. Although she was shivering she didn't really register the December cold. The news team continued to film as she leant forwards to catch his strained words.

"Wow, Miss Clancy, a sight I've been waiting my whole life to see! Did you get him?"

"Well, don't get too used to it. And yes, he won't be troubling us any more. It's time for a holiday, Tim.

Barbados or the super yacht, your choice, what do you fancy?"

The only reply he could manage at this time was by way of a rapid but shallow breathing.

She rubbed her arms against the cold and the Paramedic stepped forward with his large jacket and put it over her shoulders. She swept it together in front of her for more warmth. The Paramedic then found her a blanket, which she partly used for warmth and partly to kneel on the concrete pavement.

"I love you, Miss Clancy, and I have since that night you came for me. I am sorry; I just can't help it. The more I try to control it, the stronger my feelings grow. Can you forgive me? One more thing, Penny," he smiled a little as he spoke the word he'd been desperate to voice for weeks, "Penny, tell me, can you tell me?"

"Of course I forgive you, don't be silly. How could anyone be sad when a man like you tells you he loves you." The tears broke through at this point and were now given free rein. Choking them back, she went on "Yes, go on, anything," she said, doing her best to alter the tone of her voice from that of one comforting a dying man to one with more optimism. Optimism for another day tomorrow: surely, youth's promise of many more to come after that. She knew this would have to be her best performance at lying. Why was it that so many tears were continuing to frustrate her efforts?

She knelt by his side holding a cold, and already lifeless, hand that he could no longer feel. She appeared as might a priest administering the last rites to a dying man.

"Tim, just ask me, whatever you want to know is okay."

"Miss, please stand away; we need to get to work; we haven't much time," came from Sister Munro.

Two huge venflons, intravenous cannulae, were inserted into his uppermost arm and to the drip, so formed; two bags of blood were connected. The paramedic squeezed on the bags with all his strength, so that they would flood into the patient's failing circulation in as short a time as possible. Tim's blood had relentlessly seeped on to the pavement and showed no signs of stopping.

"Miss, please stand aside, we need to get to his neck to put a central line in," suggested Sister Munro.

"We haven't got time to get him back to the hospital," agreed Mr Charles and continued, "I'm going to need to stop the bleeding. I just wonder if I dare try to clamp the splenic artery here. Maybe if we get him into the ambulance and use Entonox?" Mr Charles thought aloud.

The Paramedic continued to squeeze the bags of blood and the supplies were rapidly running down. Sister Munro prepared some plasma expanders for use when all the blood had been used. It was being consumed at a rapid rate.

Mr Charles put the central line in and more blood was run in as fast as the lines would carry it. The additional emergency crew had arrived in the ambulance; they pushed away the taxi to gain more room and hopefully a rapid transfer of the patient into the back. They reversed the ambulance to be near their patient and opened the rear doors. A motorcyclist was on his way with further supplies of 'O' negative blood, which was universal donor blood that could be used for anyone.

"Readings are dreadful," sister Munro said, "we are losing him. The blood transfusion is just not helping. I still can't get a BP."

The surgeon made ready to attempt to clamp the splenic artery; he looked longingly at the flat surface and bright light in the ambulance, wondering if they had time to get him in the back. Removing Tim's belt and the sodden cardigan, he tried to look for the offending artery, using suction and swabs by the score, to soak up the blood. The more suction he applied and the more swabs he used – the more blood that appeared.

"Miss, I won't tell you again, we are going to have to get him in the ambulance if he is to have a chance." Clancy decoded these last words, for she knew they were now redundant and pitched to provide false hope. She could tell that chances had run out because there was no conviction behind the sister's words, or even expectation that they could save him.

Tim stirred; he brought his neck up a little so he could gaze into those beautiful eyes for one last time.

"Penny, I just need to know. Can I ask you, do you love Toby? I just need to hear it from you. It will be our secret, I promise," came from Tim with urgency. Then, between rapid, short, sharp breaths he somehow managed more words. "Do you think you could have ever loved me? I'll dream of that kiss forever. My life began the day you came for me." He knew he was in the last seconds of his young life.

Eyes that rarely cried, switched from studying him with intense concern, to become like twin rivers overflowing. She realised that he was dying and, in that minute, she understood that he had guessed it too; for his questions were now delivered with urgency. These were the last things he was ever going to learn. Without doubt, it was to be his final request – his very last wish.

She'd lost so many good agents and friends in the past few weeks, all of those losses grievous to her. And yet it seemed this one was even more painful than all those that had come before. In that moment, she knew why.

She made to get up, but she knew there were two things she had to say.

"Toby is my friend, like a brother, or even a father."

"And it's you, Tim. I came for you. It was *me* who came for you. I talked Toby into it. I pestered him for weeks to let me run the mission. The more I saw of you, the more I liked what I saw. I *just* had to come and get you. I begged Toby to let me get you from that Casino.

It always was you, Tim, and nobody else – because I love you. I always have and I realise that I always will."

She kissed him – his lips now cold.

"Miss, go now, or we'll lose him," the plaintive cry from the sister.

Clancy's words hung in the ether and they comprised endearments that he'd waited all his life, or so it seemed, to hear.

And yet here, at its end, they were words that he could no longer register. Moreover, his deep, honest and open eyes now stared wide, they became even paler than life could support, meaning they could not even see those pretty lips as they formed them.

Sister Munro looked away; she could see that it had gone against them. She knew that it was unprofessional to cry, but somehow the loss of this young, almost angelically handsome man had defeated such discipline. Mr Charles caught her eye, a gaze that he was unable to meet.

"He's flatlined," Sister Munro said, through the tears that she gave up trying to quell.

The distress was firmly etched to Clancy's face with illimitable intensity. She gripped the cold and lifeless hand, holding it to a cheek that was awash with tears.

"Tim, don't leave me, just when I've found you. I beg you."

"Please don't leave me here all alone, because I love you, Tim."

"It was always you, and just you. Forgive me for not being able to tell you sooner."

She stood. The tall, supremely fit and strong woman, in that moment, reduced to a collapsing tower of tears. Through all her pain and suffering, the cruellest thought came to claim her with obliterative menace – she wondered with even more distress just what could she possibly say to his poor parents.

She screamed at the film crew, just as Sister Munro rose, too, in order to comfort her.

"Can't you leave the poor man to die in peace?"

They hung their heads, and their cameras, in a study of perfect shame.

THE END